MW00978505

THIRTY-SIX POINTS

A Novel
of the Korean War

by
Samuel Martin Kier

FIRESIDE FICTION
2005

FIRESIDE FICTION

AN IMPRINT OF HERITAGE BOOKS, INC.

Books, CDs, and more – Worldwide

For our listing of thousands of titles see our website

at

www.HeritageBooks.com

Cover photograph of Able Company, 5th Infantry Regiment
by Regimental Photographer Arnold Chang
Courtesy of the National Archives

Published 2005 by
HERITAGE BOOKS, INC.
Publishing Division
65 East Main Street
Westminster, Maryland 21157-5026

Copyright © 2005 Samuel Martin Kier

All rights reserved. No part of this book may be reproduced or transmitted in any form or by any means, electronic or mechanical, including photocopying, recording or by any information storage and retrieval system without written permission from the author, except for the inclusion of brief quotations in a review.

International Standard Book Number: **0-7884-3487-X**

AUTHOR'S NOTE

THIRTY-SIX POINTS is a novel. It is the story of two American soldiers; Private Ben Stewart, who was drafted following his sophomore year in college, and his platoon sergeant, SFC Rob Palmer, a career soldier. The story is also a chronicle of some of the exploits of the Fifth Regimental Combat Team during the fluid part of the Korean War, primarily July 1950 through April 1951, and the more static, outpost phase of the war from November 1952 through July 1953. Throughout the book there is a mix of historical fact and human drama. In general, the men below the rank of battalion commander are fictitious characters. An exception was made for those men who were decorated for heroism in battle. In such cases, real names were used. Major events in the lives of members of the Fifth Regimental Combat Team, as revealed in command reports, battalion journals and after-action reports, served as grist for much of the story.

Thirty-six Points is presented in three parts. In Part One, the reader is introduced to Ben Stewart, college student, and Rob Palmer, combat infantryman. In Part Two, a parallel is drawn between the military training of Ben and that of his Chinese counterpart, Private Hua Xing, a member of the Chinese People's Liberation Army. Their lives, and that of Corporal Iannis Karsatos of the Greek Expeditionary Force, merge during the intense fighting in the Chorwan Valley during June 1953. During Part Three the war comes to its conclusion and its survivors struggle to recover from the experience. Each of the three parts is preceded by an historical narrative to give the reader an understanding of the larger context.

The United States Army in the final months of the Korean War was, to a large part, composed of a generation of young Americans who had been born in the early 1930's. Two-thirds of them were drafted, subject to the Universal Military and Training Act of 1951. As children, during World War II, they played soldiers, built fighter plane models and collected scrap paper for the war effort while their fathers and uncles fought in Europe and in the Pacific. They knew that they, too, would one day don uniforms and serve their country. As they grew into young manhood, most hoped that their hitch in the military would come during one of those rare times when the world was at peace.

Despite the unpopularity of the draft, there was no organized draft resistance movement during the Korean War. The incidence of draft evasion was no greater than it had been for World War II. One reason for the lack of an anti-war or anti-draft movement may have been the preferential treatment given those traditional troublemakers, the college students. A student was deferred from military duty as long as he earned a designated qualifying scholastic test score and maintained a required grade point average. Another reason for a lack of resistance to being drafted was the young man's life-long expectation that he would serve his country once he reached military age.

The newly inducted soldier was given a serial number. At that time, the number bore no relation to his social security number. The draftee's number began with the initials "US" rather than the "RA" (Regular Army) designation assigned to enlistees. "RA" soldiers enlisted for particular branches of the Army and their requests were generally granted provided they were found suitable. "US" soldiers were assigned wherever they were needed. Their requests generally fell on deaf ears.

Following the war, draftees did not write books about their experiences in Korea. Their educations and civilian careers had been interrupted and they just wanted to get on with life. *Thirty-six Points* (the number of rotation points that the soldier had to accrue in order to come home from Korea) is an attempt to portray the war from the perspective of the draftee.

ACKNOWLEDGMENTS

I AM GRATEFUL to Michael Slater, whose book, *Hills of Sacrifice,* rekindled my interest in the proud history of the Fifth U.S. Infantry. Thanks, also, to Korean War veterans and dear friends Dick McFarland and Bob Quinn for reviewing earlier versions of my manuscript and to John Daniel for his fine editorial analysis. Their advice and encouragement were much appreciated. Thanks to my mother, Mary Kier Tyler, for preserving letters that I wrote home from college and from the Army. Without them I would have had a difficult time remembering what goes on in the mind of a twenty-year-old.

The photograph of Able Company, Fifth Infantry Regiment, used for the cover, was shot by Regimental Photographer, Arnold Chang of Honolulu and is the property of the National Archives. It was selected by Michael Slater for inclusion in his book, *Hills of Sacrifice.*

The principal characters in this story are fictional. Of course, they are composites of the traits of people that I have known but no attempt was made to portray an actual living individual.

Thanks to the old sergeants, whose names I've forgotten, but whose stories of the bleak days of 1950-51 have remained with me for fifty years. This book is dedicated to them and to the nearly one thousand members of the Fifth Regimental Combat Team who perished in Korea.

Samuel Martin Kier
Pacific Grove, California
June 2004

The author as a young soldier in 1954

PROLOGUE

THE GIRL who walked into the lobby at Encina Hall did not look one bit like the Mary Ellen Rawlings that Ben Stewart remembered from his childhood. That Mary Ellen had been a little blonde tomboy with pigtails and oatmeal-scented breath. This young lady approaching him from across the lobby was no tomboy. She was a full-grown woman. The pigtails had been replaced by a short bob that framed her lovely, tanned face. She strode up to him, held out her hand, flashed a bright smile, looked at his six-foot, two-inch frame, and said, "Ben Stewart! You haven't changed a bit."

They both chuckled. They hadn't seen each other since the summer following their sixth grade year. That was the summer that the Stewart family had sold their home in Walnut Creek and moved to the Sacramento area.

"Well, you've certainly changed," said Ben. "Very nice changes, I might add."

"Thank you...uh...my mom said to give you her best when I ran into you. She heard about your admission to summer quarter through the conniving mothers message service."

"Yeah, I heard about you through the same network," responded Ben. "How about a coke? We've got six years of catching up to do, Mary Ellen."

"It's Ellie, Ben. Everybody calls me Ellie, now."

Ben and Mary Ellen had been admitted conditionally to Stanford during summer quarter of 1950. Conditional admission was reserved for applicants who had very respectable, but less-than-perfect, high school grade point averages coupled with high entrance test scores and had demonstrated leadership qualities in student government, athletics and other high school activities. If they were able to demonstrate acceptable scholarship during the twelve-week summer quarter, they would be re-admitted for the following winter quarter.

The summer quarter students had registered for classes on Friday, June 23. The freshmen spent Saturday attending residence hall orientation meetings and moving into their rooms. The men were assigned to Encina Hall and the women to Lagunita Hall.

A social gathering involving the residents of the two halls was held at Encina on Sunday afternoon to allow the sexes to mingle before classes began on Monday. It was at that event that Mary Ellen and Ben renewed their friendship.

Mary Ellen put her empty coke glass on a tray and said, "Well, I best be going. I want to finish organizing my things and I imagine that you do too."

"Mine are in pretty good shape already," responded Ben. "How about I walk you back to Lagunita?"

"That would be nice," she said. "I want to hear more about your decision to go pre-med, why you want to be a doctor."

As they walked, Ben talked about Bill Granstedt, his family doctor in Orangevale. Bill was a Kansas-bred Navy vet who kept up with the latest medical developments but continued to prescribe enemas, mustard-plasters, and any time-honored treatment that could still do the job. Dr. Granstedt had been pleased to hear that Ben was interested in taking pre-med courses and had had several conversations with the youngster, noting that there would be a place for Ben in Orangevale when he became Dr. Stewart.

When the couple reached the women's dormitory, they prolonged their stroll by circling the small lake to the west of the building. As they did so, Mary Ellen rested her hand on Ben's arm. Misinterpreting the gesture, he bent to kiss her and was somewhat embarrassed when she drew away and said, "It's a little early for that, Ben."

"But we've known each other since we were little kids."

"Well, that's no reason for you to act like a little kid," she chided, good-naturedly. "I'm just not ready for that."

"I'm sorry. That was stupid of me," said Ben as he turned to walk back to Encina Hall. "Maybe I'll catch up with you in Western Civ tomorrow morning." Mary Ellen smiled and waved.

Monday morning, as Ben pulled on his Levis, he was catching some music on Wally King's morning show on KPO, San Francisco. As he reached under his bunk for his loafers, the music format was interrupted by a newsbreak:

Yesterday morning the U.S. State Department was informed of an outbreak of hostilities on the Korean Peninsula. According to reports we've received, armored and infantry units from North Korea crossed into South Korea at 4:00 A.M. Korean time, Sunday morning. The main thrust is moving south along the Pochon-Uijongbu corridor toward Seoul, the capital of South Korea. There are additional invading forces driving down the east coast toward the mountain town of Ch'unch'on.

South Korean troops, amounting to five under-strength infantry divisions, have moved north to attempt to block the attack. It is understood that the South Korean Army is vastly outnumbered by the Communists from the North. In addition, South Korea has no armored units and no air force. It is not known whether President Truman will authorize the commitment of U.S ground troops to assist the South Korean people. However, the U.S. ambassador to the Republic of Korea, John Muccio, has ordered all non-essential American Embassy personnel and all U.S. dependents to evacuate to Japan. Stay tuned to Radio KPO, throughout the day, for further developments.

Since there seemed, to Ben, to be nothing earth-shaking going on anywhere in the world, he turned off the radio and headed toward the "Quad" for his 9:00 o'clock section in the history of western civilizations. When he arrived at the classroom, Mary Ellen was already seated, flanked by her two roommates. Ben winked at her and smiled and found an empty desk at the rear of the room.

The first morning of class was taught by a young graduate assistant. He quickly previewed the quarter's work and then launched into a short summary of ancient Greek contributions to current thought. Their first outside reading assignment would be Euripides' tragic drama, *The Trojan Women.*

"Did any of you get to read *The Trojan Women* in a classics course in high school or did anybody just read it for your own amusement and amazement?" asked the instructor.

Several hands went up rather hesitatingly. Mary Ellen spoke. "I didn't read it thoroughly but I recall that it involved Helen of Troy and was quite bloody."

"You're right, Helen played a major role in the story. Just off hand, might there be any connection between the play and the events of a few hours ago in Korea?"

The student seated next to Ben said, "Keep a look out for a large wooden horse rolling south across the border?"

"I doubt that they would try that ruse again," chuckled the instructor," but you might have something there. The people from the two Koreas are the same, ethnically and linguistically. The North Koreans could easily infiltrate the south dressed as farmers and refugees. I personally think that *Trojan Women* is one of the earliest pieces of anti-war literature in existence. Let me know what you think about that on Wednesday. There are plenty of copies in the Reserved Book Room. I guess, that does it for today."

Ben and Mary Ellen met that evening at the Reserved Book Room. They checked out copies of Euripides' play for the two hours allowed and studied quietly until 9:00. As Ben walked Mary Ellen back to Lagunita, he held her hand. He met no resistance. As they approached the front door to the dormitory, she said, "So, what do you think?"

"What do I think?"

"What was the point of our reading *The Trojan Women.*"

"I don't really know," Ben responded. "I couldn't keep my mind on it. I'm distracted a little by this Korean thing. I wouldn't be surprised if I end up there before it's over."

"Don't be silly, Ben, you're a seventeen-year-old kid. They'll have the whole business over with in less than a year."

"I hope so, Ellie, but maybe you should start being nicer to me just in case."

"Okay, soldier," she said as she stood on her toes and gave him a goodnight kiss.

PART I

JUNE 1950 - MAY 1951

The nation of Korea, a frequently invaded buffer state in the Far East, had been under the domination of Japan since 1910. In 1943, U.S. President Franklin Roosevelt, Britain's Prime Minister Churchill and Chiang Kai-shek, the leader of Nationalist China decreed that, following the defeat of Japan, "Korea shall become free and independent." However, when Japan surrendered in the summer of 1945, Harry Truman, Roosevelt's successor, suggested that the surrender of Japanese forces in Korea could best be expedited by the Soviet Army north of the 38th Parallel and by the American troops south of that boundary.

The Soviets were quick to agree to Truman's suggestion. As soon as the Japanese units north of the line capitulated, the USSR sealed the border. Unexpectedly, Korea had been divided into a Communist north and a democratic south.

For the next five years, the North Korea People's Army was trained and equipped by the Soviet Union. In the south, the United States trained and equipped an army for the Republic of Korea. The officers and NCOs of the seven divisions of the NKPA were largely veterans of Manchurian guerrilla warfare and the Chinese Civil War. Their Soviet mentors trained them rigorously and supplied them well with small arms, artillery, armor and fighter aircraft.

In late spring of 1950, the North Korea People's Army faced a much smaller ROK Army, both in personnel and firepower, south of the 48th Parallel. The South Koreans had only five infantry divisions and no tanks, no artillery and no tactical air force. At midnight on June 25, 1950, the Communists had 90,000 combat troops poised to pounce on South Korea. Four hours later they attacked.

On Friday, June 30, President Truman authorized commitment of U.S ground troops to combat in Korea. He signed Public Law 599, extending the Selective Service Act until July 9, 1951, apparently feeling that a year would be more than enough time to resolve the Korea problem. He also moved to authorize the call-up of Army Reserve and National Guard units for up to twenty-one months of active service.

One of the regular army units to receive an immediate alert was the Fifth Regimental Combat Team at Schofield Barracks on Oahu. The Fifth RCT consisted of the Fifth Infantry Regiment, an old-line regiment originally organized in July 1798, the 555th Field Artillery Battalion, and the 72nd Engineer Company.

Veteran members of the Fifth RCT were familiar with Korea. The Fifth Infantry had been inactivated in 1946 following a period of occupation duty in Germany but North Korea's military build-up prompted re-activation of the Fifth on January 1, 1949 in Seoul, Korea. Its mission was to train the ROK Army and to maintain outposts along the northern border of South Korea.

Morale soared in April 1949 when the severely under-strength Fifth RCT was alerted for shipment to Hawaii. Two months later, as they moved to Inchon to embark, many Communist sympathizers showed their lack of appreciation and respect for the Americans by screaming insults, throwing rotten fruit and spitting at them. When the troops arrived at Pearl Harbor, young ladies from the Hawaiian Visitors Bureau draped colorful leis around the necks of the grateful soldiers while beautiful hula girls danced on the piers. As the soldiers moved into Schofield Barracks, they felt like they were in heaven.

The unit morale improved greatly, under the command of Colonel James Simpson, and replacements continued to fill the vacancies in the ranks. In the spring of 1950, training took place in the morning hours and the afternoon was reserved for team sports. America was at peace. When monthly paydays arrived, the privates would draw their $75, don their colorful aloha shirts and head for town.

Following its being alerted for return to Korea, the Fifth RCT received last-minute transferees from the U.S. Army of the Pacific, primarily Hawaiians. Many had just completed basic training with the Fifth Provisional Training Company. The new folks had just enough time to fire their newly issued M-1 rifles and throw one grenade each before boarding the transport ships bound for the Far East.

SUMMER 1950

PFC ROB PALMER stood on the deck of the USNS *General Hugh G. Gaffey* watching the lights of Pusan's harbor approach. It was late at night but Palmer couldn't sleep. He was tingling with excitement. The Detroit native had enlisted in the Army in 1948 at the age of seventeen. Since completing basic training at Fort Knox, Kentucky, he had been transferred from one stateside infantry post to another. But, finally, this was Korea. Hawaii was fun but he now was going to get a chance to do what he was trained to do. He tossed the butt of his cigarette out into the breeze and watched its glowing end float down until it disappeared in the inky water.

Once ashore, the troops formed up on the pier and then route-stepped in a column of twos toward their bivouac area, a nearby bean field.

"Hey, haole boy. Where you from?"

Rob looked up into the smiling face of the huge Hawaiian who was walking beside him. "Michigan. I grew up outside of Detroit."

"You still got family deh?" Kauahilo's voice had that characteristic island lilt to it in contrast to Palmer's flat Mid-west twang.

"No. My parents died when I was little. I grew up in an orphanage."

"No brah, no seestah, no pretty wahine?"

"Roger that, buddy. No family. No girl friend," replied Palmer.

"Well then," concluded Eddie, "Nobody to give a shit when you get your head blown off. You one lucky brah."

"You're probably right," responded Palmer.

The Reverend and Mrs. Laughlin who ran the orphanage were the closest thing that he had to parents. They offered their charges tasteless food, strict discipline and a rigid daily schedule. When Reverend Laughlin signed the parental waiver permitting Robert to enlist, the seventeen-year-old was already well prepared for the drabness and regimentation of army life.

On August 2, when morning broke over the bean field, Sergeant Veenstra instructed the platoon to make a light pack. They would be leaving their personal duffle bags at the bivouac area. Rob noticed that Eddie wasn't making any headway with the assignment.

"You need some help, Pardner?"

"Yeah, man, I don't have a clue. I must have gone fishin' the day that they taught this crap."

"Stow a change of socks and underwear, a clean set of fatigues and your mess kit and toilet articles in your pack. That's all you'll need."

As Eddie stuffed his pack, Rob rolled Eddie's blanket lengthwise, inside his shelter half, showed him how to lash it to his backpack, legionnaire-style, and how to strap his entrenching tool to the back of the pack. He hoped that Eddie's apparent gaps in training and lack of concern were not typical of the new Hawaiian recruits.

Once they were packed, the men of Second Battalion were rushed by train and then by truck convoy to Chindong-ni, a coastal village situated on an important road junction eight miles west of Masan. The Sixth Division of the North Korean People's Army was rapidly advancing south in an attempt to flank them.

When Second Battalion arrived at the dusty little village, Companies G and E were ordered to dig in on an arc facing northwest. Rice paddies covered the low land and corn grew part way up two hills that were designated 342 and 255. Whoever controlled the pair of hills controlled Chindong-ni. Word quickly passed to Rob and Eddie and the other members of George Company that they would be assaulting Hill 342 the following day. Occasional small arms fire from the crest of the hill suggested that 342 was inhabited by unfriendly folks.

The sun was high in the sky and the heat was already sweltering; well above 100 degrees, when Rob's platoon began to climb the hill. He soon felt dizzy and disoriented. When they were halfway to the crest of the hill, they began to receive heavy automatic weapons fire. George Company was pinned down with no place for cover. When they received the order to fall back, Rob took a few labored steps and collapsed.

Eddie Kauahilo had remarkable stamina and speed for a big man thanks to several years of grueling football practices at Roosevelt High School in Honolulu. When he reached the road at the bottom of the hill, he noticed that Palmer wasn't with the group taking refuge in what shade could be found at the edge of the cornfield. Without hesitating, Eddie ran back up the hill until he came to Rob who was lying beside the trail, grimacing and hanging on to his helmet with both hands. The Hawaiian dropped down beside him.

"Are you hit, Palmer?"

"No, not yet." the prostrate soldier responded weakly.

"Then get the fuck up and let's shag ass."

"I can't get up. Something's wrong with me."

PFC Kauahilo threw his one hundred and fifty pound comrade over his shoulder and ran down the slope. Bullets kicked up the dust on both sides of him.

When they reached the relative cover of the cornfield, Sergeant Veenstra intercepted them. "Did Palmer get hit?"

"Nah. He sick or somethin'"

"Probably just heat exhaustion. Get him into the shade and start splashing some water on him."

Eddie's canteen was empty but Rob's still contained a couple of inches of water. Eddie slapped handfuls of the warm liquid on his friend's grimy face, saving a little so the groggy soldier could have a drink. Rob was able to pull himself into a sitting position.

"Thanks, Eddie, but you probably should have just left me there. You could'a been killed. This embarrasses the hell out of me. I feel like such a pussy. Never happened before."

"C'mon, ain't no big t'ing, brah. Get up, you scrawny little haole." Eddie helped Palmer struggle to his feet. "Who knows, tomorrow you may have to pack me down off the hill."

George Company returned to that morning's point of departure, filled their canteens from the water buffalo, and dined on some peanut butter and jelly sandwiches that had just been brought forward in the mess truck. Rob ate about half of his, handed the remainder to Eddie and promptly dozed off.

During the relative cool of the night, Fox Company climbed Hill 342. When they reached the crest, they were greeted by intense small arms fire. They returned rifle and BAR fire, aiming at the enemy's muzzle flashes. Mortar fire support was requested and was soon falling on the North Korean positions. As the men of Fox Company pushed forward, the enemy soldiers panicked and ran. Company F christened their objective Fox Hill.

On the following morning, Rob awoke as the sky was brightening over the Sea of Japan. There was a mist rising from the rice paddies and the smell of cordite lingered from Fox Company's assault of the hill and its subsequent efforts to blunt counterattacks by the angry North Koreans, who were incensed because, for the first time, their rapid drive toward Pusan was being challenged. Palmer felt hungry. He was fully recovered from his heat exhaustion. Regimental S-2 had notified all unit commanders to expect a high of 110 degrees. The flies and mosquitoes were already revving up their engines.

During a morning formation, Sergeant Veenstra told the men that they had one hour to get something to eat and pack-up.

"So what's happenin', Sarge?" said one of the men."

Veenstra replied, "I understand that we're heading west to a little village called Tosan. First Battalion has been assigned the job of securing a road junction near there and we'll just support their attack. Eventually we're supposed to link up with the 35th Infantry and the 5th Marines."

"Are there a lot of Gooks over there, Sergeant?"

"There's a whole damn NKPA division waitin' for us. Now, no more questions. That's all I know for now. Just be ready to move out by 0630."

When the riflemen of Second Battalion fell in on the Chindong-ni - Tosan road they were missing a third of their number. Fox Company had been relieved on Hill 352 by a platoon from the 5th Marines in order to join the attack but when Lt Col Throckmorton, the battalion commander, realized that the company had lost fifteen KIA, he ordered them to get some rest.

By the time the hot, dusty hike to Tosan was over for George Company, First Battalion had secured the road junction. Therefore, Second Battalion received orders to attack a ridge north of the village. With the absence of Fox Company, the job would fall to Easy and George on the morning of August 9.

When morning came, the countryside was shrouded with fog. As Rob sat down with a mess kit full of powdered eggs, Sergeant Veenstra detected a smile on the young soldier's face.

"What are you so happy about, Palmer."

"I was just thanking God for the fog. It sure beats the heat."

"I don't know. I don't like it," responded the older man. "It's going to keep the fly boys from plastering the top of that hill and it will interfere with adjustment of the artillery. Then, to top it off, we were told last night that somebody forgot to pack us any recoilless rifle ammo so we can't even turn to those for support so it'll be all M-1s, BAR's and grenades doing the talking. I don't like it."

"Maybe they'll call off the attack," said Rob hopefully.

"That's unlikely." grumbled the sergeant as he rose and ambled off to clean his mess kit.

Veenstra was right and by noon the attack had bogged down. Easy and George Companies found themselves under heavy enemy fire with little recourse. Lieutenant Colonel Throckmorton pulled them off the hill. Rob was relieved to pull back but was somewhat crestfallen. In terms of missions accomplished, his company was batting 0 for 2.

As darkness fell, they formed a skirmish line and started back up the hill. This time, three tanks, the battalion's 81-mm mortars and an attached platoon of 4.2-inch mortars provided some muscle. It wasn't long before the North Korean defenders began abandoning their positions on the crest.

As he sat on the top of the hill, which had been wrested from the enemy with very little blood shed, Rob felt a sense of exhilaration. The sky was full of stars and he could hear the sounds of the Third Battalion moving up on their flank. This was more like it. He'd had no further problems with the heat and fate had placed him in the best damn infantry battalion in the U.S. Army. In the morning they lined up to continue to press the attack westward toward Much'on-ni. A woefully under-strength Fox Company and five Sherman tanks took the point. The rest of the battalion followed. They were flanked, on the right, by First Battalion and by Third Battalion on the left or south side. The movement of men and vehicles kicked up such a cloud of dust that many of the men wore their gas masks to keep from choking. Eddie Kauahilo had developed cramps and diarrhea after breakfast and had dropped out a little before noon.

Suddenly the relative quiet was shattered by two quick explosions and the rattle of small arms fire. The noise was coming from the front where the column had just entered the eastern end of Chinju Pass. A 45-mm anti-tank gun had just knocked out the lead tank. The driver of the second tank tried to turn his Sherman around but it slipped into a deep gulch. The two dismounted tank crews and about fifty Fox Company survivors climbed onto the three remaining tanks and headed back to the main body of the Second Battalion.

Sergeant Veenstra ordered the company off the road and into the high ground on the south side of the pass. After the first few shovels full of dirt flew, one of the men yelled, "Sarge, there's nothing here but hard pan. What are we going to do?"

"Gather up loose chunks of shale and build a wall. It'll provide some protection from grenades and small arms. Better than nothing."

Eddie Kauahilo reappeared at dusk. He seemed uncharacteristically quiet but had no difficulty downing a can of unheated lima beans and ham. Twice during the night, he got up, grabbed his entrenching tool and wandered off to do something about the rumbling in his stomach.

In the pre-dawn darkness, large elements of the NKPA 6th Division emerged from abandoned mine shafts. Around 0400, Rob could hear fire-fights all around them as the North Koreans attacked regimental headquarters, as well as the First Battalion and the 555th Field Artillery Battalion positions which were still east of the pass. Sergeant Veenstra moved among the men, making sure that all were awake. "Lock and load. Make sure you've got one in the chamber and your safety's off. We're about to entertain some company."

As the sun came up, North Korean infantry attacked Lieutenant Colonel Throckmorton's command post. The headquarters personnel were on the verge of being wiped out when Easy Company arrived and repulsed the attack.

Soon it was George Company's turn to ride to the rescue. Heavy Mortar Company was trying to beat off an attack with small arms and was being overrun.   Sergeant Veenstra ordered everyone down to the road where twelve vehicles, a mix of ¾- ton trucks and armored personnel carriers, awaited them. Privates Palmer and Kauahilo scrambled into the same truck as the first sergeant.

The relief convoy was within a half-mile of Heavy Morter Company when firing erupted from both sides of the road but particularly from a nearby rice paddy. Veenstra yelled at the men to follow him. They had gone just a few yards when they heard North Korean voices. The sergeant lobbed a couple of grenades in the direction of the sound and it was soon apparent, from the muzzle flashes, that George Company was horrifically outnumbered. The men dove into a roadside ditch and began to pour fire in the direction of the rice paddy. The North Koreans were bunching up in preparation for an attack on the ditch.

At this point most of the convoy was burning except for one nearby personnel carrier and a jeep and trailer. A 50-caliber machine gun was mounted on the personnel carrier. As Sergeant Veenstra bounded onto the truck, tracers were flying all around him. He cocked the charging handle of the machine gun a couple of times and then began slaughtering the North Koreans.

Although Rob was intent on his own problems, he was close enough to the truck that he could hear Sergeant Veenstra swearing at the enemy, then swearing at the gun until he cleared a jam, then as he emptied the first box of ammunition, cursing whoever set up the gun without placing the extra ammunition within reach. Rob could see bullets slamming into the truck as the surviving North Koreans tried, with everything they had, to put the crazed sergeant out of business. Another soldier brought the rest of the belts of 50-caliber ammunition to Veenstra and then scrambled back to the ditch. The sergeant reloaded and, once again, unleashed a torrent of bullets and profanity.

While the North Koreans were involved with Sergeant Veenstra, a lieutenant, who had been wounded in the foot, was able to unhook the jeep from the trailer, turn the jeep around and pile the wounded on the vehicle. That accomplished, he headed east through the pass toward the battalion aid station.

Rob had just tossed a full clip of 30-caliber cartridges to Eddie and was in the process of firing his last clip, when Sergeant Veenstra gave the order to "haul ass."   He had fired every available round of 50-caliber ammunition; the wounded had been evacuated, so there was nothing more that could be done. They ducked down as they trotted along the bottom of the ditch and then turned off in the paddy fields to the south and headed for home.

A giddy, panting Eddie Kauahilo said, "Guess we creamed those motherfuckers!"

"Who's we?" responded Rob. "I'll bet nearly every one of those Gooks took a fifty-caliber slug. Sergeant Veenstra was the wrath of God. It was like he had an invisible shield around him. I'm sticking real close to the Sarge after this. I figure that's the only way I'm going to get home in one piece."

It was mid-morning when George Company got back to the Second Battalion area. Orders had come down from regiment to hold until nightfall and then complete the movement through the pass. The men spent the day cleaning weapons, restocking cartridge belts, slaking their thirst and trying to find some shade.

That evening they filed down to the road to join the regiment's advance guard. Shortly after moving out they began to take small arms fire from the left and right front. Machine gun tracers coming from the hills ricocheted off the road and the sides of the canyon. The files of infantrymen returned fire. Wounded men were loaded into the trucks and the column continued to move. In an hour Second Battalion was west of the pass. Two hours later the entire column had cleared Chinju Pass.

For the next couple of days, First and Second Battalions tried to regain control of the pass, destroy the surrounded enemy and recover abandoned vehicles and bodies. It finally took air strikes to destroy much of the equipment. Most of the bodies, including those of four members of George Company, would not be recovered until late September when the 25th Division broke out of the Pusan Perimeter.

The battle of "Bloody Gulch" was over and the Fifth RCT returned to its line of departure at Chindong-ni. The NKPA had won a tactical victory but their offensive toward Pusan had been stalled.

As the dispirited rifle company assembled on the bank of a dry riverbed near Chindong-ni, they learned from Sergeant Veenstra that the regimental commander, Colonel Ordway, had been relieved of his command. He would be replaced by their battalion commander, John Throckmorton. The men were elated. The "Rock" was their guy. He wouldn't lead them into a mess like Chinju Pass.

Following "Bloody Gulch" the combat team was assigned a defensive sector of ridgeline on the left flank of the 24th Infantry Regiment. To its front, an even higher ridgeline, Sobuk-san, was in the hands of the North Koreans. There were too few men to occupy every meter of the MLR (the main line of resistance or front line) so the rifle companies formed strong points on select pieces of high ground, doing their best to cover the numerous gaps with overlapping fire. The First Battalion dug in on the right, the Second Battalion was in the center, and the Third was on the left flank. First Platoon of the 72nd Engineers served as the RCT's only reserves.

On 20 August the first seventy-three KATUSA's (Korean Augmentation to the US Army) were assigned to the RCT. Mainly untrained draftees, they were issued a uniform and a rifle and paired with an American GI who was supposed to teach them how to soldier.

George Company, however, was fortunate to receive the services of Sergeant Kang Sin Kwan. Sergeant Kang's military career began in 1941 when he was conscripted into the Imperial Japanese Army. He served in Manchuria and was then sent to the Philippines where he was captured by American forces in August 1945. At the outbreak of the Korean War, he joined the ROK Army and was eventually assigned to the 5th RCT as an interpreter.

George Company was assigned to a sector of high ground which protected the main supply route from Pusan to Masan. The topsoil was deeper than they had encountered on the edge of Chinju Pass, so they dug a series of two-man foxholes as they set up their defensive position.

Privates Palmer and Kauahilo shared a foxhole near the center of the company line. The week had been uneventful and, during darkness, the big Hawaiian had been catching up on his sleep. Rob would discover his buddy asleep when it was supposed to be Eddie's turn to be on watch. Whenever he could, Palmer would just let him sleep.

The North Korean Fourth and Sixth Divisions were still operating in the area and there had been some commotion a couple of nights before in the sector defended by Third Battalion, so Palmer did his best to remain alert. But shortly before dawn, on September 4, he began to lose the battle against fatigue and boredom. He couldn't have dropped off for more than a few seconds when he was startled by the sound of small arms fire and cries of *manzai* as North Koreans assaulted the foxholes on the perimeter. He grabbed his M-1, slammed in a clip, put a round in the chamber and kicked the bottoms of his partner's bare feet.

"Wake up, Eddie. We've got a little problem here. The Gooks are comin' from all over!"

Kauahilo awakened instantly, grabbed his helmet in one hand and his loaded Browning automatic rifle in the other. They began firing at every shape that was above ground, trusting that everyone in G Company had sense enough to stay in their holes.

The enemy soldiers were everywhere. It wasn't long before some of the G.I.'s on both sides of Palmer and Kauahilo jumped out of their holes and broke for the crest of the hill.

"Where are you guys goin'?" yelled Rob.

"Time to haul ass, Palmer."

"Did we get an order to bug out?"

"Fuck it. Don't need no order. It's damn right unhealthy around here," said their neighbor as he scrambled out of his foxhole.

"Then we're stayin' you chicken haole bastard," yelled Kauahilo.

"It's your ass, soldier boy, suit yourself." The frightened rifleman headed for the crest of the hill.

As the fleeing troops descended the friendly side of the hill, they were ordered to halt by Lieutenant Don Krause, Executive Officer and SFC Fred Knowlton. The two leaders managed to scrape together a counterattack force of twenty-seven men, including a few from the company command post. Krause ordered mortar support from weapons platoon and from Heavy Mortar Company and the men formed a skirmish line and retraced their steps up the hill. When they reached the crest, the North Koreans ran, not so much from the sight of twenty-seven U.S. soldiers, but from the arrival of big 4.2-inch mortar rounds from the tubes of Heavy Mortar Company.

With the first **w-o-o-oumpt** from an exploding mortar round, Rob and Eddie crouched as deeply in their foxhole as they could, praying that they would be spared a direct hit. As the barrage lifted they resumed their task of killing the enemy soldiers that were still within close range. Those North Koreans that had withdrawn first were soon being slaughtered by fire from the 555th Field Artillery.

When it became quiet and light enough to move about the forward slope of the hill, the survivors of George Company surveyed the damage. They counted a hundred and twenty enemy dead littering the surface. In the foxholes around the perimeter, lay the bodies of fourteen fellow G.I's and two KATUSA's, Mun Son Ja and Song Yong Shik. Many of the hill's young defenders had been killed as they slept.

Rob wiped his face on his sleeve. For the first time, he began to think longingly of the day when his current enlistment would be fulfilled. Perhaps, he thought, he didn't have what it would take to face twenty years of such exhausting and disheartening work.

* * *

Ben walked into the kitchen of his family home, carrying the morning mail in his hand. He put the stack of letters down on the kitchen table, where his father was drinking a cup of coffee.

"Here they are," Ben announced. "My grades. Let's see how I did." He opened the letter from the registrar's office and felt a grin stretching across his face as he read the news aloud: "History of Western Civ, B, biology, D, English, A, Spanish, A, phys ed, A. All right! That's better than a 3-point GPA. I'm in for winter quarter!"

"That's great, Benjy," said Bill Stewart with a weak smile. "But what happened in biology?"

"I just couldn't figure out what they guy wanted, Dad. He was pretty disorganized."

"Well I may be just a high school graduate, son, but it would seem to me that good grades in biology would be required for entrance to med school."

"They are, Dad. Don't worry, there aren't going to be anymore D's in science classes." Ben began to bristle. "I realize how important they are."

"As a matter of fact, it's not really biology that I'm worrying about, Benjy. I just don't know how you're going to afford Stanford. You know I haven't had a steady income since I left Jorgensen Steel. Things are tough right now."

"Don't worry about it. I can make it on my own. I'm making ten bucks a day on the dredger. I'll have more than enough saved for winter quarter tuition and room and board by January. I can get a hashing job on campus. I can do it, Dad. You just take care of things here and don't worry about me."

Bill Stewart said nothing as he stared into his coffee cup. Ben noticed his father's pathetic expression but it didn't effect his elation. As far as he was concerned, things were looking great.

"I think I'll call Ellie and see if she's received her grades," said Ben. "I hope she made the cut." He got up and walked to the phone on the wall. He could tell from his father's expression that the man hadn't heard him.

"Dad, I want to call Ellie Rawlings and this is the only phone in the house. Do you have something else you could be doing?"

"Oh, I'm sorry, son. I'll get out of your hair." Bill refilled his coffee cup and headed for the upstairs bathroom.

Ben had a brief conversation with Mary Ellen's mother, supplying one-word answers to her questions. Finally, the young woman came on the line.

"Hi, kiddo. Did you get your grades?" asked Ben.

"Yeah, they came yesterday."

"So how did you do?"

"Well, I went plus 6. So I guess I'm eligible to come back," she responded.

"What did you get in bio?"

"I got a C."

Ben was stunned. "You copied my notes and you got a C? That guy gave me a D."

"What happened?"

"Beats me. Anyway I'm happy that you will be back at Stanford. We're going to have a wonderful…"

"I'm not going back to Stanford, Ben," said Mary Ellen. "I don't think it's the right place for me. I went into Oakland yesterday and picked up an application for Holy Names College. Have you heard of it?"

"Yeah. I've heard of it. It's that women's college by Lake Merritt. But I can't understand how you could turn down the chance to get a Stanford education. Geez, I'll bet there are one hell of a lot of Nobel prize winners teaching at Holy Names," said Ben sarcastically.

"Please understand, Ben, I just think I'll be more comfortable there."

"But what about us? You're my little study buddy. I'm going to miss you."

"I think you're going to study better without me. You'll probably get straight A's if I'm not there to bother you. We can see each other on weekends."

"Well I guess if you're not around where I can keep my eye on you, I would just as soon you attend an all women's college. "I'm going to have to hang up now and get ready for work. Talk to you later. Bye-bye, Ellie."

"Bye, Ben. It's good to hear that you're a little disappointed."

* * *

Natomas Gold Corporation operated several gold dredgers on former farmlands on the south bank of the American River near Folsom. Ben had been initially hired as a laborer but when a vacancy occurred for a stern oiler on one of the "boats" he had readily accepted the opportunity, even though the job was from 4 P.M. until midnight. His hourly pay went from $1.16 to $1.25. His social life was suffering but his bank account was thriving.

As Ben drove his mother's '40 Chevy to work, his phone conversation with Mary Ellen was on his mind. He wasn't terribly disappointed by her decision. Things were really going rather well. He would be going back to the "Farm" in January. There was no radio in the car so he filled the vacuum with his own crooning of *I Want a Sunday Kind of Love.* Then he chuckled and said to himself, "I'll be lucky to get that."

FALL 1950

BEN PARKED THE CAR in front of Bonham's Department Store on Folsom's Main Street. He went into the store, browsed in the music section for awhile and then selected a couple of Benny Goodman singles.

"Are these to be a gift?" the clerk asked as she took Ben's money.

"For me. Birthday present," Ben said. "I just turned eighteen today."

"Happy birthday," the clerk said. "Do you feel like an adult?"

"Not yet, but I will soon. I've got to go over to the drug store now and register for the draft."

"Do you think you'll get called up? Korea?"

"Not much of a chance of that," Ben answered. "I'll apply for a student deferment when I get back to school." He grinned and added, "Stanford."

* * *

In mid-September, the Fifth RCT ended its service with the Twenty-fifth (Tropic Lightning) Division and, after five short days in reserve, was attached to the First Cavalry Division. The combat team was assigned the mission of spearheading the tactical breakout from the Pusan Perimeter in the vicinity of Waegwan, a small town located on the eastern bank of the Naktong River approximately fourteen miles northwest of Taegu.

On the morning of 18 September, the Fifth RCT launched a full regimental attack. For the next twenty-four hours they encountered stiff resistance and then, suddenly, it lessened. Apparently the news of the X Corps' successful landing at Inchon, four days previously, had filtered down to the NKPA company level. The enemy had the U.S. Army in front of him and another horde of American soldiers and marines approaching his rear. It was enough to ruin his day. Lieutenant Colonel Throckmorton was able to establish the regimental command post in Waegwan the evening of the 19th.

At 1800 hours on the 19th, the Fifth Regimental Combat Team was detached from the First Cavalry and assigned to the Twenty-fourth Infantry Division replacing the 34th Infantry Regiment. Only one hundred and eighty-four of the two thousand men of the 34th Infantry that had arrived in Korea in July were still fit for duty. The few survivors were distributed among the division's other two regiments, the 19th and the 21st. Later that evening the Fifth RCT crossed the Naktong River in assault boats, meeting little resistance.

At daylight on 24 September, the combat team attacked northward toward Kumchon. The NKPA 849th Independent Anti-tank Regiment fought a stubborn rearguard action to prevent the Fifth from entering Kumchong until the following day. By nightfall on the 25th the road to Kumchong and the town had been cleared of enemy soldiers and mines. Morale in the Fifth RCT was soaring.

After Kumchong there was a brief lull in the fighting. The Fifth Infantry received two hundred and thirty-two replacements and sixty-nine returned-to-duty personnel along with two hundred additional KATUSA's. Despite these reinforcements, the regiment was still thirteen hundred men below authorized strength.

Throckmorton devoted several days in October to realistic training in combat attack, defense, and withdrawal. The best third of the KATUSA's were integrated into the RCT's line companies and the remainder was transferred to the ROK Army.

Since the liberation of Kumchong, distressing rumors had been circulating throughout the Eighth Army that the job was not done. The North Koreans had been sent packing but the G.I.'s wouldn't be going home. General MacArthur and the politicians in Washington agreed that the two Koreas should be reunited. At 0900 on 9 October, the Eighth Army invaded North Korea. The Fifth RCT remained south of the 38th Parallel until 15 October when sufficient motor fuel could be brought forward.

The plan of attack called for the Eighth Army to advance in the west along the railway line and main highway linking Seoul with the North Korean capital of Pyongyang and for X Corps to make an amphibious landing on North Korea's east coast at Wonsan and march north toward the Chosin Reservoir and the Yalu River. These two independent field commands would be separated by seventy-five miles of high, nearly impenetrable mountains. Impenetrable, that is, to all but the Chinese peasant soldier.

On the morning of 15 October, when the Fifth RCT advanced into North Korea, the Chinese Fourth Field Army crossed the Yalu River to come to the aid of their Communist brethren.

Douglas MacArthur continued to assure President Truman that China would not enter the war.

As the combat team moved northward, supplies dwindled. On 21 October, LTC Throckmorton announced that meals would have to be restricted to two per day or to three meals at two-thirds quantity. By the end of the month, the typical ration was a slice of Spam and a half canteen cup of grapefruit juice twice a day. The regiment had received enough winter sleeping bags for the rifle companies but the tankers, artillerymen and headquarters personnel would have to continue to make due with blankets and ponchos. There was frost on the ground every morning but no winter uniforms had arrived. The X Corps' Wonsan operation had diverted much fuel, equipment and food to the east coast.

* * *

Palmer jerked a piece of toilet paper from his helmet liner band, crumbled some dead leaves in his hand and rolled a smoke. He lit up. The foul tasting mess was not a satisfactory answer to his craving.

He scratched his arm and felt his new stripes. He was a corporal now; a squad leader, the toughest job in the Army. If they were ever to get back up to strength, he would bear full responsibility for the behavior of eleven other men. LTC Throckmorton was being paid a hell of a lot more for dealing with five battalion commanders. He guessed that he'd have to stay in now and work his way up the ranks if he wanted to reduce his workload.

His men were continually griping about the cold and the hunger and the shortage of cigarettes. Eddie Kauahilo dreamed about food, night and day. He spent considerable time roaming the villages foraging for eggs, chickens and beer and, in the few cases where they had something to share, the North Koreans would give it to him. This was in sharp contrast to the South Koreans who wanted big money for their produce.

Rob didn't join the gripe sessions. He'd accepted the fact that army life is a feast or famine situation. He regretted that he couldn't keep his guys happy, but it was enough to make sure that they had functioning weapons, sufficient ammunition and were doing their best to protect their hands and feet from cold injuries. He was proud to assume such tasks and there was certainly no resentment on the part of the other PFCs in the squad. They respected their squad leader, whom they described as "R.A (regular army) all the way."

LTC Throckmorton continued to get reports of Chinese forces in the area. When the RCT captured Taechon on 29 October, two of the prisoners were Chinese Peoples Volunteers. These were the first Chinese troops to be captured in Korea. Throckmorton sent them to the rear, but the folks at Division and higher did not believe they were Chinese. General MacArthur had staked his professional reputation on his firmly stated belief that Red China would not intervene in a lost cause.

From Taechon, the Fifth RCT attacked northwest toward Kusong. The Third Battalion led the advance on 30 October and soon came under mortar and self-propelled artillery fire. Then Throckmorton ordered the First Battalion to come up on the Third's left and flank the stubborn defenders. The enemy withdrew slowly. Later, Sergeant Kang identified many of the dead as Chinese.

Kusong fell after a fierce fight on Halloween. NKPA minefields, small arms and mortar barrages slowed the attack until Air Force B-26s blasted the defenders. That allowed Third Battalion to overrun the burning town. The Fifth RCT suffered eight killed and ten wounded before the end of the day.

On November 1, the regiment attacked northwards up a narrow valley into fierce automatic weapons and mortar fire. Its objective was a road junction a few miles north of Kusong where a combined force of five thousand CCF and NKPA soldiers were dug-in.

That night, Able Company infiltrated through the hills and came in behind a Chinese company in foxholes on the forward slope of a ridgeline. They wiped out the surprised Chinese. By sunset, the combat team had killed approximately four hundred NKPA and CCF soldiers.

Late that afternoon a courier plane dropped LTC Throckmorton a message ordering him to stop the combat team's advance. A few hours later they received another message to "how able" (haul ass) and withdraw to the south. The Eighth Army had unknowingly entered a massive, intricately planned Chinese trap. By mid-November the Eighth Army would face 180,000 Chinese troops.

The Fifth RCT was rushed to Kunu-ri, a small town surrounded by rugged mountains. Kunu-ri straddled an important road junction that had to be held until the battered ROK II Corps could pull its men and equipment from the mountains north and east of town.

The combat team had just arrived around noon and had not yet dug in when the thick fog lifted exposing a mass of Chinese infantry heading their way. The Triple Nickel slammed hundreds of 105-mm high explosive rounds into the ranks of the Chinese. Weapons companies mowed them down with 50-caliber machine guns, 81-mm mortar and 75-mm recoilless rifle fire but on they came. Whenever they could see, Air Force fighters would roar down and strafe and rocket the attacking forces. The defending infantrymen were happy to endure the clink of the shell casings that fell from the skies and hit their helmets. The Fifth RCT's stand at Kunu-ri allowed the Eighth Army to stabilize its hard-pressed lines.

* * *

November 16, was a quiet and uneventful day. Rob Palmer returned from an NCO meeting around noon and pulled the squad together.

"What's up, Rob? Did they tell you when we're going home?" said one of the privates.

"No, there's been no word on that. That's not what I've got to tell you and that is that Sergeant Veenstra was killed this morning," said Rob, choking back a sob.

"That can't be true, Rob. There's been no firing along the line."

"It's true, all right," responded Palmer. "Graves Registration has already picked up the bodies of the sergeant and his driver, Corporal Bly."

"What the hell happened?"

"The report was," explained Palmer, "that they were out in the jeep and hit a land mine. The jeep was hurled over a five-foot mound and dropped into the canyon below. It blew up. Both of 'em were killed instantly."

No one said anything for a few seconds and then Eddie spoke. "Well, after Bloody Gulch we thought that Sergeant Veenstra would live forever. Since then we've learned that nobody's indestructible. I could see him dying during a fire-fight in the middle of pile of dead Gooks but not hitting a mine. It's a fuckin' shame." There was a murmur of agreement as the squad dispersed.

Despite the fact that the regiment suffered nine battle casualties and one hundred and nine cases of severe frostbite during the stand at Kunu-ri, General MacArthur considered the period a lull and directed the Eighth Army to retrace its steps and advance to the Yalu River without delay.

Indian summer hit Korea on Thanksgiving Day when the thermometer rose to a scorching 40 degrees Fahrenheit. Service Company took advantage of the above-freezing temperatures to operate the shower point. Despite the relative warmth of the day, Eddie Kauahilo envied the smaller men in the company who joined the chow line dressed in North Korean winter uniforms that had been liberated from a warehouse during their advance to the Yalu. He confronted the short Hawaiian standing in front of him.

"Hey. Why you guys wear da Gook suit on a warm day?" He enjoyed lapsing into pidgin English when he conversed with one of his Hawaiian compatriots.

"Don' know, Brah. Dey feel good is all. You no got da kine Gook suit?"

"Nah. Warehouse no got my size," countered Eddie. "Gook Army no got to fit big Kanaka like me."

A mess kit heaped with turkey, stuffing, gravy and sweet potatoes soon took some of the sting out of Eddie's feelings of deprivation. In addition there was canned corn, olives, mince pie and candy. In a way though, Eddie could thank the wonderful feast for his exposure to the cold. Shipments of cold weather clothing sat on a loading dock in Pusan so that all available transportation could be used to carry turkeys to the troops for their Thanksgiving dinner.

The men were thankful for the shower and the turkey and for the forty-degree weather but they weren't thankful for the orders that arrived that day. The communication stated: *24th Division will attack west in zone from present position 24Nov50 and destroy enemy forces in zone. Seize line Taesan-dong, Nakchong-jong, Won-ni. Prepare to attack on order to south bank of Yalu River.* The Eighth Army's order of battle from west to east, from Korea Bay to Tokch'on, was: US 24th Division (and 5th RCT), British 27th Commonwealth Brigade, ROK First Division, US 25th Division, US 2nd Division, the Turkish Brigade, and the ROK II Corps.

After dinner, as Eddie cleaned and oiled his M-1, his brooding continued. "Here we go one more time. Every time we go we lose more boys. I hear we're some thousand guys short of TO&E for an infantry outfit. I've got no winter clothes and when there is a shitty job, we get it."

"You got it, Eddie," responded Palmer. "We're a bastard outfit. They're always jerking us around. The big brass don't appreciate us. It's enough to make a guy really proud of his unit." Eddie, not quite sure if he caught Rob's drift, continued griping and preparing for the forthcoming attack.

WINTER 1950

WHEN THE FIFTH RCT left the line of departure, on 24 November, it advanced on the Eighth Army's extreme left flank. There was sporadic, light small arms and mortar fire, but hardly enough to impede their progress. MacArthur's "Home by Christmas" offensive was proceeding nicely in the 24th Division sector.

At dusk on the twenty-fifth, tens of thousands of Chinese infantrymen closed on the American and ROK positions in the center and right of the line. They attacked to the sound of blaring bugles, their way lit by parachute flares. By 26 November, MacArthur realized that he was losing the battle. He changed the name of the "Home by Christmas" offensive to a "reconnaissance in force." At 2200 hours on 27 November, I Corps issued orders by radio to all units to withdraw the following morning.

LTC Throckmorton's plan called for First Battalion to disengage and head south at 0430, 28 November, to an assembly area north of Anju on the Chongchon River. They were to be followed by Second Battalion at 0500. Third Battalion was instructed to cover the disengagement and then proceed south.

There were two bridges spanning the Chongchon River north of Anju. The Fifth RCT was directed to proceed to the bridges and dig-in on the north bank. They were to protect the two spans until the Eighth Army was across.

As Palmer directed the placement of his squad, the afternoon wind whipped him savagely. The temperature dropped to twenty-two degrees below zero, wind chill factor, as the battered remains of the Eighth Army limped across the bridge. He could not remember ever having been so cold. He hoped that eventually the generals would run out of shit details to assign to the Fifth Infantry. He ordered everyone to change into their dry socks and nagged them repeatedly to keep their fingers and toes moving.

The Second Infantry Division had been assigned to serve as rear guard for the withdrawal. But when the Indianhead Division turned to follow the rest of the Eighth Army, they found that the Chinese had surrounded them.

An entire enemy division lay between them and the river. That afternoon the Second Division suffered three thousand casualties, lost most of its equipment and abandoned all of its artillery. The grand old division from Fort Lewis had been rendered combat-ineffective. When word reached the rear that the Second Division had been badly mauled, panicky supply sergeants torched piles of badly needed parkas and other cold weather equipment.

When the few survivors of the 23rd Infantry Regiment had crossed the bridge, Rob received orders to pull his men out of their positions and fall in with the rest of the company.

As he slung his M-1 over his shoulder, he yelled "Time to haul ass, you guys. They're going to blow this bridge."

It began to snow as the freezing men joined the rest of the column and headed south.

Looking back over his shoulder, Eddie said, "I hear that the Chinks that are chasing us are wearing U.S. Army winter uniforms."

"Where did you hear that bullshit, Eddie?" said Rob.

"I heard it from a guy that heard it from another guy in the Triple Nickel that heard it from a forward observer. He said, 'I shit you not'. They're all bundled up in U.S Army parkas."

"Hmm," said Rob, "What we need is a good Chink supply sergeant. They're doin' a hell of lot better job than ours."

Throughout the withdrawal, the combat team's battalions leapfrogged through one another. Upon reaching a piece of key terrain, generally high ground, the advance guard would dismount their trucks and form a perimeter defense. Once the main body and rearguard battalion had passed through their perimeter, the advance guard would assume the mission of rearguard and the process would be repeated. Their destination was Uijongbu, a city south of the Thirty-eighth Parallel.

Along with orders to blow the bridge at Kunu-ri, John Throckmorton had received congratulations on his promotion to the rank of colonel. It would be the first of many promotions in the Fifth RCT.

On 16 December, Colonel Throckmorton sent 24th Division G-1 a request for twenty-two officers and 829 enlisted men to bring the Fifth Infantry up to its authorized strength. The Division G-1 finally agreed to replenish the combat team's ranks with an infusion of replacements. There were plenty of vacant NCO positions for the veterans. Corporal Robert Palmer's positive attitude and good care of the men in his squad had not gone unnoticed. Palmer was bumped up to assistant platoon sergeant. Even Eddie was promoted.

"So, Corporal Kauahilo," said Rob, "I hear you're going to take over the squad."

"You better believe it, man. I've got the power now," boasted Eddie.

"So what are you going to do with all your power?"

"The first responsibility of the squad leader is to kick some ass around here and demand warm clothes and chow for his boys," responded Eddie.

"You really know how to hurt a guy, Eddie."

"Nah. No big t'ing, Rob. You did the best you could for us. I just have the feeling that things are gonna get better. Santa Claus is coming to town."

Later, at a platoon meeting, Colonel Throckmorton's Christmas message was read to the men. He wrote, in part:

As members of the team each of you may well be proud of your accomplishments during the past year. Your individual and collective efforts in training and in five months of combat have established the Fifth Regimental Combat Team in the ranks of the Army's finest. During the coming year it will be our responsibility to maintain the "Fighting Fifth's" reputation for efficiency, discipline and gallantry.

* * *

"So Big Ben," Nick said, pouring another beer from the pitcher. "Still hung up on little Mary Ellen from the College of Homely Dames?"

Ben had been convinced to put his books aside for the evening and relax for a couple of hours at the Oasis in Menlo Park with Nick Shymansky and Carl Butler. Now he wasn't quite sure that he'd made the right decision.

"I really don't know how it'll work out. I didn't see her during vacation. We wrote a few notes and talked on the phone a couple of times. I'm going over to Walnut Creek next weekend and she's coming over for the Frosh Frolic."

"Is she putting out for you?" asked Carl.

"Well, it's not really that kind of a relationship yet," said Ben. "But we have fun."

"Sounds like a waste of time to me," snorted Carl.

"Yeah, you're sure getting a lot lately, aren't you, Butler?" responded Ben, somewhat annoyed.

Nick decided that it was time to change the subject. "So, Ben did you turn in an application for your draft deferment to the Dean's office?"

"Yeah. How about the two of you?"

"We don't have to," said Carl. "We both got into Air Force ROTC. We're deferred unless we flunk out of the program."

"In a way, I kind of wish I didn't have a deferment," said Nick. "I'm not that crazy about school. I think I'm ready to go at any time. They'd probably take my military school background into account and slot me for OCS, anyway."

"Well, it sounds like the pitcher of beer you've almost finished is giving you brain damage, Shymanski," said Ben. "I say let's go back to the Village. It's getting late."

"Okay. Let's go. But there's something I need to pick up first."

Nick "laid rubber" as they pulled out of the Oasis parking lot and tromped on the accelerator once they were headed south on El Camino Real. As he did so, a Palo Alto policeman made a U-turn, flicked on his chase lights and siren and came after them. Nick pushed down heavier on the accelerator.

"Pull over, Nick," pleaded Ben. "You're just going to make things worse."

"No way," he responded. "Those idiots already nailed me for a moving violation this month. One's enough."

As they passed the eucalyptus grove by Stanford Stadium, Nick let up on the gas and pulled to the side of the road. "Aaah Fuck it! Let's see what his problem is."

Ben rolled down his window as the patrolman approached the passenger side of the car.

"I clocked you guys doing sixty right back there." He looked through the window at Nick and said, "Let's have your license, son." Ben relayed Nick's wallet to the officer. The cop made a few notes and then asked to see some identification from Ben and Carl.

"What's this all about, Officer? I wasn't driving," complained Ben.

"We're keeping a list of smart-ass Stanford kids at the department. It's simply a warning. We assume that you're smart enough to keep your nose clean from now on. You understand me?"

"Yeah," said Ben.

"By any chance do you mean 'Yes, sir?' "

"Yes, sir."

In early December Ben had received a notice from the University Housing Office that there would be no on-campus housing for those men who had entered Stanford during summer quarter. He had been assigned to a four-man room at Stanford Village. The university had leased a de-activated, rambling, pavilion-type army hospital several miles north of the campus. Ben shared the former hospital ward with his friends Nick and Carl and another acquaintance, Sherm Kohler, a pre-med student from an up-scale Oakland neighborhood called Piedmont.

Following the December Chinese offensive, there was a dire need for whole blood and plasma in Korea, so on a gloomy Friday in January, the four roommates joined hundreds of Stanford students in a school-wide blood drive. Rows of cots had been set up in the basketball pavilion and Red Cross workers harvested the precious fluid. There was a moment of drama when an Army helicopter landed on the lawn between Encina Hall and the gym and quickly whisked the crates of filled pint bottles to their next destination.

At four in the afternoon, the Freshman Frolic Committee, which included Ben, Carl, and Don Stern, their resident assistant from Stanford Village, was able to get back into the gym and begin decorating for the following evening's dance. The Frolic Committee had booked Louis Armstrong and Ella Fitzgerald for the occasion. It was planned that the students would enter the room through the mouth of a large crepe paper replica of "Satchmo's face." Ben and Carl spent several hours stuffing crepe paper into the chicken wire base for the face. When they finished they were rather pleased with their creation.

Mary Ellen arrived at around noon on Saturday. She was wearing one of her father's white shirts, Levis rolled up below her knees, white bobby sox and saddle shoes. She had lost her summer tan but she looked great to Ben. They greeted each other with a quick, self-conscious hug.

"Gosh, it's good to see you," Ben said. "How long has it been?"

"It's been a whole week, silly. You know, Ben Stewart, weekend's are a good time to hit the books."

"The books will be there. I don't want to think about studying. I asked you over here to go to the dance, not nag me about studying."

"Dance, that's all?" she asked.

"That plus whatever else you'll let me get away with."

Mary Ellen smiled and said, "C'mon. We need to check in with Miss Ostergard. She insists on interviewing all overnight guests and their dates."

The couple entered Roble Hall and found the office of Abigail Ostergard, the Director. The older woman assured Mary Ellen that she was welcome to stay but that she would have to abide by the rules of the residence hall. Then she glanced threateningly at Ben, who nodded that he understood. Since it was Saturday night, the front door would remain unlocked until 2:30 A.M. If she weren't in by that time, it would reflect badly upon her friends, Marge and Boop, and she would not be welcomed back again to Roble Hall.

The sky was cloudy but the rain was holding off, so Ben and Mary Ellen walked up to Lake Lagunita. The lake had been dry during the fall but had been replenished by the winter rains. They sat on the beach and talked until Mary Ellen complained that she was getting chilly. As Ben walked her back to Roble, it occurred to him that the complaint about "getting chilly" might have been an appeal to cuddle a bit. He was angry with himself for blowing the opportunity.

Ben and Mary Ellen double-dated with Carl and Boop. The theme for the Frosh Frolic was *Mardi Gras*. The dress was Stanford informal rather than the elaborate costumes that one associates with the Mardi Gras celebration in New Orleans. The men wore blazers, ties, slacks and penny loafers and the young ladies wore skirts that reached the required six inches below the knee, cashmere sweaters and small strands of pearls.

The foursome was thrilled to be in the presence of Lady Ella and the great Satchmo. During Ella's vocals, Louis Armstrong kept interjecting remarks like, "Come on, Lucy. Let's get juicy." The dancers loved the performance of the two jazz greats.

After the dance, Carl dropped Ben and Mary Ellen off at her car so that they could have some time to themselves before the 2:30 lockout. The young couple had pretty much exhausted their topics of conversation during the afternoon and evening, so they whiled away the minutes keeping each other warm and listening to Jimmy Lyons on the car radio.

"I think we ought to try and get together every weekend," said Ben.

"Well that would be nice but we'd probably both flunk out." said Mary Ellen.

"But it would be worth it."

"Not if you lose your deferment," said Mary Ellen. "You'd be shipped off to Korea and I'd be short one boyfriend." She pulled his face down close to hers and gave him a long kiss.

When they came up for air, Ben made his throat as gravelly as he could and said, "C'mon, Lucy, let's get juicy."

Mary Ellen laughed. "What makes you think I'm not. C'mon, Benjy, it's 2:25."

"Just one more kiss," he pleaded.

"At the door," she promised.

* * *

The Dean of Men looked up from his desk. Then he looked down at the sheet of paper in front of him.

"Yes, Mr. Stewart, what can I do for you?"

"I received a letter from your office, Dr. Baugh, suggesting that I'm in danger of losing my 1-S draft status, if my grades don't come up."

"What seems to be the problem? What's giving you difficulty?"

"Chemistry and physics, primarily."

"Maybe pre-med is not your cup of tea."

Ben bristled at the Dean's suggestion. "No, that's not it at all. I really want to study medicine. I know that I'll be a good med student and a good doctor, if I can only do something about the physical sciences. Is there any way of giving me a chance to bring my grades up before notifying my draft board. Probationary status or something."

"Not that I know of, Mr. Stewart. The best way for you to stay out of the Army is to buckle down and do something about your grades," said the older man.

"Well, I've got a question about grades. Stanford limits its admissions to folks who are in the upper five percent of their high school classes and then grades them on the curve. That means that a lot of Stanford students who are used to getting A's come here and have to settle for B's, C's and even D's. Is that taken into account when you decide whether to notify my draft board? If I were down the road at San Jose State, I would very likely be pulling down A's and B's and wouldn't be in this mess."

"Do you want to transfer out of this "mess" and go to San Jose State?"

"No, that's not the point. It really doesn't seem equitable. I mean with the draft board and all."

"The point is, Mr. Stewart, that you are not living up to the agreement that we have with Selective Service. As a matter of fact they don't even have to listen to our recommendation for deferment, although they usually do. If you don't want your education interrupted by the Army, you'd better do something about it. Have you talked to the professors in the classes where you're having the most difficulty?"

"No. What good would that do? They'd probably just tell me to hit the books harder. Well, thanks, Dr. Baugh, for your time."

"Not at all, Good luck, Stewart."

* * *

In every letter from home, Ben was asked whether he had investigated the various Reserve Officer Training Corps programs at Stanford. It was common knowledge that students enrolled in ROTC programs were exempt from the draft as long as they remained in school. Ben had checked with the Navy and Air Force programs and found that their rosters were full. They were not taking new enrollments until fall. He wasn't interested in the Army ROTC.

During the week following his meeting with the Dean of Men, Ben kept an appointment with a recruiter for the Marine Corps' Platoon Leader Class. The young officer, resplendent in his dress blues and reeking of cologne, explained the details of the program.

"The PLC program won't impact your study time here at Stanford at all, Mr. Stewart," explained the recruiter. "There are no classes or drills during the school year. If you are accepted to the program you will attend summer training at Quantico, Virginia for the next three summers. When you graduate from college, you will be commissioned a second lieutenant in the Marine Corps Reserve."

"Then what?" asked Ben.

Then you'll have weekly meetings and further summer training but you'll remain safe from the draft. Of course you could be called for active duty at anytime during the eight years following graduation. But, we can't promise that since the Korean conflict is winding down."

Ben nodded that he understood while the young marine inspected him carefully. "Tell me, Mr. Stewart, why do you want to be a marine?"

"Well, I haven't given it a lot of thought, really. The Air Force and Navy programs, on this campus, are full. I need to do something about a deferment until I finish school. I guess if I have to be in the military, I'd rather be a marine officer than an army private."

The recruiter, rustling some papers, looked like he was having indigestion. "Thanks for dropping by, Mr. Stewart. I'll submit your application along with my recommendation." The two young men had been mutually unimpressed.

Fortunately, Ben had a good outlet for the stress generated by the physical sciences and his shaky deferment status. He had signed up for the track and field team and reported to work-outs each week-day afternoon at Angel Field. In his senior year in high school, he had taken first place in the Sac-Joaquin Conference 180-yard low hurdles event. His high school coach had written a very glowing letter of recommendation to the Athletic Director at Stanford.

When Ben turned out for track at the beginning of winter quarter, he was surprised to find that the Stanford coaching staff did not treat him with the level of respect that he had anticipated. In fact, they actually ignored him during his afternoon workouts and he made no overtures toward them. He worked out his own training schedule based on his high school program. Two upper-classmen, Bob Mathias and Bobby Bryant, took him under their wing and saw that he got some instruction and encouragement.

* * *

General Walton Walker, Eighth Army Commander, was killed in a jeep accident on 23 December. General Matthew Ridgeway was summoned from Washington to take command. Ridgeway was disappointed to find that the Eighth Army, on the whole, was a demoralized wreck. He quietly relieved numerous physically exhausted commanders and replaced them with fresh, innovative and vigorous men.

Ridgeway brought a new tactical and operational perspective to Korea. In his opinion, Korea was excellent tank country. He viewed the tank's mission as that of a mobile, armored assault gun that could shrug off hits while battering the enemy's defenses. He demanded that his commanders commit their tanks and infantry as teams. He beefed up the American and

ROK artillery, believing that too many guns had been disgracefully lost during the withdrawal.

The new Eighth Army commander was appalled by the living conditions of his soldiers and took immediate steps to increase supplies of tents and cold weather clothing. He forbade his units from establishing bivouacs and command posts inside vermin-infested homes and buildings. General Ridgeway restored the American soldier's confidence in his ability to fight the Chinese. His leadership would turn things around.

On New Year's Eve, the Chinese crossed the Thirty-eighth Parallel and invaded South Korea. They directed their main effort against the Eighth Army's left flank because that sector had been assigned to ROK divisions. The ROK positions promptly collapsed. Ridgeway reluctantly issued orders to withdraw.

* * *

When the Chinese divisions hit the U.S. Twenty-fourth Division on opening night of the offensive, the First and Third Battalions of the Fifth RCT advanced northward, determined to hold their blocking position long enough to cover the 24th Division's withdrawal. The Second Battalion was placed under the command of the hard-pressed 27th British Commonwealth Brigade.

On New Year's Day the sky suddenly cleared and waves of FEAF fighter-bombers caught the Chinese advancing in the open. In the next five days the Air Force flew twenty-five hundred sorties; bombing, strafing and rocketing the exposed Chinese infantry. They inflicted an estimated eight thousand CCF casualties. The 555th Field Artillery, using white phosphorous shells to adjust their fire, joined the carnage whenever the Chinese got too close.

The march south was nearly six weeks old when George Company reached the outskirts of Seoul. Although he didn't express it, Rob Palmer was becoming as tired and angry as the rest of the men in the platoon. He resented having to retreat but there were just too many Chinese and too few G.I.'s.

Eddie Kauahilo had been experiencing a bad cough for a couple of weeks. It had become so bad that he felt like his back was breaking whenever he went into a coughing spasm. Cough syrup laced with codeine gave him momentary relief. He obviously was running a fever and the medic was trying to deal with it with APC pills.

Colonel Throckmorton had continued to order the practice of leapfrogging throughout the withdrawal. When the Fifth RCT entered Seoul, Third Battalion was the vanguard. The capital city was a smoldering heap of ashes. The destruction of familiar landmarks rendered the advance party's maps useless. Fortunately the battalion chaplain had worked in the city prior to the war. Chaplain Dick Oostenink took the point and led the RCT south to the Han River.

General MacArthur had directed General Ridgeway to not risk the destruction of the Eighth Army in a futile defense of Seoul. The army crossed the Han, blew the bridges, paused momentarily and then continued marching south. The Fifth RCT stopped and set up a blocking position at Changhowan-ni on the Thirty-seventh Parallel. They had retrogressed three hundred miles since November 28.

Replacements began to arrive in increasing numbers, with five hundred and three new men joining the unit on 21 January alone. Earlier in the month, Sergeant Palmer had been temporarily dispatched to the rear to help train the new troops.

When Palmer returned to G Company, he discovered that Eddie Kauahilo had been diagnosed with pneumonia and had been evacuated to the Thirty-fifth Station Hospital in Kyoto, Japan. He was also informed that his platoon sergeant had received a battlefield commission and that Rob had inherited the platoon. During an NCO briefing he learned that the company, reinforced with tanks, heavy weapons and a couple of squads from the battalion intelligence and reconnaissance platoon would be patrolling north of the MLR on the following morning.

When George Company reached Inchon, after making no contact with the enemy, Palmer's patrol was ordered to advance to the south bank of the Han. At that point they were the northern-most United Nations unit in Korea. They captured two Chinese infiltrators and rejoined the company.

The following day the entire Second Battalion along with the 7th Cavalry Regiment and supported by Tank Company and the 555th FAB conducted a reconnaissance in force north of the MLR. They made no contact whatsoever with the Chinese. The commander of the Twenty-fourth Division was so encouraged by this report that he directed the Fifth RCT to move to Inchon and prepare to attack northward toward a series of ridgelines on the far side of a wide valley.

Colonel Throckmorton studied the snow-covered terrain from the rear seat of an L-5 Piper Cub. He would order the First Battalion to seize Hills 475 and 406. Second Battalion was assigned Hill 256. Third Battalion would remain in reserve.

At 0500 on 29 January, Palmer moved among his men and gently shook those squad leaders who were still asleep. The new replacements would not need waking. They had lain awake most of the night wondering what awaited them on Hill 256. Rob reminded the squad leaders to check weapons and ammunition and to ensure that everyone was equipped with field jacket hoods and gloves. It promised to be a cold hike.

George Company, lining up on both sides of the dirt road, moved out at 0730. The ground fog was very thick and concealed the column of troops wending its way to the northwest. The quiet men, each one occupied with his own thoughts, were able to proceed safely for the entire morning. At times, patches of snow slowed the advance.

The fog lifted at 1330 revealing the two attacking battalions quickly moving from marching files to a skirmish line. Rob hustled the men of First Platoon into line abreast of Second Platoon and the two groups led the attack. The company commander, his staff and Weapons Platoon followed closely and Third Platoon brought up the rear.

As soon as they came within range, Chinese automatic weapons and small arms began to chatter. The platoon leader was killed instantly and command of the platoon shifted to Palmer. He yelled at the men to take cover until the supporting artillery fires and air strikes had had a chance to stifle the machine guns. By nightfall George Company had secured its objective on the lower part of a long ridgeline emanating from Hill 256.

The artillery and air support made little noticeable impact on the fortified hill. Word came that First Battalion had cleared their two objectives by 1630 but Second Battalion was still facing stiff resistance. With darkness approaching, the men dug in as best they could in the frozen ground.

The thick ground fog returned on the morning of the 30th. By now the guns of the 555th FAB were well registered on Hill 256 and fired intermittently during the morning to encourage the Chinese to keep their heads down.

Company E was assigned the mission of passing through George Company and attacking and occupying the hill that afternoon. Easy Company hesitated just long enough for the FEAF to scorch the top of the hill with napalm and then began their ascent. They fought to within a hundred and fifty yards of the crest of the hill by nightfall, dug in for the night and fought off repeated enemy probes. The following morning, in bitter hand-to-hand fighting, they chased the Chinese from the hill.

During the first week in February, the Fifth RCT fought the Chinese near Sobuk. The CCF were well fortified in bunkers that tunneled from the rear to the front of the ridgelines. The combat team gained ground slowly up the steep hills. They depended on accurate 75-mm recoilless rifle fire to knock out the enemy's automatic weapons. FEAF fighter-bombers did a good job of preventing the Chinese from reinforcing those defending the ridges.

The Chinese resisted for more than a week and then, on 9 February, they suddenly disappeared. The next day, Inchon and Kimpo Airfield were back in UN hands. On the 16th, the combat team was temporarily attached to the 25th Infantry Division for the duration of an offensive, the mission of which was to cut enemy supply lines and destroy all enemy forces in their zones of action. The attack warranted and received massive and destructive artillery support. When the Fifth RCT reached the Han River they discovered four to five hundred dead Chinese lying in demolished bunkers and foxholes.

The combat team crossed the Han River on 5 March and beat off an enemy counterattack that night. They were heavily engaged with CCF forces on 6 March near Yangpyong. Then enemy resistance seemed to diminish and by 10 March the Eighth Army had succeeded in outflanking Seoul. The combat team went into reserve until the 16th. During that period of rest, Eddie Kauahilo returned from his hospital stay in Japan.

SPRING 1951

BEN WALKED over to the bulletin board at Angel Field. He had just completed his first workout since returning from spring vacation. He found the roster for Saturday's dual meet with San Jose State and read the list three times. His name wasn't on it. He stormed off the track and headed for the athletic building. He encountered the track coach in the hall outside of his office.

"Coach, I noticed that my name wasn't on the roster for the San Jose State meet."

"What is your name and what's your event?" asked the older man.

"I'm Ben Stewart. I run the two-twenty low hurdles."

The coach scanned his clipboard. "Have you run a full flight of the two-twenty lows?"

"Not yet. No one asked me to. That's the problem. I've really had to do my own thing around here."

"Were you here during spring break, Stewart?"

"No, I went home."

"Well, the rest of the team remained here preparing for the San Jose meet. That's when we made the event assignments."

"That's news to me," Ben said, as his voice became louder. "How was I supposed to find out about that?"

"It seems that everybody else did. You're going to miss the San Jose State meet, Stewart. But if you do a better job of reading the bulletin board and showing us what you can do, there should be plenty of opportunities to run hurdles before the season is over."

Ben turned without saying a word and headed for the shower room. He was really angry. "Screw the track team," he thought. "I can put my afternoons to better use." He showered and turned in his red and white uniform, sweat suit and spikes. He still had time to drop track and enroll in another P.E. class before it would affect his grades for the quarter.

After dinner Ben called Mary Ellen to tell her about his run-in with the track coach and that his weekend schedule had changed so they would be able to see each other after all.

"I'm sorry, Ben," she said. "I thought you had a track meet this weekend, so I made other plans."

Ben was tempted to ask what her plans were but decided that he really didn't want to know. He hung up after promising to call back at mid-week.

* * *

On 18 March, Palm Sunday, the Fifth RCT resumed climbing hills. King Company met stiff resistance on the 19th. Two days later the combat team was relieved in place by the 35th Infantry Regiment and the Turkish Brigade. They withdrew a short distance to rest and reorganize and then resumed the attack at 0800 on Good Friday, the morning of the 23rd.

The mission assigned to Second and Third Battalions was to secure a series of ridges and destroy all enemy forces in the area. First Battalion remained in reserve. The two assault units secured all objectives by noon and a counterattack against Third Battalion was repulsed by 1330.

When darkness came, Chinese artillery and mortar rounds slammed into the Third Battalion. An attack around midnight knocked a K Company platoon out of its position. The platoon counterattacked and was back in place by 0430.

At dawn, the exhausted GI's moved forward again. Air strikes and artillery blasted a path for the infantry. Efforts by Fox Company to seize Hill 814 were hurled back until the Chinese withdrew from the hill before dawn on Easter morning, March 25.

The Fifth RCT continued northward, taking one contested hill after another until they had pushed the Chinese back across the Thirty-eighth Parallel. The rearguard of the CCF 226th Regiment, 76th Division, 26th Army suffered heavy losses, primarily from air strikes and artillery fire, as they endeavored to screen the arrival of fresh CCF armies gathering in North Korean assembly areas in preparation for a new offensive.

At the end of March, the Eighth Army stood poised on Line Idaho, just south of the Thirty-eighth Parallel. Colonel Throckmorton established his command post at Pisi-gol. Then on 5 April the RCT moved north to Phase Line Kansas and relieved the 21st Infantry on the line. This new line commanded high ground north of the Thirty-eighth Parallel and included, in its center, the large water barrier of the Hwach'on Reservoir. Line Kansas ran 115 miles from Munsan-ni on the Imjin River to Yangyang on the Sea of Japan. It served as a base of operations to threaten the Chinese build-up in the Iron Triangle, a heavily fortified valley surrounded by Ch'orwan, Kumwha and Pyonggang.

Army Secretary Frank Pace visited the front on 12 April. Shortly after his arrival at "Domino," the code name for Colonel Throckmorton's command post, a call came to the regimental switchboard asking for Frank

Pace. The operator's initial response was that there wasn't anyone in the Fifth RCT by that name. Fortunately the error was caught and moments later Pace was informed that General Allen, the Eighth Army Chief of Staff, had been trying to contact him. Pace was soon on the line with General Allen in Taegu. Allen was relaying a message from Washington. Pace was instructed to fire MacArthur.

Secretary Pace ushered General Ridgeway outside in the midst of a hailstorm and informed him that he, Matthew Ridgeway, was now supreme commander in the Pacific Theater. A week later, Douglas MacArthur delivered his "old soldiers never die" speech to Congress.

The relief of General MacArthur was not as newsworthy an event among the GI's as it was on the home front. Generals come and generals go. It doesn't make a damn bit of difference. However, there was an exciting rumor circulating throughout the regiment. There was much talk of an imminent rotation policy. If it were true, those soldiers who were deployed from Schofield Barracks in July 1950 would soon be leaving Korea. Sergeant Palmer was told to submit a list of men from the platoon that would be eligible for rotation.

One afternoon, Rob returned from a briefing at battalion. Gathering the men around him, he said that he had good news and bad news. There was a chorus of groans amid a sprinkling of "What's up, Sarge?"

"It looks like the scuttlebutt about a rotation policy is really true. I've been asked to submit a list of you guys who deployed from Schofield last July. You'll be the first to leave." He looked around at the faces and realized that his list would be short. Less than half of the men were from the original platoon and many of them were back on duty after recovering from wounds.

"And the bad news is that we're going to pack up and head north again," whined a disgruntled PFC.

"Actually, it's worse than that," replied Palmer. "Colonel Throckmorton has been offered a new job as an aide to General Collins at Eighth Army Headquarters and he's going to take it. His replacement is a guy named Williams or Wilson or something."

"Never heard of no battalion commander named Williams or Wilson in the Fifth," observed one of the men.

"He's not from the Fifth," responded Palmer. "All they told me was that he's a West Pointer and his combat experience was with an airborne outfit."

"Has he commanded a regiment?"

"Apparently not," said Palmer.

"Why didn't they give the job to our battalion CO, Colonel Ward?"

"Colonel Ward has been promoted to regimental exec. I guess he just didn't have enough pull with General Ridgeway to get the top job. At least the new colonel will have somebody close by who knows what he's doing."

"Shee-it! Put me at the top of your rotation list, Rob," said Kauahilo. "Colonel Throckmorton is the reason most of us are still alive. I don't want to work for some green West Point ring-knocker."

"Colonel Throckmorton is a ring-knocker, Eddie."

"Yeah, but he's a straight-leg infantryman, not some airborne fairy. Please put my Kanaka ass on the next boat to Hawaii nei."

Palmer turned and walked away, putting an end to the conversation. He, too, placed West Point graduates and airborne soldiers in the same category as warm beer and wet toilet paper but the brass had their reasons for making certain decisions and who was he to question them. As for the rotation policy, he yearned for the comforts of civilization but he couldn't help worry about the fate of the regiment in future battles. The draining of experienced men from its units would leave the war in the hands of draftees; young men whose only interest was self-survival. God help them!

* * *

"Ben, old buddy, if you're invited to pledge SAE, say yes. You'd be a fool not to join us." Nick Shymanski had invited his former roommate to dinner at his fraternity house.

"Yeah? Why is that?"

"Number one because Carl and I are here. Number two, it's the closest house to the Quad, so you can get a couple of minutes more sleep in the morning. Number three…Edna's a great cook…

"The way I see it," interrupted Ben, "Number one, I'd probably get less studying done. Number two, the ramped up social life would require more bucks. At Toyon Hall, the afternoons are quiet and I can study. I really need quiet afternoons and evenings to study since I want to see Ellie on the weekends."

"…Number four," continued Nick, "we have a lot of parties with the women's houses here and the sororities at San Jose State. We'll fix you up with a local lady and you'll save time and money. No more trips to the East Bay. No more wasted weekends. The brothers will see to that, Ben. Oh, and you can hash at the house to reduce your board bill."

Ben was skeptical about the benefits of fraternity life but Nick had him half convinced. He thought about it as he walked back to his dormitory room. When two of the older members of the house dropped by his room a couple of days later and invited Ben to join Sigma Alpha Epsilon, he readily accepted.

* * *

The Fifth RCT dug in around nightfall on 22 April on a six thousand meter front in the vicinity of Unjimal. The MLR, manned by the First and Second Battalions, straddled a narrow valley between two rugged ridgelines. The broken nature of the terrain made it nearly impossible for the companies to connect. Easy Company, on the extreme left, tied in with King Company of the 19th Infantry while Able Company on the extreme right tied in with the ROK 6th Division. One rifle platoon from Item Company was dug in on an isolated hilltop about two thousand yards to the rear of First Battalion to cover the right flank in the likelihood that the South Koreans would bug-out.

The razorback ridgelines, covered with dense vegetation, reduced the visibility of the defending riflemen. One platoon of Sherman tanks and one of 4.2-inch mortars was attached to each of the forward battalions. The Third Battalion and the 555th FAB were on the valley floor, twelve hundred yards south of the MLR. The Triple Nickel had hastily registered its defensive fires. If needed the Third Battalion would face several hours of hard climbing before they could reach the MLR; not exactly what one would call a rapid reaction force.

* * *

Second Battalion's deployment began with Easy Company at the top of Hill 795 and moved downhill to the east with Fox in the center and George on the right where they tied into the left flank of First Battalion on the valley floor. The position seemed very vulnerable to Palmer and he moved back and forth urging the men to dig fast and deep.

"Do you think we're going to get hit, Sarge?" inquired a recent replacement.

"Probably, but there's nothing to sweat. We've got Fox on our left and Charlie Company on our right. They're all good men. The guys I worry about are the ones in Able Company. They have the ROK's on their right and can't even tie in with them because of the terrain. The Chinks will head straight for that hole in the line and the ROK's will run as soon as they smell them coming."

At 1835, Chinese 150-mm artillery and 120-mm mortar rounds began to drop around the company positions and up and down the line. Three hours later, Chinese infantrymen were spotted moving south along the ridge toward Hill 795. The platoon manning Second Battalion's outpost scampered back to the MLR.

As darkness fell, Palmer could hear the racket from isolated fire fights up the hill to the left as Chinese patrols probed Second Battalion. At 2120 the men heard the alarming sound of bugles and, within seconds, twenty thousand Chinese infantrymen slammed into the U.S. Twenty-fourth Infantry Division, which was comprised of the 19th and 21st Infantry Regiments and the Fifth Regimental Combat Team.

In the light of the full moon, men from Second Battalion could see hundreds of peasant soldiers descending the hill, moving through the underbrush, and driving straight for the boundary between Fox and George Companies. After fifteen minutes of exploding grenades, the chatter of burp guns and the crack of rifles, the Chinese wedge had penetrated between the two companies of GI's. Fox Company mounted a counterattack and restored the line.

At the top of the hill, 19th Infantry's K Company was soon overrun leaving Easy Company of the Fifth RCT dangerously exposed. The men of Palmer's platoon could hear a terrible fire fight on their left but could see no targets in the densely wooded, broken terrain. In a few minutes a handful of survivors came running into Second Battalion's positions yelling that the Chinese were right behind. Five minutes later the Chinese hit Easy Company from three sides. The company stood its ground killing scores of enemy soldiers with rifles, BAR's and machine guns.

After an hour of steady fighting, the MLR began to buckle. When it became obvious that the CCF had enveloped the combat team's left flank in great strength, LTC Wilson ordered Second Battalion to withdraw down the hill. Company E's second platoon was directed to cover the withdrawal. It was to pull back as soon as it had run out of machine gun ammunition.

Around midnight, however, it became apparent that the combat team was no longer in danger of being surrounded. Both flanks had been secured. Third Battalion, saddled with weapons, ammunition, water, rations and equipment, climbed to the top of the western ridgeline and occupied blocking positions behind the Second Battalion companies on the line. Easy Company was still in position but had lost at least fifty men since it had been surrounded the previous evening.

Intense fighting continued on both ridgelines until 0915, when the 24th Division commander ordered the Fifth RCT to withdraw through the 21st Infantry and occupy an assembly area in the rear. King Company covered the withdrawal from a high point on the western ridgeline.

As the Fifth Infantry awaited orders, LTC Wilson knew that it was only a matter of time before the combat team would be covering the withdrawal of the 24th Division from the deteriorating situation on the MLR. The First and Second Battalions pushed patrols forward on 24 April to identify possible blocking positions. The Third Battalion dug in on high ground east of Ukkalgye to protect the eastern flank of the main supply route from Chinese units moving south through the shattered ROK 6th Division's sector. All through the day the 555th FAB provided artillery support for the hard-pressed 19th and 21st Regiments.

Shortly before midnight, strong Chinese units skirted the right flank of the 24th Division. With the collapse of the 6th ROK Division, there existed a thirteen thousand meter gap between the right flank of the 24th Division and the left flank of the First Marine Division. There had also been a penetration on the left flank between the 24th and 25th Divisions.

General Van Fleet, the new commander of the Eighth Army, ordered withdrawal to Line Lincoln, a few miles north of Seoul. The plan was to have the 19th and 21st Infantry Regiments pass through the Fifth RCT and then the combat team would serve as divisional rearguard for the withdrawal. The Third Battalion remained on top of its hill east of the MSR. The Second Battalion with Tank Company, Fifth Infantry, and Company D, 6th Tank Battalion moved north a short distance to block a possible Chinese advance down the valley floor. The First Battalion moved out at 0300 to occupy a blocking position on a hilltop on the western side of the main supply route.

Upon withdrawal, the Third Battalion would take the point and Second Battalion would serve as rear guard. They waited throughout the morning for the 19th and 21st Regiments, who were withdrawing under pressure, to pass through them.

As they waited, several men of George Company observed troops moving past them on the high ridge that ran parallel to the road south. Rob Palmer approached Eddie Kauahilo to see why the big squad leader was pointing frantically to the east. Then he saw the cause of the commotion. Their right flank was being enveloped by elements of the CCF 60th Division. He glanced to his left and saw the same scene taking place along the western ridge. The news was quickly relayed through the channels to regiment S-2 but the intelligence officer said that there was nothing to worry about. As far as he knew there was no evidence that the Chinese were conducting such a maneuver.

"So what's the skinny, Rob?" said Kauahilo.

"S-2 says not to worry. Says they're probably just some refugees trying to keep one jump ahead of the Chinks."

"They're not refugees," observed Eddie. "Refugees don't wear green uniforms."

"I agree," replied Palmer, "but they'll run smack into Third Battalion in a little bit. By now the Third will have dug in on some high ground south of here."

But that was not the case. LTC Wilson was not familiar with Colonel Throckmorton's practice of leapfrogging the battalions during a withdrawal. His orders were to have the column push straight south and he made no plans for protection on the flanks. Unimpeded the Chinese columns continued until they reached Pisi-gol where they set up an ambush on both sides of the road.

It was after 1700 before the soldiers of George Company were ordered to climb on the back of six Patton tanks of D Company, 6th Tank Battalion and ride south. They were the last company to leave that day's position and were unaware that the middle of the column was just minutes away from receiving intense automatic weapons fire from both sides of the road.

When Major Baker, the First Battalion commander, reached the pass near Pisi-gol, the Chinese sprung their ambush. His driver died as the jeep turned over. Infantrymen piled out of their trucks and tried to form for a counterattack while artillerymen tried to unlimber their 105's. The Triple Nickel's gunners died next to their guns. The scattered efforts by the infantrymen lacked coordination and artillery support. They were quickly picked off by the Chinese.

As the column ground to a halt, Palmer could hear the rattle of small arms fire to the south. He jogged over to a point in the road where Sergeant Kang was talking to some refugees that were heading north. Kang nodded to Palmer as he approached.

"These folk say they not go south, Sergeant Rob. They walk south this morning but run into many Chinese near Pisi-gol. They say they go home."

Suddenly men were yelling and remounting the Pattons. Little was known other than that there was a roadblock and First Battalion was in dire straits. Their task was to fight their way through the block and re-open the road.

The mounted infantry pushed forward until they began receiving Chinese mortar and automatic weapons fire. Palmer had no difficulty convincing the platoon that the time had come to abandon their perches on the tanks and take cover. The men jumped down and began returning fire to both sides of the road. SFC Young, one of the charter members from Schofield, climbed into a half-track armed with quad-50's and poured fifty-caliber machine gun fire into the Chinese until the vehicle took three direct hits from mortar fire.

Colonel Wilson, CO of the Fifth RCT, and LTC Stuart of the 555th FAB had gone forward to investigate the roadblock at the mouth of the pass. Wilson had no idea what could be done to save his command. Then Stuart remembered that there was a dirt road that led west from the main supply route (MSR) that had been improved by the 72nd Engineers during the previous month. Wilson contacted Major Baker to confirm if the alternate route was still open and, after checking it out, Baker responded that as far as he could tell the Chinese had not sealed it off. Wilson ordered the combat team to break contact and take the alternate route.

George Company and the six tanks retained their job as rear guard. They stayed until the survivors of First Battalion and the Triple Nickel had cleared the trap. The pressure became more intense as there were fewer and fewer GI's to provide return fire. Finally they were alone and it was time to mount up and leave. They withdrew under cover of darkness.

As they headed west and entered a cut in the road the lead tank was hit by a bazooka round and burst into flames. The infantrymen quickly abandoned the other five tanks and sought cover, directing their fire toward muzzle flashes on the hillside above them.

The five surviving tanks tried to bypass the burning leader but, they too, were hit by bazooka rounds and set on fire. Their crew members were killed by automatic weapons fire as they attempted to crawl through the hatches.

Palmer, realizing that little could be done for the unfortunate tankers, found Eddie Kauahilo and his squad and directed the small group to run between the burning tanks and the bank until they were clear of the cut. As tracer bullets snapped the air around them, they ran across a fallow rice paddy and eventually stumbled on the dirt road that headed south, paralleling the ambush route.

It was well after midnight when the exhausted band of GI's ran into a First Battalion outpost and knew that they had made it home alive. At the company command post, Palmer was able to contact the Second Battalion to report his return and to account for his twelve survivors. Following that he curled up on the ground and slept for four hours. This was a remarkable feat considering the coolness of the early morning hours and the fact that his sleeping bag had been incinerated at sun-up when the Air Force finally arrived and destroyed the tanks, artillery and vehicles that had been abandoned in, what would come to be known as, "Death Valley."

* * *

The spirit of the Chinese soldier cracked toward the end of April. His confidence collapsed in the face of overwhelming American firepower and inadequate food supplies. Approximately seventy thousand CCF troops had fallen killed or wounded in the spring offensive. Thousands of their comrades perished from exhaustion, starvation and disease. Ignoring their plight, Chairman Mao directed his commanders to launch another major offensive.

As Mao's armies prepared for another massive assault on the Eighth Army's line, the men of the Fifth RCT had little time to lick their wounds after Death Valley. On 4 May they received orders to establish a regimental-sized outpost line of resistance in the vicinity of Masogu-ri, a rubble-strewn village approximately three miles forward of the 24th

Division's sector of the MLR. Each battalion was deployed on a hilltop astride the Pukhan Valley. Their mission was to seek out the enemy, attempt to determine his plan and to deceive him as to the location of the division main line of resistance.

During the first half of May, Rob Palmer led four patrols north of the OPLR without making contact with the CCF. On the 15th, the young sergeant's final patrol, a Chinese soldier strolled up to the squad of GI's, with his hands on his head, and made it known that he had information to trade for rice and cigarettes. Sergeant Kang determined that the man was a member of the 191st Division, 64th CCF Army.

According to the hungry soldier, his unit had been fighting in Korea just since February but had been badly mauled by the ROK First Division near Seoul. They were now currently massing for an offensive against the Fifth RCT.   Sergeant Kang accompanied the young Chinese to 24th Division G-2 where he was interrogated further before being transported to the prisoner-of-war pen on Koje-do, a small island off the southeastern coast of the peninsula.

Forty-eight hours passed before the prisoner's information became a reality. At 0015 on 17 May, Love and Item Companies reported that they were under small arms fire.

At 0130, the platoon manning George Company's outpost and listening post, came in with a strange report. They had observed a long column of enemy soldiers coming down the road mounted on Siberian ponies. They estimated that it was at least a battalion of mounted infantry. At first the rest of the company wondered what their buddies had been sniffing but the lingering light from a few mortar flares revealed the rare sight. Once discovered, the Chinese dismounted their Mongolian ponies and the battle was joined.

After two hours of fighting, Colonel Wilson contacted division headquarters and requested that the Fifth RCT be allowed to withdraw to the MLR. General Bryan passed the request up the line to IX Corps G-3, Colonel Kunzig, who replied, "Hold until daylight and further instructions will be issued." Major General William Hoge, IX Corps Commander, was concerned that a night withdrawal might turn into a disaster. He reiterated that it was Army doctrine to avoid night withdrawals. He ordered the combat team to draw into tight perimeters and hold their positions until daylight.

The most intense fighting occurred about 0530. The night sky was brilliantly illuminated by flashes of weapons of all sizes. Tracers filled the air. Minutes later the crisis peaked. Pressure decreased on the Fifth RCT as the main Chinese assault took place further to the east; in a strike against X Corps units dug in on No Name Line. As usual, the ROK's broke, but the rest of X Corps held on and slaughtered the Chinese. X Corps artillery blasted entire CCF battalions and regiments into oblivion firing 105,000 rounds between 16-19 May.

On 20 May, the Eighth Army counterattacked to take some pressure off of X Corps. The Fifth RCT advanced in driving rain, humping heavy combat loads up and down the steep ridgelines, fighting constantly as they moved forward. Large numbers of Chinese soldiers laid down their arms.

Two veterans of George Company missed the counterattack. On the afternoon of 19 May, SFC Rob Palmer and Corporal Eddie Kauahilo climbed into a supply truck bound for Inchon to begin their journey home. Palmer felt some feelings of regret that he couldn't be part of another victorious drive north but, then, he'd already had that pleasure a couple of times. Other young men needed that kind of morale lift. Eddie, on the other hand, had no regrets about leaving. He desperately needed four weeks of warm sand and rum and fish and poi and a pretty wahine to revive his soul.

As the truck pulled out, Rob began to snooze. Eddie kicked the bottom of his friend's boot. "So brah, what you t'ink? You going to re-up?"

"I already have. Sent the papers through Regimental S-1 yesterday. How about you?"

"I don't know. Sometimes I t'ink I've had enough of this shit and other times I wonder what else I'd do. Maybe I'll wait and see if I can get off these orders to Germany."

"Why would you want to do that?"

"Sounds like another cold place to me and I suppose there are a whole bunch of fuckin' Germans there."

"I would guess you're right about that." Rob closed his eyes and returned to his own thoughts. He wondered how his life would be in California. He'd never been there. He had received orders to the Sixth Army Training Command at Fort Ord where he hoped to serve as a field first sergeant in a basic training company. He would rather do that than be part of the instructor cadre. As for Eddie, Rob suspected that once they left Japan, he would never see his big Hawaiian buddy again. That's the way the Army works. You make friends, share food and misery with them, depend on them and then, suddenly, they're gone.

PART II

The Eighth Army offensive continued into June as United Nations ground troops advanced to Line Wyoming in the Iron Triangle area. They could have kept going but there seemed to be little point in more bloodshed. The major players, with the exception of Syngman Rhee, realized that the two Koreas were not going to be reunited. There would be no victory, in the usual sense.

On 27 May, elements of the Fifth RCT counterattacked an enemy force that was attacking the command post of the 21st Infantry Regiment and, in so doing, captured 1,141 Chinese prisoners. A month later the combat team relieved the 32nd Infantry on Line Wyoming. The unit was relieved on 8 August and placed in reserve.

On 23 June 1951, Jacob Malik, the Soviet UN delegate, proposed cease-fire discussions. Within a week both President Truman and the Communist commanders, North Korea's Kim Il Sung and China's Peng Teh-huai agreed to begin talks.

These discussions between senior military officials, on both sides, immediately ran into trouble because the Communists seemed intent on saving face and portraying themselves as the victors. Two weeks passed before the two sides could agree on an agenda.

On 5 August the United Nations Command suspended the talks because communist armed troops were present in the neutral area. On 10 August the talks were resumed but were halted again on 22 August because the neutral area was violated by UN aircraft. They did not resume until 25 October.

During the suspension of the talks, the fighting resumed with a new ferocity. The UN troops fought and died at formerly obscure points on the map that we now know as Bloody Ridge, Heartbreak Ridge and Old Baldy.

The Fifth RCT joined the IX Corps offensive on 13 October 1951 to secure Line Nomad. After a series of limited objective attacks, it advanced to positions just south of Kumsong. The combat team remained there until it was relieved by elements of the California National Guard's 40th Infantry Division in February 1952.

FALL 1951

BEN RETURNED to campus one week before fall quarter registration with a healthy balance in his checking account. He had spent the summer working on the survey crew that was laying out the roads and building sites for the new Aerojet Engineering plant beside Highway 50. The new plant, a subsidiary of General Tire Corporation, would be producing, among other things, the JATO booster units that were used to increase the thrust of aircraft that were required to take-off with heavy loads at high altitude airports.

Ben loved the work. The hot Sacramento summer didn't bother him as long as he started the day in the cool of the morning. He was very pleased with the $1.65 an hour and enjoyed watching his bank balance grow as he worked twelve-hour days and occasional weekends. Day after day, he helped punch lines through the old dredge rock tailings along the highway. He was fascinated by the sight of men and heavy equipment turning the survey lines into roads and buildings.

He would have liked to take advantage of every day of the vacation but, as an SAE pledge, he was required to return to campus to participate in a week of cleaning, painting and gardening. The old Georgian-style fraternity house and the twin concrete lions guarding its entrance were to be "standing tall" before the previously-initiated "actives" returned to school.

Not long after the work week, the pledges began meeting to plan a sneak attack against their older brothers who had deprived them of a week of precious vacation. These meetings were usually held at the end of evening training sessions during which the pledges were exposed to the history and traditions of the fraternity.

On a Saturday evening, after most of the actives had left, a flat-bed truck pulled into the parking lot behind the fraternity house. It was loaded with eighty burlap bags filled with horse manure. Ben, because of his physical size, had been assigned to a tie-up crew. He and his fellow conspirators moved through the second and third floors of the house and subdued and bound any of the older brothers who were among the unfortunates that had decided to spend a quiet evening in their rooms.

While that task was being accomplished, the manure crew rolled up the carpets and scattered the horse apples throughout the downstairs. Every mattress in the house was tossed from the sleeping porch to the parking lot below and was loaded on to the truck. Then the truck moved out, followed by a caravan of cars, and all headed for a night of revelry on San Gregorio Beach on the San Mateo County shore.

The night seemed long to Ben. He had a couple of beers beside the fire and then crawled into the back seat of Carl's convertible to try to keep warm and get some sleep. However, sleep evaded him.

Ben doubted that the excitement of the pledge sneak was really worth the retribution that would surely follow. It wasn't. The uncomfortable night spent by the active brothers inspired the design of many tortures that were carried out during Hell Week, a week when Ben's self-control got a good workout.

There was not a lot of study time during Hell Week and Ben was struggling with physics, organic chemistry and another chemistry course entitled inorganic quantitative analysis. His mother constantly urged him with notes and phone calls to meet with his professors, hire a graduate student to tutor him, or do something other than waste his time. Ben finally made an appointment to see Dr. Noller, his organic chemistry professor.

Despite Ben's physical stamina, the combination of his anxiety and the long climb to Professor Noller's office on the fourth floor of the chemistry building, left him winded. He finally found the door, knocked on the glass pane and was instructed to enter.

"Dr. Noller, I'm Ben Stewart. I have an appointment with you to discuss the organic chem class."

"How do you do, Mr. Stewart? I'm glad you did come in. You're barely passing the course."

"I was wondering if you thought it would help if I had someone tutor me. Bob Jepson, a senior in my house is a chemistry major."

"Yes, I know Mr. Jepson and, no reflection on him, but I think it might be a bit late for tutoring. The final exam is just three weeks away."

"Well, what would you suggest, sir?"

"Let me see your notes, Stewart." Ben handed Dr. Noller his notebook and the older man began to peruse the notes, tapping his pencil on the pages as he read.

"These are very good notes, Stewart. Very complete. But it's a lot of detail. I would suggest that you go through them and condense the organic compounds under four headings: preparation, reactions, physical properties and industrial uses. I think that a tutor would just tell you what you already have in your notes. You could spend your time more profitably memorizing the material arranged in the matrix that I've suggested." Dr. Noller noticed the confused look on Ben's face. "Do you understand me, Mr. Stewart? Here, Please make a note of those four headings. You're making me nervous." Noller grinned as he handed Ben his notebook.

Ben replied sheepishly. "Oh, yeah...preparation, reactions, physical properties and industrial uses. Anything else, sir?"

"Why are you taking organic chemistry, Mr. Stewart?"

"Because I need it to get into med school."

"Why do you want to be a physician?"

"I live in Orangevale, a farming community northeast of Sacramento. The area is served by two doctors. Our family doctor is a good doc, a navy vet, but he's overworked. The other man makes so many mistakes that patients flee his practice and go to our doctor. I want to get through med school and go home and help Doctor Bill. He's been very encouraging. I'd hate to let him down."

"It's very doubtful that you will get into medical school with D's in chemistry, Stewart. You might really want to look at other options."

"There is no other option, Dr. Noller. I've thought about this for a long time."

"Very well. Good luck on your final."

Despite this last exchange, Ben felt some encouragement from his meeting with Dr. Noller, so he held a less helpful conference with Dr. Kirkpatrick in physics and managed to get some time alone with Dr. Skoog in quantitative analysis. That evening he attempted to update his mother by phone. She wondered why he didn't ask about a tutor for quantitative analysis.

"It's not a lecture course, Mom. My grade will depend entirely upon the lab results that I hand in at the end of next week. Right now, I'm failing the course. A tutor can't help me get good lab results."

"What are these lab results?"

"Well, we're given chemical compounds to analyze. Our job is to determine what percentage of certain elements they contain and then identify the compound."

"So what's the problem?"

"If I add one more drop of the test solution than is necessary, I'll get the wrong results. If my calculations are wrong, I'll screw up the results. There's a lot of luck involved. A tutor can't help me there. The results that I turn in next week are sort of up to God."

"It sounds more like it's sort of up to you, kid. You've got some thinking to do."

"About what?"

"About your abilities and your weaknesses and what it all means. Med school might not be your cup of tea."

Ben squeezed the telephone receiver in his hand until he thought it would break. "It's my cup of tea, Mom. Just let me worry about myself."

"Cool down, honey. We just want you to be successful. That's all."

"Yeah, I know, Mom. Good night. Love to everybody."

SPRING 1952

DESPITE EARNING A's and B's in English, French, Spanish and history, Ben's science grades continued to wreak havoc with his grade point average. Spring quarter was well underway before he finally decided to deal with his dilemma. Ben phoned Mary Ellen. He needed to talk and he needed to put his arms around someone soft and sweet.

"Ellie, what do you have planned for next weekend?"

"I've got a tough midterm on the following Monday, so I plan to study," she replied. "What are your plans?"

"I've got to see you. The pressure is really getting to me," said Ben.

"Well, the pressure's going to get to me, too, if I go into that midterm cold. You'd be better off hitting the books yourself."

"Well, maybe it wouldn't take all weekend," he suggested. I could catch the Del Monte to the city from Palo Alto at 9:00 on Saturday morning and then take the Greyhound to Walnut Creek. We could have lunch at Lommel's and then I could go back to San Francisco in time to catch the Del Monte at 4:00. So what do you think? I really need to see you."

"I think that sounds crazy" replied Mary Ellen. "Sounds like too little time and too much expense. Let's do it some other weekend when I have time to drive you back to campus on Sunday evening. I really do want to see you but not next weekend. Sometime soon."

Ben did go out to Walnut Creek a couple of weeks later. He saw Mary Ellen as someone who really had her head on straight and he wanted to see what she would think about his taking a leave of absence from Stanford for a year. He was thinking that it might be a good idea to get away and think about whether he should continue in pre-med and, besides, he really needed to work full-time for a year in order to finance his last two years of college.

She listened to what he had to say and then said, "You know that you'll be out of school about six weeks before your draft notice arrives."

"Probably. But the way things are, I can be drafted right out of school or right off the job. It doesn't matter where I am. One option would be declaring my major to be something like history or Romance languages and pulling down straight A's and getting my deferment back. But that's not what I want. I really do want to be a doctor."

Ben drove Mary Ellen's Plymouth convertible back to campus on Sunday afternoon. The drive gave the two of them more time to talk. When they pulled up in front of the fraternity house on Lasuen Street, she kissed him and said, "I'm going to miss you, soldier."

"No you aren't. Just think of all the studying you're going to be able to do when I'm half way around the world. Besides, it's probably not going to happen and, if it does, things have really wound down in Korea. I would probably be there no more than a few months."

"Promise? I've grown rather fond of you," she said.

"Love you, too. I'll call you later." Ben slammed the car door, bounded up the stairs and turned and waved as Mary Ellen drove away.

* * *

Stanford's post office was located across the street from the SAE House. During Dead Week, the week before spring quarter finals, Ben crossed the street to check his mailbox. There were two letters in it that were postmarked from Sacramento. He leaned against the Post Office wall and opened the envelopes, one at a time. The first was from Aerojet Engineering Corporation and the other from the Selective Service Office. The personnel director at Aerojet wrote that he was delighted to hear from Ben and that there was a job waiting for him on the survey crew as soon as could get there.

The second letter negated the first one. It informed Ben that he was to report to the Greyhound Bus Depot in Sacramento at "0600 on 6 Jun 1952" to be transported to the U.S. Army Induction Center on Van Ness Avenue in San Francisco. The letter went on to enumerate all the penalties that Ben would face if he failed to appear. These threats, of course, triggered his Scots-Irish temper but his solitary tirade was of short duration since he had known that there had been a real possibility of his being drafted. He was just going to have to suck it up.

Ben's draft notice was very unwelcome news for his parents. He tried to convince them that the Korean Conflict had turned into a rather benign stalemate. The media focus was on the negotiations at Panmunjom. The Stewarts suspected that the fighting and dying were continuing but that the press was tiring of that aspect of the story.

Ben's mind was not on dying. His chief concern was what was going to happen to his wavy crop of hair. As soon as he got home, he went to Mac's Barber Shop on Greenback Lane and instructed the barber to give him an inch-long flattop. Mac insisted that Ben would just be wasting

$2.25 because the Army would not be impressed. The Fort Ord barbers would not leave him unmolested just because his hair was short. But Ben insisted, so Mac fired up his clippers.

SUMMER 1952

WHEN BEN boarded the bus at the Greyhound Bus Depot at Sixth and J Streets, it was nearly full. He tossed his workout bag in the overhead rack and spoke to the young Black inductee sitting next to the window.

"Good morning, trooper. Is that seat taken?"

"No, it's yours as long as you skip the "trooper" business. There's still a chance that it might not happen. Until I pass the physical, I'm just going to enjoy being <u>Mr.</u> Grady Williams."

"You don't look like you're going to have any trouble with the physical."

"I've developed a tricky ankle playing football and I've got letters to show the army doctors. The coach at Cal did his best to save my deferment. Nothing doing."

"Oh, you're that Grady Williams. Ran one play ninety-eight yards from scrimmage against Stanford last fall."

"Oh, you read about that, did you?"

"No, I was in the stadium, Grady. I was in the rooting section wearing my red sweat shirt."

"It's a good thing you didn't wear it today," said Grady with a grin. "Nobody's going to sit next to me in a red shirt."

"Well, it looks like we're all going to be wearing the same color now. I'm Ben Stewart, by the way."

Grady shook Ben's hand. "We'll see about that. I'm Grady and the big albino across the aisle from you is my teammate, Dick Goodman."

As Ben grasped Dick's hand, the big blonde athlete said in his best Julia Child impersonation, "What is a Stanford man doing on this bus?"

"I requested a limo but they turned me down," retorted Ben, "so I'm afraid I'm stuck with you jokers."

The three found a lot to chat about as they traveled west on Highway 80. It was after nine when the bus finally reached the U.S. Army Induction Center at 100 Van Ness Avenue. As the passengers trooped in, they were met by a staff of doctors and technicians who put them through a two-hour physical.

When the medical staff was through, the young men were given chits that could be redeemed for food at a couple of nearby lunch counters. After lunch, they yawned their way through a lengthy battery of aptitude tests. Ben demonstrated his remarkable ability on language tasks and his mediocrity on items that involved spatial and numerical concepts.

At four o'clock the inductees lined up to be sworn into the Army of the United States, the official title of that branch of service that was reserved for young Americans conscripted for military service. Ben stepped forward and became Private E-1 Benjamin Stewart, US56245290. Dick and Grady were sworn in as well. The latter's letters of appeal had not impressed the government doctors.

It was past the dinner hour before the bus to Fort Ord was ready for boarding but there had been no food chits issued and no permission granted to leave the Induction Center. On the way to Fort Ord, there was a lengthy stop in Gilroy to pick up several more passengers, use the restroom and purchase snacks.

It was well after 9:00 P.M. when the nation's newest soldiers arrived at the Fort Ord Reception Center. They were immediately ushered into a mess hall where they were served a glop of stringy canned beef on a hard round biscuit and a cup of black coffee. There was an undercurrent of grumbling from the group who were used to Mom's cooking and had routinely downed a half gallon of milk daily. But Mom was a good four-hour drive away for most of them and their milk drinking days were over.

After finishing their "mystery meat," they were herded across the street to a supply room and issued a barracks bag, two olive-drab cotton herringbone twill fatigue uniforms, a couple of fatigue caps, towels, bed linens and a blanket. They then marched down the street, were assigned to barracks and were told to choose a bunk and go to sleep. They were advised that an orderly would come through at 0500 hours and rouse a few "volunteers" for KP.

Ben glanced around at his twenty roommates and decided not to make a spectacle of himself by wearing the pajamas that he had packed in his work-out bag. After making his bed, he crawled beneath the sheets in his skivvies. It had been one of the longest days he could remember. He soon fell asleep to the sound of the showers and the chatter in the latrine.

Ben crawled out of his bunk shortly after 0500, grabbed his toilet kit and towel and headed for the latrine. Once there he stretched to place his bare feet on the few remaining dry spots as he worked his way to the shower.

At 0600 the contingent stumbled into formation outside the barracks. The early morning air at Fort Ord, which had appropriately been nick-named Fort Pneumonia, was cold and damp from the summer fog. Ben was amused as he surveyed the group of men in their wrinkled fatigues, floppy, unblocked caps and civilian shoes of every size and description. He predicted that the Army would have its hands full trying to make soldiers out of this crew.

When all were assembled, they shuffled off to the mess hall for cold cereal and pancakes. Ben, Grady and Dick were chatting over breakfast and hadn't noticed that the other recruits were quickly vacating the large room.

The mess sergeant approached them and said, "You fellows enjoy your breakfast?"

"It was okay," answered Ben.

"You're the last three here," observed the sergeant.

"We're not in any rush," Dick said.

"I'm glad to hear it. C'mon in the kitchen and I'll show you where we keep the brooms and mops. You're not leaving until this mess hall is standing tall. Since you guys like to take your own sweet time, you may wind up pushing a broom every morning."

The three Sacramento recruits learned their lesson. From then on they ate quickly in order to evade the prowling mess sergeant.

The next ten days in the Reception Center went by quickly. On day two the men were marched to the barber shop where Ben's stylish flattop gave way to "white sidewalls" with a short mane on top. He had indeed wasted $2.25. The ensuing days were spent at the immunization clinic, the dental clinic and the vision clinic. There were a couple more sessions of aptitude testing and a trip to the clothing warehouse where all were issued heavy socks, three sets of underwear, two pairs of brown combat service boots, a pair of brown oxfords, a field jacket, an olive drab garrison hat and an overseas cap. Finally, they were measured for their olive drab, woolen (Class A) uniforms with waist-length "Ike" jackets.

Midway through the second week the Reception Center non-coms made quite a ceremony of marching the recruits to the post office so that they could, as ordered, mail home their civilian clothes. There was something so final about relinquishing those last trappings of youthful freedom.

When Ben got to the front of the line, he handed his tagged work-out bag to the mail clerk. "Hey," he said. "You're Pete Grolier!"

The clerk grinned. "Hi, Ben. Welcome to Fort Pneumonia."

"I haven't seen you for awhile. Do you miss the SAE House?" Ben asked.

"Not really. The Army is pretty much the same thing. A hell of lot more brothers, though, and the Army bathroom is a little more sanitary. Things really haven't changed that much."

"How did you end up here?" said Ben.

"This was my first assignment after clerk-typist school. I had hoped to be assigned to the post newspaper but the Army, in its wisdom, saw mail clerk written all over me. Six days from now, I'll have only nine months left to go. At that point, I won't be eligible for overseas shipment. So I can't complain."

From the rear of the room, one of the Reception Center cadre members roared, "Knock off the bullshit, you two, and keep this line moving."

Private Grolier dismissed Ben with a wave. "Well have a good time in the Army, Brother Stewart. By the way, I like your haircut."

Pete Grolier had been a reporter on the *Stanford Daily* staff when he received his "greetings" from the draft board. Once settled at Fort Ord, the former journalism major mailed a weekly column to the *Daily* entitled "The Private Life of Pete Grolier." He painted a humorous picture of basic training and clerk-typist school for many Stanford students who were destined to share similar experiences.

On 18 June, the band of inductees bid goodbye to the Reception Center and marched several blocks east to the area of buildings assigned to Company D, Sixth Combat Engineer Battalion. They were greeted noisily by the cadre of non-coms that would be their mentors and tormentors for the next eight weeks.

"You!"

"Me?" Ben responded, keeping his eyes straight ahead."

"You see me talking to anybody else?"

"No, but…"

Corporal Howell moved into Ben's field of vision and stood with his arms crossed and a scowl on his face. "What's your name?"

"Stewart. Benjamin Stewart."

"I heard your left eye-ball click, Stewart. The moving of eye-balls when one is at attention is forbidden in Dog of the Sixth, Stewart. When you are at attention, I don't want to hear growling guts, clicking eye balls, nor any other noxious and nauseating noises. Do you understand me, Stewart?"

"Yes, Corporal." Ben was feeling more curiosity than intimidation from his encounter with Corporal Howell. The man's command of English seemed a little out of place. Ben suspected that the corporal might have gone beyond the eighth grade in school.

Howell moved along the line and stopped in front of Dick Goodman. He scrutinized Dick's face until he found, or imagined that he found, some golden stubble on his chin. Dick was dispatched, on the double, to the barracks to get his razor. When he returned, Corporal Howell instructed him to dry-shave his chin and the rest of his face until it met Dog Company's standards.

The entire afternoon was spent in ranks in the company street. No one escaped verbal abuse for imaginary misdemeanors. Some of the new troops found the experience stressful but Ben, Grady, Dick and other former high school and college athletes, had survived many previous attempts at humiliation. They just did what they could to face forward, remain invisible and keep their eyeballs from clicking.

Dog Company was housed in the same type of barracks as those in the Reception Center; two-story, beige-colored frame buildings. Each floor held sixteen double bunks stacked on each side of the center aisle. Ben chose one of the bottom bunks and arranged his underwear, socks, and shaving gear in the top tray of the foot locker that was pushed against the foot of his bunk. Dick took the upper bunk. His footlocker was against the wall under a window. There was a clothes rod on the wall for their extra set of fatigues and their khaki shirts and pants. Their Class-A wool uniforms would also hang there when they arrived from the warehouse.

Each soldier was issued two rubber stamps; his full name and serial number on one and the initial of his last name and last four digits of his serial number on the other. All items in the foot locker and on the clothes rod were required to be stamped and placed in the locker or hung on the rod in a prescribed fashion. It other words, Ben's toothbrush and handkerchiefs were placed in the same location in the footlocker tray as those of every other soldier in the company and all of his shirts were hung so that the right shoulder was facing the center of the room.

The latrine was located at the south end of the building. There were six toilets against the inside wall and six wash basins on the opposite wall. To the left was the shower room with four shower heads.

The following morning the men cued up outside the supply room and were issued the M-1 rifle that would be their constant companion throughout basic training. They were also presented with a web cartridge belt, which carried an eight-round clip of .30 caliber ammunition in each of its ten pockets, a resin-coated nylon poncho to serve as a raincoat or ground cloth, and an M-1 bayonet and scabbard. This naturally led to a morning of instruction in the manual of arms and an afternoon of "dismounted" drill.

There was a class that evening after chow. Before dismissal, Corporal Howell, asked that all men with first aid or medically-related experience to remain for a few minutes. Dog of the Sixth needed two aid men. Dick was a former ski patrol member and Ben had been a football manager during his first two years of high school so he had a lot of experience taping ankles and dressing cuts and scrapes. The two decided to stick around and see what the job entailed. Ben was willing to grab any experience that might enhance his possibility of being assigned to the Medical Corps.

When they gathered at the rear of the room there were no less than five candidates for the two company medic slots.

One of the candidates was a regular army enlistee who had had some first aid training with the Army Reserves. He had enlisted for the medical corps and would be sent to Fort Sam Houston in San Antonio following basic training. He sauntered over to Ben and Dick.

"You guys might as well head for the barracks. I've got this job in the bag. I enlisted for the medical corps. You two won't get shit. You're "U.S.""

When Corporal Howell arrived he listened to each man's pitch and finally pointed to Dick and Ben. "You guys are hired. Get to company supply in the morning and pick up your blue helmets and medical bags. There's also a footlocker full of supplies. Pick that up too."

The medical corps enlistee objected to Howell's choice. "Permission to speak freely, Corporal Howell, I signed up for three years to become a medic. I deserve more consideration than these draftees."

Howell took his time responding. He wanted to say that he didn't really want any regular army dickhead second guessing him but he was able to calmly respond, "With all due respect, Private, I'm "U.S" myself and I think these men can do the job."

The "promotion" entitled Ben and Dick to quarters in a small two-bunk cadre room. They were exempted from KP. There would be no more nights listening to twenty different snoring patterns. The room, however, was barely big enough to hold their bunks, personal foot lockers and the third locker filled with first aid supplies.

Following morning formation, one of the two medics would escort the men who reported to sick call to the brigade infirmary. When one had sick call duty, the other would strap on the medical bag and join the remainder of the company in that morning's training activities. They discovered how important it was to communicate with each other one evening when Ben answered a knock on the door and ushered in Private Rudy Aguilar. The visitor, seeing that both medics were there, seemed somewhat nervous.

"Hi, Doc. I need some more of that cough syrup. This damn cough is still hanging on."

"That's the third bottle in three days, Rudy," said Ben.

"Like I told you, this cough is terrible." Rudy began to hack and doubled over. "But it's getting better, thanks to that syrup."

"Wait a minute," Dick said. "You got three bottles from me, too."

"What's with you guys," Private Aguilar snapped. "I'm sick and I'm entitled to medicine."

"It looks like you've been shittin' us, Rudy," said Ben. "You don't have a cough. You just want to get strung-out on codeine. If you're so sick, go to the infirmary."

"I don't need to go to the damn infirmary. Just gimme the syrup. Come on, you guys."

"I'm going to give you one more bottle, Rudy, just to get you out of here," said Ben. "If you ever ask for another, I'll report it to the infirmary. From now on you can deal with them." Private Aguilar grabbed the bottle of cough syrup and left without saying a word.

"That wasn't very smart, Ben. We should turn that guy in," said Dick.

"I suppose so. Hopefully he won't try to snow us again."

Toward the end of the second week, Ben was summoned to the personnel office. He welcomed the chance to talk to someone in authority about his future in the Army. Ben was fairly confident that those in charge would value his keen interest in medicine and send him to Fort Sam after basic.

"You made really high scores on your tests, Stewart," began the personnel sergeant as he showed Ben the test summary. "These scores and completion of basic will make you more than eligible for Officers Candidate School at Fort Benning. How do you feel about that?"

"That's really not the way I want to go. I was pre-med at Stanford and I would like surgical technician training or something similar."

"The problem is," said the sergeant, chuckling, "the Army needs a lot more platoon leaders than it does medics. Your needs take a back seat to those of the Army."

"How would OCS affect my two-year active duty obligation?" queried Ben.

"Your two years would begin as soon as you're commissioned."

"Well thanks for the suggestion, Sergeant, but I think the Army should take a cue from the California prison system. Time served while waiting for trial and sentencing is usually counted. I guess I can head back to my company now." The sergeant smiled and nodded.

For the first two weeks of basic training the recruits were forbidden to leave the one-block company area. They were assured that all of their needs would be met by the cadre of Company D. Private Luis Meyer, from nearby Carmel Valley, was able to exploit this period of quarantine. Meyer was the descendent of a German sea captain and the daughter of the Spanish land grant owner who had owned much of Carmel Valley during the early nineteenth century. The descendents had remained in Carmel Valley where Luis' family owned a small grocery store.

Twice weekly, Luis' older brother would pull up on the street behind the barracks area and provide his younger sibling with another few cartons of chewing gum, candy bars and cigarettes. The young entrepreneur would then stow this stock under the tray in his footlocker and pass the word around that the store was open. To keep things simple, he charged fifty cents for candy, gum or a pack of cigarettes. In the summer of 1952, most candy bars and packs of gum cost a nickel. Smokes were twenty cents. The customers complained but Luis would simply shrug and refer to the principle of supply and demand.

When they were in quarters, Ben and Dick generally left the door to their barracks room open. One Sunday evening as they sat on the bunks engaged in a bull session with Grady and with Neil Wade, a dropout from a Jesuit seminary, a soldier stumbled through the door, clutching his arm, the bill of his fatigue cap pulled down over his eyes. He mumbled the typical soldier's plea for aid, "Hey medic, my arm's all fucked up. You got some shit to put on it?"

Ben stood up, jerked the man's cap back, and burst into laughter, as he revealed the face of John Mitchell, an early childhood friend of his from Walnut Creek. John had just begun basic training with Charlie Company of the Sixth Combat Engineers.

"How did you know I was here?" chuckled Ben.

"I ran into Dusan Bradovich at the Post Exchange." During their pre-teen years, John, Dusan, Ben and George Preston had been inseparable as they enjoyed summer vacations in Sutter Creek, an historic little town in California's mother lode area. John continued, "He said that you were right next door in Dog Company. I'm going up to the Phone Center to call home. Why don't you come along and do the same?"

"What do you hear from Preston?" said Ben, as they approached the Phone Center.

"He just finished his second year at West Point," said John. "Fortunately, we'll both be out of the Army before he gets his commission. Wouldn't that be a kick. Having to lick Georgie's boots."

"I can't imagine having to deal with that," said Ben. "I just think it's rather interesting how...no matter where boyhood chums wander, as our families move from place to place, we can always depend on Uncle Sam to bring us back together again. Kids can say with certainty, 'See you someday at Fort Ord.'"

The days of basic training flew by. They were devoted to daily drill, bayonet practice and physical training. There were classes in map reading, communications, first aid, water safety, chemical warfare, and the detection and disarming of mines. The trainees were taught to disassemble their rifles by feel rather than by sight so that they would be prepared to clear a jam that might occur during darkness.

Ben, Dick and Grady all qualified at the sharpshooter level, with the M-1 rifle, on the rifle ranges in the sand dunes just west of Highway One. The M-1 was accurate at five hundred yards as long as the windage screw didn't become loose during protracted firing. They learned to chant that this, most basic of infantry weapons is a gas-operated (little manual cocking required), semi-automatic, 30 caliber rifle. It accepted an eight-round clip of cartridges. Woe unto the recruit that referred to the weapon as his "gun." He would be ordered to raise the 9.5 pound piece in his hand, grab his crotch with his left hand and chant, "This is my rifle and this is my gun; one is for shooting, the other's for fun."

The process of becoming skilled marksmen had not come easy. Prior to firing live ammunition, the trainees spent several hours learning to coordinate breathing, aiming and squeezing the triggers of their weapons so as to avoid jerking. Actual firing, while lying in the sand at the rifle range, proved to be somewhat more challenging. Ben got so much sand in the receiving chamber, where the cartridge clip is inserted, that he was having difficulty inserting the clip. When he finally succeeded and squeezed off a round, his rifle wouldn't reject the empty cartridge automatically so that he had to pull the bolt back by hand. He had to repeat this process for the next few shots and was completely out of sync during rapid-fire trials. He was relieved to note that he was not the only one having trouble.

The training cadre at the rifle range were incensed, acting as if this were the first time in history, that such a collection of "eight balls" had occupied the firing line. As they formed up to march back to the barracks, Corporal Howell threatened them with all sorts of punishments and restrictions.

When they reached the company street, the formation stood at attention to listen to the day's announcements from Lt. Maletis, the company commander. During their day on the range, the company area and barracks had been visited by post inspectors. Dog Company had placed second best in the battalion and fifth best in the regiment. Nothing more was said about their "disgraceful" performance on the rifle range.

Following the first week of firing on the KD range (known distance), Dog Company was assigned the task of pulling targets for Easy and Mike Companies of the First Infantry Regiment. This required lowering the targets upon the command of the range officer, finding the bullet holes, and re-raising the targets so that the shooters could be shown, with a black disc on a pole, where the bullets had impacted.

Late one morning, as Ben pulled targets, a solder that was several targets away from him dropped to the sand and stiffened making a hoarse cry. In response to a chorus of "Holy shit, Medic. Magnuson's been hit!" Ben raced to the man's side. Private Magnuson's eyes were rolled back. He was very pale but there were no signs of bleeding.

"Thank God," mumbled Ben. "Looks like he's just having a seizure." Ben fumbled in the medical bag until he could find a tongue depressor to keep the soldier from biting his tongue. However, Private Magnuson's jaw was so rigidly shut that Ben couldn't force it open. A few seconds later the soldier's body and extremities began to jerk.

Corporal Howell came running along the line. "Stewart, what the hell's goin' on? What's the matter with him?"

"Magnusen seems to be having a grand mal seizure, Corporal Howell. He's unconscious now but he'll probably be okay."

"Well he doesn't look okay and I've called for an ambulance. When it gets here, you go to the hospital with him. Understand?"

By this time the advanced infantry trainees along the firing line had all been pulled back, wondering what kind of catastrophe had occurred down in the pits. Soon an olive-drab ambulance was making its way down the dirt service road between the ranges, heading toward the target line on the beach.

By the time the ambulance reached the north end of the target pit, Magnuson was awake and his color was improving. Ben noticed that the pupils in his eyes were returning to their normal size. Dazed, he asked, "What am I doing on the ground?" Then he glanced down at his crotch. "Oh hell, I've wet my pants."

In a near whisper, Ben said, "You've done more than wet them, Billy, but no big deal. They probably have a pair of clean britches for you at the hospital."

Ben sat beside Magnuson as the ambulance wound its way to the old World War II era, pavilion type hospital on Third Street. He wished that the vehicle would get a move on so that he could get out and get a breath of something besides Magnuson's feces.

"Do you remember feeling anything before you blacked out, Billie?"

"Right after we got to the target pits, I felt like I was getting sick to my stomach."

"Anything else: Heart burn, lump in your throat?"

"I can't remember."

"Did you ever have a seizure before?"

"No". At this, Magnuson turned his head as the color drained from his face. Ben tried to move his feet out of the way but the vomit plastered his boots. He reached in his medical bag for gauze compresses and proceeded to clean Magnuson's face and the side of the gurney before he attended to himself. The ambulance now smelled like someone had had a bowel movement in a brewery.

"I'm really sorry, Stew. I couldn't stop it."

"I know it, Billy. No problem." Ben was relieved to note that the ambulance was now backing into the emergency entrance. As he sprang from the rear of the ambulance, an orderly told him to go find the receiving waiting room and stay there until he was summoned. The doctor would want to speak to him.

Ben was glad to see that there was a restroom off the waiting room where he could find paper towels and water and finish cleaning his boots.

Then he dropped on to a plastic-covered couch and began to mentally rehearse his testimony for the neurologist. He soon feared he was going to suffocate in the eighty-degree heat of the unventilated room. However, as he got up to go outside, a medic entered the room and spied him.

"You the guy that came in with the epileptic fit."

"No, I'm the guy that came in with the guy that had an epileptic seizure."

"Come with me, smart ass, and I'll show you the way to Neurology."

Ben was ushered from the cool hall into another stifling room, the office of Major Bryan. The doctor asked Ben to sit.

"I understand that you were with the private during his episode. Please tell me what you saw."

"Well," began Ben, "it was a pretty classical grand mal seizure. He felt an aura of nausea and by the time I got to him he was about to move from the tonic phase into the clonic."

"Let's start again. Private Stewart, isn't it? I'm the doctor. I make the diagnoses. You're the dogface who was down in the pits pulling targets. Tell me exactly what you saw. Cut the medical jargon."

Ben apologized and gave Dr. Bryan the details. After a bit the doctor relaxed and thanked Ben for his good observations. He told Ben that Magnuson's was the third epileptic seizure that he had seen that week and that none of the three could remember having previous seizures. Ben asked him if there were anything at Fort Ord or anything inherent in basic training that could lead to an onset of first-time seizures. Dr. Bryan felt that one contributing factor might be that a number of young soldiers were having their first experience with alcohol now that they were free of parental supervision. Ben, remembering the smell of the vomit-spattered ambulance, agreed that that may well have been the case with Billy Magnuson.

Magnuson never did return to the company. Ben and the others were not privy to what had happened. His disappearance was similar to the case of Private William Ivory, a small, effeminate, apparently homosexual, soldier who just disappeared one weekend. There was no explanation of the matter by the cadre. Some subjects just weren't open for discussion.

The war in Korea was being fought primarily at night because the Communist forces wanted to avoid the wrath of the U.N's air power. Therefore there was an emphasis placed on nighttime training at Fort Ord and other basic training facilities.

When the day arrived for crawling the infamous infiltration course, the recruits spent the afternoon learning to breech barbed-wire entanglements by scooting under the wire on their backs with their rifles resting on their upper bodies; rifle bolt down to avoid getting snagged. When night fell, Dog Company filed down a trench beside the course and waited until the machine guns began to fire streams of red tracers overhead. They were then given a whistle command to move forward under the wire in the direction of the guns.

Corporal Howell had given instructions that every man was to report to him when he had finished traversing the course. Ben wasn't listening carefully to this order. When he completed crawling the course, he found Grady and Dick and sat down with them to await the trucks that would take them back to the barracks.

Corporal Howell approached the three, glanced at his clipboard and asked, "Stewart did you check in with me when you finished?"

"No, Corporal, but I did finish the course."

"Did you not hear me say that I wanted every swingin' dick to report to me as soon as he finished."

"Nope, Corporal, guess I missed that."

"Well, you get your ass back in that trench, Stewart, and crawl the course again. If you're not back by the time the trucks leave, you can hike back to camp. The cool night air might improve your hearing."

Ben stumbled down the dark trench cursing Howell with every breath. At this point the machine guns were no longer firing and the floodlights had been switched off. After crawling about twenty feet, it occurred to him that the infiltration course was no longer lighted so he stood and moved forward in a crouch, stepping over the wire strands and occasionally snagging his fatigue pants. He reached the end of the infiltration course in record time and reported to Corporal Howell.

Around 2200 hours, it was apparent that the trucks would not be coming so the company fell into a marching column for the long hike back to the barracks. To raise the spirits of the tired youngsters, Corporal Howell belted out a Jody cadence and the troops sang the response in time with the crunch of their footsteps. As he listened to "Sound off, one, two, cadence count, three, four," it occurred to Ben that "one, two" sounds enough like "fuck you" in a group that he probably could get away with the substitution. So that's how he responded to Corporal Howell's command to sound off and when he got back to the company area around midnight, he felt purged of his anger.

Corporal William Howell had been a high school English teacher in Santa Barbara when he received his draft notice in June, 1950. He arrived in Korea in November of that year and was assigned to the Fifth Cavalry Regiment. He survived the year of retreating and counterattacking north and south of Seoul and was then sent home and assigned to the Sixth Army Training Command at Fort Ord.

Howell had been a very demanding English teacher and, as field first sergeant for Dog of the Sixth, was even more demanding as he trained young warriors. His insistence on perfection applied to himself as well.

He consistently fired at the expert level on the rifle range. He could pitch one grenade after another through the third story window of the one-dimensional fake buildings in Fort Ord's back country. He could out-jog, and rack up more push-ups and pull-ups than Grady, Dick or any of the other jocks in the company. He wore a snow-white helmet, crisp, starched fatigues, spit-shined cordovan boots, and a large shiny belt buckle fashioned from a scrap of brass from a mortar shell.

Ben quickly recovered from his feelings of animosity toward Howell, and would go to the dayroom one or two evenings a week to participate in literary discussions led by the field first sergeant. These meetings were open to any men in the company who were interested. An evening's discussion might revolve around Ernest Hemingway's life and how it influenced his writing of *Farewell to Arms* and *For Whom the Bell Tolls*. Howell led the discussions, in part, to keep his sanity in an intellectual wasteland. He was a good teacher and a good soldier.

On Friday, August 10, the last full day of basic training, the company marched to the blood clinic and contributed two hundred pints to the war effort. That afternoon, orders came and were read to the men by SFC Miller, the administrative first sergeant. The regular army enlistees were all assigned to the branches for which they had enlisted. A few of the draftees were assigned to Cooks and Bakers school at Fort Ord. Ben and Dick were among the multitude who would report back to Fort Ord and the First Infantry Regiment, in thirteen days, to begin Advanced Infantry Training. Grady was as bewildered as Ben was disappointed, when it was announced that Private Grady Williams was being assigned to Fort Sam Houston where he would train as a combat medic. The Army, in its infinite wisdom, had spoken. The men of Dog Company lined up in front of the orderly room to pick up their written orders.

There was a graduation parade on Saturday morning and an open house for families and friends in the company area. An obviously hung-over William Howell delivered a lengthy farewell address to those assembled. He would report the following Monday to the Separation Center, would be a civilian again by Wednesday, and would resume classroom teaching in January.

Ben hoped that Mary Ellen would arrive too late for the parade and the open house, so that he could change into civilian clothes before she arrived. But her Plymouth convertible rolled into the parking lot near the parade ground just in time for her to witness the entire battalion pass in review.

She finally found Ben as the formation broke up. "Hi, soldier, you look so cute in your uniform. I must have shot a whole role of film during the parade trying to find you."

Ben kissed her and said, "I can't wait to get out of here. Just give me a chance to get out of the old "crude suit" and into my civvies. I'm already packed."

Ben's mother had invited Mary Ellen to Orangevale for a couple of days. Mary Ellen had offered to drive Ben home following his graduation from basic training. He threw his barracks bag in the trunk of the convertible, got behind the wheel, and they were soon on the road to Pacheco Pass. Ben was very quiet for the first few miles.

"So what's going on in your little scalped head, Benjamin? You usually have a lot more to say when we haven't seen each other for awhile."

"Well, things just aren't working out like I thought they would"

"You're not going to be in the Medical Corps, are you?"

"How did you know that?"

"Figure you would have told me if you had some good news. So what's the verdict?"

"I'm to report back to Fort Ord in a couple of weeks to begin advanced infantry training."

"What's advanced infantry training?"

"Well, it's another eight weeks of the same stuff, but it means that my MOS or military occupational specialty will be light weapons, infantry. I'll just be a rifleman."

"Oh, darlin', that sounds bad," she said. "That sounds like Korea."

"Not necessarily. There are infantry outfits in Europe, especially Germany," explained Ben.

"Aren't there infantry posts in this country."

"A few. But this country is pretty busy right now protecting South Korea and keeping the Russians out of Western Europe. I'm sure I'll be going overseas."

"I'll pray that you get sent to Germany then."

They stopped in Santa Nella for gas and some lunch and then pushed on arriving at Ben's home around dinnertime.

On Sunday morning, Ben and Mary Ellen went with the rest of the Stewart family to take communion together at Trinity Episcopal Church in Folsom. Ben's mother, Mary, was sure that her son would be sent to the Far East, so she had insisted that her 48-year-old husband, Bill, a back-slid Methodist, take catechism and be confirmed so that he could come to the communion rail with them. Father Castledine had agreed that he would give Mr. Stewart the "short course." Mary promised Bill that if he did this for the family that she would never again require him to go to church. He agreed as he assured her that there would never be a return trip.

* * *

In many ways advanced infantry training was more of the same elements covered in basic training but there were some differences. More of the training was scheduled at night, a good time to practice patrolling, the platoon in attack, battlefield lighting, covering fields of fire, and moving back and forth quickly between combat outposts and the main line of resistance. Much time was devoted to stringing and unstringing barbed wire, filling and emptying sandbags and digging bunkers in the dark Monterey top soil.

Many of the night firing exercises involved more powerful killing implements than the M-1. The troops qualified on the Browning automatic rifle, a 20-pound veteran of World War II, that fired clips of twenty 30-caliber bullets. They were introduced to 50-caliber machine guns, 60-mm and 81-mm mortars and 57-mm recoilless rifles that were light to carry and could be mounted on a jeep or on a tripod.

The recoilless rifle had been developed at the end of World War II as an anti-tank weapon but had proved useless against the powerful Russian T-34 tanks used by the North Korean Army. Nevertheless it proved to be effective against machine-gun emplacements and other field fortifications. The recoilless rifle gave the infantry company its own direct fire artillery.

After breakfast on Fridays, Ben would apprehensively approach the bulletin board outside the company orderly room to see if he had drawn KP or guard duty over the weekend. He pulled each duty once during the eight weeks. He split his free weekends between his folks in Orangevale and Mary Ellen in Walnut Creek. Both destinations involved going beyond the fifty-mile radius from Fort Ord allowed for weekend passes.

Dick Goodman brought his car down for AIT and on every other weekend Ben would link up with him after Saturday morning inspection. The young AWOL's would get a little rush of adrenaline when they reached the 50-mile mark near Gustine in Merced County and then breathe a sigh of relief when they reached the same point on the return trip Sunday evening.

The eighth week of advanced infantry training was devoted to a road march along the crest of the Santa Lucia mountain range from Fort Ord to Fort Hunter Liggett and back. Burdened by packs, blanket rolls, shelter halves, entrenching tools and weapons, the men tired quickly so there were frequent rest stops.

To Ben's disgust, Dick had recently developed the wide-spread habit of smoking and would light up at each rest stop. When the order came to fall in, Dick would field strip his cigarette butt just like a veteran soldier, by tearing the paper, scattering the unburned tobacco and rolling the remaining paper into a tiny ball which he deposited in his pocket.

The Hunter Liggett hike was well-timed weather-wise. It took place during the tail end of Monterey County's Indian summer. Daytime temperatures were in the eighties, but nighttime sleeping temperatures were in the comfortable range.

October 12 was the last day of the AIT course and orders arrived on the sixteenth. Dick rejoiced when he discovered that he had been assigned to the Sixth Regimental Combat Team in Berlin. Ben found, as he expected, that he would be heading in the opposite direction. He had no clear assignment other than that he was being sent to the Far East Command with an MOS of 4745, Light Weapons Infantryman. He and the majority of the newly trained riflemen were ordered to report to Camp Stoneman in the San Francisco Bay Area, on Monday, 22 October.

FALL 1952

THE MID-OCTOBER DAYS were becoming wintry as Hua Xing rode north to Manchuria on a troop train. The unheated car was packed with noisy, excited new "volunteers" for the People's Liberation Army, but Private Hua sat quietly, immersed in his own thoughts. His young wife and baby boy were uppermost in his mind.

Xing had once hoped that his responsibility for his family and his high school teaching position in Changsha, Hunan Province would entitle him to a deferment from army service. But, as fate would have it, the American puppets, the South Koreans, had invaded the People's Republic of North Korea in June of 1950. He had been rather fortunate to avoid the army for the past two years. Then in June of 1952, a recruiter for the People's Liberation Army came to Changsha, met with the town elders and other civic leaders and presented them with notice of their annual quota for the army. Every family must contribute at least one son.

He recalled being summoned to the office of his principal and the man saying, "Mr. Hua, I have observed a number of situations where you could have bridged from your lectures to the barbaric behavior of the American murderers."

"I am grateful for your suggestion, Mr. Yao," responded Xing. I did put up a poster in the classroom. The one showing the red-haired American soldier bayoneting a defenseless Korean woman and her children."

"Yes, Hua Xing, and that is commendable. But I don't feel that you have a passion for teaching the truth. Perhaps a brief period of army service would make you a better teacher."

Xing had not shared Mr. Yao's hatred for the Americans. Americans were, he felt certainly inferior, in all respects, to the Chinese, but they are a notch above the Koreans, who are the scum of the earth. He didn't believe reports that the Americans were as brutal as the dwarf bandits from Japan who had occupied his country when he was a young boy.

The idea of going to the rescue of the inept and cowardly North Korean Peoples Army was a difficult one for Hua Xing to embrace. To him it was rather like risking your life to rescue an epidemic of jock itch. He would gladly and proudly give his life to wrest Taiwan away from its American puppet government and restore it to the motherland but he didn't want to lose one hair for Korea.

On the way home from school that day, Xing stopped by his father's grocery store. When he encountered the older man, he could tell from his face that something was wrong. He observed, "You seem troubled, Father. What is it?"

"Third Cousin paid a visit today. He said he had some family business to discuss," began the senior Mr. Hua.

"And what was it?" pressed Xing.

"He said that he had been summoned to the Mayor's office and was asked to approach our family about the advisability of your volunteering for military service."

"What! What's so advisable about that? What about Mei and little Xing?" protested the younger man.

"Perhaps 'advisable' was the wrong word," responded Mr. Hua. "According to Third Cousin every family must contribute in a time of national emergency. He informed me that we can either contribute a son to the army or the taxes on our business will be tripled. Since you are our only son, I have no choice. I must find the money somehow."

"I can help you, Father, from my teaching wages."

The older man smiled sadly and said, "The annual taxes are already equivalent to your teaching salary. Thank you, Son, I must be alone now to think."

"I will also do some thinking, Father." Xing bowed and left his father's office.

The following morning, Hua Xing visited Principal Yao and explained that he needed the morning off to visit the recruiting office of the People's Liberation Army. Mr. Yao was delighted to grant his request. He was already relishing the opportunity to replace Xing with someone more loyal to the revolution.

The paper work at the recruiting office was handled expeditiously. Xing was informed that his only option was to enlist for the duration of the PLA's intervention in Korea. He was given two weeks to put his affairs in order.

Mr. Yao expressed his immense pride in Xing, as the young man signed his request for an indeterminate leave of absence. As Xing returned Yao's fountain pen, he was tempted to suggest what the principal should do with the writing implement and then thought better of it. He might really want his job back someday. That done he went home and began making preparations to move a devastated Mei and little Xing to her parents' home. At the end of the fortnight, he kissed them goodbye and reported to his assigned company's training garrison in a nearby village.

Young men from a village, or neighborhood were formed into a local training company. Several companies from a community would compose a regiment. Older veterans, many of them former Chinese Nationalist troops, were there to greet and help mentor the new recruits. These units would then go on active duty status when the forty days of basic military and political training had been completed. This localization of army units was one way of dealing with China's language problem. Those who spoke Cantonese would be in different units than the Northerners who spoke Mandarin, or the Mongolians who spoke neither. In addition it was felt that young men who had grown up together, who were already supportive of each other, were happier more effective soldiers.

Assignment to a nearby base was a blessing for Xing, enabling him to be with Mei and his baby boy on Sundays. Sometimes she was able to schedule a mid-week evening visit with her husband although that was rare. It was difficult for Xing to get permission to see her. His superiors felt that such visits only postponed the emotional break that he needed to make from his former life in order to develop the spirit of a good Communist soldier. Of course they wouldn't say so to his face. Xing just found himself suddenly assigned to details that served to preclude his seeing Mei.

The great majority of the "volunteers" were farmers from nearby villages. For the most part, they were illiterate. They were in awe of Xing's knowledge but had little in common with him, so they usually ignored him. Many had enlisted quite willingly as their families were still trying to recover from the recession of 1951.

Xing would have been able to enjoy day after day of quiet introspection and self-pity had it not been for the three-by-three squad organization plan. He had been assigned to a rifle squad composed of a squad leader and three three-man groups. An older private named Chu Tien was designated Xing's group leader and a peasant named Ho Hua, several years younger than Xing, rounded out the trio.

Private Chu had been a soldier in the Red Army since 1934. He was a luke-warm Communist Party member and had held higher rank during the Civil War but had gotten drunk and violated the army's moral regulations with a somewhat reluctant farmer's wife and had been subsequently demoted. Chu's only home was the army and he hoped to get back in its graces by serving a hitch in Korea. Xing held him in high esteem and felt lucky to have been assigned such an experienced mentor. Chu didn't return the admiration and usually referred to Xing as "Turtle's Ass" and Private Ho as "Dung Heap." Nevertheless, since his life might depend on their military skill someday, he was determined to make soldiers of them.

Not all non-coms were qualified to serve as trainers, since many of them, like Chu, were illiterate. Groups of trainers traveled the circuit of training garrisons lecturing and demonstrating the techniques they had learned in sixteen years of continuous combat. The emphasis in Xing's training was on rifles, grenades and bayonets, especially grenades. The Chinese soldier needed to learn to handle grenades well, since they were a cheap and plentiful home-grown weapon. Belts loaded with potato-masher concussion grenades, the young trainees would march out to a nearby gully to practice. A twenty-yard toss was acceptable but a thirty-five yard toss was commendable. The training cadre members were always on the alert for new talent; someone who might go on to win the all-army grenade throwing contest.

There was a couple of days of training on the planting, arming, detection, and disarming of mines. Most of the time was devoted to the domestic 10" x 10" x 4" box mines that were filled with nitrocellulose. They also studied several types of Soviet mines from the YaM-5 antitank device, packaged in wood and set for pressure detonation, to the PMD anti-personnel mines that guarantee bloody wounds from wood splinters and glass fragments.

Rifle marksmanship was not an area of real concentration. Ammunition was very scarce and there was a critical need for it at the front. China had no munitions industry. They bought most of their ammunition from the Soviet Union, who demanded cash or foodstuffs on delivery.

At the end of the third week of training, the men in the Changsha Company were issued old Japanese Gimo and U.S. Springfield rifles. By the end of basic training, Xing and his fellow recruits had fired no more than fifty rounds each. It was of little importance since they would probably be issued sub-machine guns if their unit were tapped for duty in Korea. The range officer's response to unfulfilled riflemen was "if you want to practice shooting, shoot at the enemy."

The major military focus in basic training was on marching. PLA troops drilled by marching in the country rather than on parade grounds. The columns marched at a route step and would have looked sloppy and imprecise to the western soldier but that's the PLA heritage. PLA commanders placed much more value on training soldiers to endure long marches and keep their weapons clean. That was the mark of a good Communist soldier. Private Chu and the other veterans engaged in the same physical conditioning activities but attended advanced classes while the new recruits learned the rudiments of soldiering.

Chao Wen, the company political officer, requested Xing's presence in his office during the first week of training. "Xing," he said, addressing the young man by his first name, "I am political officer Chao. I asked you to come see me so that we can get better acquainted. I'm here to help you whenever I can. Are you having any problems here at camp or maybe at home with your family?" Xing indicated with a shrug that he had none.

"It's not so difficult, Political Officer Chao. Sometimes being a soldier is better than trying to control a classroom of teen-agers," responded Xing. He had been instructed to refer to officers by their job titles rather than their rank. So it was Political Officer Chao, Company Commander Chen and Platoon Leader Hsiao rather than Captains Chao and Chen and Lieutenant Hsiao. Emphasis on rank was antithetical to the egalitarian thrust of Communism. Rank existed solely for pay purposes and for the element of command.

Chao smiled, "Well maybe we can find an aspect of soldiering that will use your intellect and your articulate language."

Xing was beginning to trust the political officer so he plunged right in. "Between my teaching experience and the bookkeeping that I did in my father's business, I was wondering if there was similar work that I could do at company headquarters."

"There are two soldiers working in the administrative section and one in the message center," said Chao. "The jobs are filled at present and, of course, those filling them are good Party members. You see, Private Hua, we must be sure that those who fill sensitive positions will be loyal and dependable."

"I understand, sir," said Xing, his heart sinking. He doubted that he could turn his back on the values of his family, just to make his life easier. His father had learned to survive by being accommodating to the Communists but never surrendering his soul. Xing had hoped to do the same.

Political Officer Chao dismissed Xing with a flick of his hand. "Well, I've enjoyed our chat, Xing. You may return to your barracks now. Be assured that I will be looking for a challenging job for you." Chao acknowledged to himself that Private Hua could be a problem and would bear watching.

* * *

The days were long at Camp Stoneman. With the exception of several daily formations, a physical exam, and some follow-up inoculations, Ben spent most of the next four days sitting on his footlocker or lying on his bunk, swapping lies with several friends that he had known since basic training. Luis Meyer kept a marathon poker game going and had pretty well destroyed the purchasing power of Ben, Jerry Holmes, a lanky basketball player from Willamette College, and Rudy Aguilar, Ben's codeine customer from basic training.

On Thursday, October 25, those men on Friday's roster for shipment to the Far East were paid. Now that he was Private E-2, Ben received $75. He was determined to hang on to his money this time. Camp Stoneman was approximately twenty-five miles from Walnut Creek and Mary Ellen had promised to come over and join him for his last evening before sailing.

Ben went to the phone center and called home and had a brief chat with his father. He promised to call later in the evening when he could catch his mother at home. Then he phoned Mary Ellen and was relieved to find that she had just arrived home from her classes in Oakland.

"About what time are you going to get here?" he asked.

"I can be there in about an hour," she replied. "Did you get a pass for the evening?"

"No. They aren't giving passes to those of us in tomorrow's shipment but don't worry, I'll meet you down by the main gate. We can go into Pittsburg for something to eat."

"'Tomorrow's shipment' makes you sound like a herd of cattle."

"You're right, Ellie. We're bound for the slaughterhouse."

"That's not funny, Ben," she said, after a moment of silence. "And what will happen to you if you get caught without a pass?"

"Nothing serious. They could put me in the stockade until another troop ship sails, but, I doubt that that's going to happen. It would involve too much paperwork."

The young couple found a little Italian restaurant in town. The minestrone and the pasta pesto were delicious but Mary Ellen barely touched hers. Ben's attempts at humor were unsuccessful. He missed the chatter and laughter and the adoring glances that had made their previous times together so special.

Ben drove the convertible back to base and parked about a block from the main gate. After such a glum evening, he was pleasantly surprised when Mary Ellen slid across the seat and kissed him passionately. Ben slid his hand under her sweater and, after much fumbling, unfastened her brassiere. As he kissed her, he gently squeezed her breast and stroked one of her nipples until it stiffened.

"I want you, Ellie. I want you right now," he whispered.

Mary Ellen stiffened and slid back across the seat. She refastened her brassiere and stared straight ahead.

Ben was not sure what to do. He'd never had to coax a woman out of a snit before. He tried to humor her with a hillbilly imitation.

"Y'all are peeved with me, ain't ya, Ellie?"

"You're damn right I'm peeved with you, Ben Stewart. I, too, love you and want you but not in the back seat of my car and not on the night before you go traipsing off to rid the world of communism."

"But I didn't volunteer to go to Korea."

"The heck you didn't. You may as well have. There are worse students than you still at Stanford. You could have worked harder to get into an ROTC program or transferred to a less competitive school. Ben, you just rolled over and passively let the draft board snatch you up."

Ben was not in the mood for a spat. He opened the car door and gave Mary Ellen a little peck on the cheek. "I guess it's time to end my AWOL. I'll write you as soon as I have a permanent address. I do love you."

"I love you, too and you'd better write me soon, Pal. We've got some stuff to talk about. Please be safe."

Ben turned and walked to the gate. He presented his identification card to the MP's and then they asked to see his pass. Ben searched in all of his pockets and went through his wallet.

"I'm sorry, man, I must have left my pass on my bunk in the barracks. I remember sliding it under my pillow for safekeeping."

"Let's see your ID again." Ben handed the green plastic card to the MP.

"When are you shipping to FECOM, Stewart"

"Uh...Monday."

"Well, okay, but after this hang on to your pass."

"Thanks, buddy. I will."

When Ben got back to the barracks, he hung up his Ike jacket, tossed his cap on the shelf and, saying nothing to his friends, lay down on his bunk. Jerry Holmes looked up from the card game and said, "Well, Benny. How did things go? Did she pinch your little inch?"

Ben turned over and glared. Holmes decided not to push it further.

* * *

The man sitting next to Xing had boarded the train with a contingent from Northern China. After an hour of silence, he turned toward Xing and, in an attempt to be friendly, introduced himself as Yang Peixing. Xing winced as he was nearly choked by a cloud of garlic-scented breath. He mumbled his name and then excused himself, saying that he needed to stretch his legs.

As Xing retreated up the narrow aisle, he concluded that if there were a lower form of life than the Korean, it was the Northern Chinese farmer. Maybe his best defense would be to develop their voracious appetite for garlic. The resulting rancid breath and body odor would encourage people to leave him alone.

Shortly after dark, the train arrived at Andong, Manchuria, the end of the line. The new and returning soldiers, stiff from the cold and inactivity, stumbled off the train and into formation. They would stop briefly at

Andong Barracks before crossing the river to Korea. It was rumored that they faced a six-day march before arriving at the front lines.

The evening meal was the first order of business. Xing, Chu and Ho joined the chow line, bowls in hand, to receive a serving of rice with a few tiny chunks of pork and some vegetables. They washed down the meal with cups of hot tea. Chu and Ho belched with satisfaction and Xing had to agree that it was not too bad for army food. He had expected worse. Ho warned him that there would be many times when that would be the case.

After eating, the new recruits lined up outside the supply warehouse where they were ordered to remove and turn in their summer uniforms. As they stood shivering in line, they were issued a most welcome woolen blanket, heavy brown quilted cotton jacket and breeches, felt leggings, fur-lined boots with cloth tops and leather bottoms and a pile hat with ear flaps. They retained their packs.

Leaving the supply warehouse, they entered their assigned barracks for the night. Shortly after staking out their sleeping areas on the cold, but apparently clean and lice-free, slate floor, a corporal entered the door and announced the guard roster for the night. Xing groaned when his name was called. He put his jacket back on, grabbed his pack and blanket and joined the others reporting for guard mount.

A light rain began to fall shortly before midnight. Xing's shift was from midnight until 2:00 A.M. As he walked his post near the supply building he couldn't imagine being more miserable. He thought of Mei in her warm bed at home and wondered how long it would be before he could share it with her. At 0200 he was relieved. He returned to the guard house, gladly accepted a cup of tea from the sergeant-of-the-guard and sat by a small charcoal stove for nearly an hour before he felt warm and dry enough to roll-up in his blanket and fall asleep.

Morning formation took place in the dark. The sky was overcast, promising further rain. After a breakfast of rice and vegetables, the soldiers were told to check the bulletin boards outside the barracks headquarters for their assignments and, thereafter, to fall in with men who were on the same roster. Xing found his company's name included with the group of replacements that would go to the 220th Regiment, 74th Division of the 24th Army Group. The 220th was currently in reserve in the Chorwan Valley, just north of the 38th Parallel. The word was quickly conveyed to the many illiterate members of the company.

There was one other order of business before their departure; the issue of weapons and emergency field rations. The latter consisted of a small sack of millet and several hard biscuits. After they had stowed the rations in their packs, they were ushered into the large armory and instructed to sit on the floor. A grey-haired armorer addressed the group. He held an unfamiliar weapon in his hands.

"Young comrades, you will be leaving in a few hours to join your glorious units on the field of battle. You see before you a different weapon than the old bolt-action Japanese shit-piece that you carried in basic training. Half of you will be issued this Type 50 submachine gun to carry on your journey to the front. It is designed to accept either this 35-round box or this 72-round drum magazine." The armorer demonstrated how the magazines clipped in place.

He continued, "It fires 7.62-mm ammunition at a rate of 700 to 900 rounds per minute. However, I can assure you that anyone caught wasting lead at that rate will be permanently assigned to a grenadier platoon. In that case, your shooting days will be over and your, usually short-lived, throwing days will begin. This submachine gun is simple to operate and maintain. It is dependable in extreme weather conditions. Even the stupidest Northern peasant can become proficient with the Type 50." There were a few subdued chuckles in response to the armorer's remarks.

On the command to fall in, the room's inhabitants sprang to their feet and formed four straight ranks. They were then instructed to count off by two's.

"Half of you will be issued a submachine gun and one ammunition belt for the march to the front. The other half will carry nine pounds of extra ammunition belts so that you won't feel neglected nor feel that you are the recipients of a privilege. Being issued a weapon does not guarantee that you will be assigned to a weapons platoon in combat. That will be left to your unit commander and your non-coms. Those of you who do not receive a weapon now may receive one when you join your unit or you may be assigned to a grenade platoon or sapper squad. In any case, all of you will receive further training with the Type 50 on your journey south. Are there any questions?" There were none, so the men were dismissed to return to their barracks where small groups of them would begin tearing down and reassembling their new "burp guns" under the supervision of the old timers.

At 0800 the column moved out of the front gate of Andong Barracks and headed for the bridges that crossed to Sinuiju, North Korea. The rumors were apparently true. They were going to walk all the way to Chorwan. Soon Xing could see the grey river and the pair of bridges spanning it.

The column of men crossed the span that had once been a railroad bridge. The tracks were now covered with planks. American air power had put the railroads in North Korea out of business. Even the two bridges connecting Andong, Manchuria with Sinuiju, North Korea had been bombed and repaired several times.

As they moved through Sinuiju, the soldiers looked at the devastation. The town had been leveled by U.N. air raids. The people who were able had fled the popular target area but the poor folks had remained and had constructed little shanties out of the wreckage. These poverty-stricken survivors barely paused to look at the Chinese soldiers who had ostensibly come to rescue them from the barbarian invaders. Xing was disgusted with the dispirited reception but kept his feelings to himself.

When they stopped around 10 A.M., Chu flopped down and lit a cigarette, Ho went to relieve himself and Xing fished a rice ball out of his jacket pocket and chewed slowly, savoring each grain. He gazed around him at the dull scene, brown-clad soldiers sitting on brown earth beneath bare, brown trees. His first impression was that Korea was indeed a dung heap.

* * *

Ben stood on the fantail of the MSTS General Daniel H. Hill and stared out into the chilly dark sky. He watched some pelicans, as they followed the ship and swooped down to retrieve garbage that was tossed overboard by the mess personnel. During the three-and-a-half week voyage, Ben often came up on deck to escape the stench of vomit, arm pits and Hexol that permeated the sleeping area below-decks. Somewhere off to the southeast was home and Mary Ellen.

"Permission to interrupt your thoughts, Stew," said Rudy Aguilar as he joined Ben at the railing.

"Permission granted, young trooper," said Ben with a smile. "I thought you would be playing poker with Luis."

"He wiped me out. Took my last buck. Hopefully, we'll get some pay when we process in Japan. But Luis won't get another dime from me."

Rudy, lowering his voice, continued, "I'm glad to have this chance to talk to you, man, without other guys around. I want to thank you for not turning me in for sippin' all that cough syrup back in basic. I was feeling all nervous being away from home for the first time. I was upset because I received a letter from my girl friend, Raquel, saying that she was gonna have a baby. The codeine took the edge off. Helped me forget. But you could have gotten me in big trouble."

"I was a little worried that it was going to be my ass in a sling rather than yours," said Ben. "Afraid that they were going to question me at the dispensary about why I was requisitioning so much cough syrup.

You know, Rudy, being in Korea is going to be a lot more stressful than being at Ford Ord. I hope you're going to be okay at times when other guys lives depend on your being sharp."

"I think I'll be fine," said Rudy. "I tend to feel a high in dangerous situations. I don't think I'll want to fuck up my head with drugs. I know it ain't gonna be a picnic there."

Maybe not, "Ben said. "But anything's better than this smelly old bucket."

Early on Thanksgiving morning, Ben went up on deck to get some air. As he leaned on the rail, the busy harbor of Yokohama gradually loomed into view. He counted twenty-nine freighters and transports moored at the piers.

In minutes, the ship's loudspeakers became active and Ben went below to get his barracks bag and stand ready to line up when his section was called. An hour after going ashore, they were aboard a small train bound for Camp Drake.

* * *

The November days grew colder as the column of PLA reinforcements moved southwest toward Chongju. Maximum temperatures averaged fifty-five degrees and nighttime lows were below freezing. The upside-down day, marching all night and resting out of sight of the US Air Force during the day, served the men well. They were able to keep moving during the coldest part of the night and sleep during the day when it was relatively warmer. The skies were usually overcast and there was some light rain but mostly at night when their bodies were warm from exertion. They were able to sustain marches at a rate of two-and-a-half to four miles an hour depending on the terrain.

Company Commander Chen would halt the march shortly before dawn. The ten man cooking crew would set up immediately, starting their fire under a tent fly. This was probably unnecessary because the sky was usually overcast, but earlier columns had been roasted by US Air Force and Marine napalm drops so Captain Chen insisted that the kitchen boys take all precautions.

While the cooks produced their mouth-watering smells, the remaining one hundred and twelve men in the company would attend meetings. Sometimes these meetings were relatively pleasant, limited to lectures by Political Officer Chao, followed by role plays and group singing. But, at least once a week, Chao would conduct a self-criticism session. At one such meeting, Chao stood and said, "I have committed an error and it troubles me. I lost my temper when I was criticizing a soldier in another platoon and I nearly hit him. I will try very hard not to lose control again." Turning to the group, he asked, "So what have the rest of you done that troubles you?"

Private Chu spoke first. "I have belittled Comrades Ho and Hua in an effort to feel better about myself. I'll try to stop doing so."

"That's a good insight, Comrade Chu," said Chao. You have been doing some serious thinking."

"I've been feeling homesick," said Ho, somewhat crestfallen. "A soldier cannot do his work well if he thinks about home."

"Yes, I've been aware of your reactionary thoughts of home, Comrade Ho," admitted Chao. Please try and drive them from your mind."

Then it was Xing's turn to confess but struggle as he might, he couldn't recall having committed an error. He sat quietly on the ground, unconsciously snapping twigs.

"And you, Comrade Hua," prompted Chao, "what have you done that is unworthy?"

"I have thought very hard about the past days, Political Officer Chao, and I'm unable to think of any errors that I might have committed."

"Perhaps you need to be reminded," replied Chao, "that you groaned and made other disrespectful sounds when you heard that you had been rostered for guard duty in Andong."

Xing was stunned. Captain Chao was not present when he had reacted so. Who had reported him? Probably not Private Ho. He's too stupid, thought Xing, to know what's right and wrong and too timid to approach any officer. It was most likely Chu. After all he is a Party member and has definitely been riding my ass at times. I've got to be more careful. Xing admitted, "Yes I do remember groaning a little. I will try very hard to do my duties cheerfully."

"And we will do what we can to help you carry out your duties cheerfully, Hua," said Chao. "But having to remind you of your transgressions make them not as excusable as they would be if you were to admit them freely. You will need to be punished so that you can learn this lesson well. What do you think, comrades? What would be an appropriate punishment for Hua?"

"Since he likes sentry duty so much," said Chu, "I would suggest posting him on duty for an entire day." Several of the others grunted and nodded their agreement.

"Yes, that would be quite appropriate," responded Chao. "Your comrades, Hua, have suggested that you remain awake after morning meal and spend the day thinking about your attitude and what you might do to become a more willing soldier in the People's Army. Report to the headquarters after you've eaten and remain there until we begin this evening's march. The charge of quarters will be able to keep his eye on you and prod you should you fall asleep. The hours of quiet contemplation will be good for you."

At 0730, Xing joined the chow line and held out his rice bowl to receive his ration of rice and vegetables floating in soup. Still smarting, he started to go off by himself and then thought better of it. By now he suspected that any non-social behavior would be reported. He walked over and sat beside Chu and Ho. The three men quietly slurped their breakfast.

Upon finishing, Chu belched his appreciation and Ho offered to take all three bowls and rinse them. When Ho returned, Chu said, "Have I ever sung *Love Thy Feet* for you two boys?" Both shook their heads. "Well, it's a good one. It was composed by a comrade on the long march in 1949. Goes something like this."

>Very useful is a pair of feet;
>Without them you can't do a damn thing.
>I am glad to learn we're marching again,
>For here comes a chance of rendering service.
>In case you get blisters,
>Gently pierce and dry them, applying kerosene.
>For heaven's sake, don't peel blisters.
>Bathe them when you camp down
>And don't forget to give them credit
>At summing up time.

Chu sang the song in a soft, clear voice. When he was through, Xing felt somewhat better. He excused himself and headed for the company headquarters.

Xing sat on the ground in the headquarters area. He started to reflect on his "reactionary" behavior but quickly decided that he wasn't going to spend the day wasting his time that way. When the CQ was busy with other matters, Xing would glance around him to see if he were being observed. When it appeared safe to do so, he would remove his bent photo of Mei and little Xing from his jacket pocket, take a quick peek and replace it. He spent much of the day communing with them, dwelling on pleasant times so that his face would not betray his heartache.

At 1600 the CQ awakened Xing with a gentle shake and told him that it was time for the evening meal. It was already growing dark. Fighting to regain complete consciousness, Xing mumbled, "I wasn't asleep. I was just thinking."

"You've been in deep thought for about two hours, Private Hua. But don't worry, no one will know about it. I would have awakened you if anyone had come around, especially that son of a pig, Captain Chao. In the Nationalist Army, you would have been beaten and that would have been the end of it. I preferred that to this sneaky tattling."

"Thank you for your kindness," said Xing. Obviously the other soldier felt that he could trust him or he wouldn't have made such dangerous statements. Although Xing felt that he could trust the man, he didn't want to increase the risk through further conversation. He shrugged and left for the chow line.

At dusk the column reformed. Five rifle squads took the point, thirty headquarters personnel took the middle and the remaining four rifle squads brought up the rear. The cooks fell in with the headquarters personnel, having quickly struck and folded the tent fly and cleaned the cooking pots. The latter hung on a carrying pole supported on the shoulders of two members of the kitchen crew.

Political Officer Chao strode over to Xing's squad and wished them all a good evening and a pleasant march. As they moved out, he announced that he would like to march beside them for awhile.

"And you, Comrade Hua, did you have a profitable day?"

"Yes, Political Officer, I see things much more clearly now."

"Good, Hua, then we are still friends." Xing responded to that ridiculous assumption with a smile and a nod of his head."

After a few minutes, Chao said, "Comrade Ho."

"Yes, Political Officer Chao."

"It would be very nice if you would lead the squad in the singing of the *Rules and Remarks.*

Ho belted out the first line to set the pitch and then the rest of the squad and soon the entire company chimed in with:

> Our rules are:
> All actions are subject to command.
> Do not steal from the people.
> Be neither selfish nor unjust.
> We are to remember these remarks:
> Replace the door when you leave the house.
> Roll up the bedding on which you have slept.
> Always be courteous.
> Be honest in your transactions.
> Return what you borrow.
> Replace what you break.
> Do not bathe nor urinate in the presence of women.
> Do not, without authority, search the pocketbooks
> Of those you arrest.

WINTER 1952-53

BY THE SECOND WINTER of the Korean War, the U.N. and communist lines of battle had solidified. The opposing forces built fortifications facing each other and spanning the entire peninsula. This situation had the appearance of the trench warfare in World War I but was actually somewhat different. In the former conflict, opposing divisions controlled relatively narrow but very deep sections of the line of contact and had friendly units on either side of them. In Korea, however, divisions controlled broad sections of the battle line (MLR), but their regiments were frequently dug in on isolated hilltops and separated from other units by hundreds of meters or more.

Little activity occurred throughout most of the summer and fall of 1952. Assaults on isolated positions, sieges of U.N. outposts, and especially heavy artillery bombardments characterized this phase. A positive aspect of this period was the revelation that ROK troops demonstrated that, when properly trained and supported, they could slug it out toe-to-toe with the communist forces.

Engagements during this period included fighting between the 7th Marine Regiment and parts of the 7th and 45th Infantry Divisions against Chinese forces at various points along the western sector of the front in early July. There were repeated communist attacks directed toward Old Baldy, Bunker Hill, and Outpost Bruce. During a Chinese attack on Outpost Kelly, the 65th Infantry Regiment from Puerto Rico suffered 350 casualties. The Oklahoma National Guard's 45th Division and its 245th Tank Battalion engaged in their most fierce fighting of the war in the area around T-Bone Hill while Chinese units attacked the ROK 9th Infantry Division on White Horse Hill and the French Battalion on nearby Arrowhead Hill.

In October, Eighth Army Commander James Van Fleet ordered a limited offensive to improve the center of the UN lines by capturing a complex of four hills - Triangle Hill, Pike's Peak, Jane Russell Hill, and Sandy Hill - northeast of Kumwha in the Iron Triangle. The U.N. forces suffered approximately 9000 casualties in this operation while accomplishing very little in the way of capturing new terrain. The Chinese continued to be willing to trade men for terrain. They suffered 19,000 casualties on Triangle Hill alone.

The Fifth RCT, which had been involved in the IX Corps offensive in October 1951, remained on the line near Kumsong until it was relieved by elements of the California National Guard's 40th Division in February 1952. The combat team was then dispatched to the POW camps on Koje-do where they pulled guard duty for three months. Following that the Fifth RCT was placed on Line Minnesota in the Punchbowl sector and was not relieved until November. They moved back into reserve at Tokkol-li in the Yang-gu Valley.

Meanwhile the truce negotiations at Panmunjom dragged off and on. In October, 1952, the talks were yet again interrupted by a Communist walkout and the war became a political football in the United States as the elections approached. Americans, tired of the war, put Dwight D. Eisenhower in the White House. "Ike" had promised to end the conflict. The truce talks did not resume until March of 1953. The uncertainty caused by Joseph Stalin's death motivated Kim Il Sung of North Korea to approve resumption of the talks and acceptance of the UN proposal to exchange sick and wounded prisoners.

* * *

It was shortly after noon when the "Toonerville Trolley" deposited Ben and his buddies at Camp Drake. The camp, an aging installation in the Yokohama-Tokyo area had originally been a military academy. It had been taken over during World War II by the Japanese Imperial Army and had passed to the control of the U.S. Army in 1945.

The young replacements spent the afternoon of their Thanksgiving holiday in their block-long barracks building, then left for a turkey dinner in the mess hall and finally retired to the beer bar. Ben, having retained much of his Camp Stoneman pay, felt compelled to buy a couple of rounds for the destitute poker players.

Saturday morning they began three days of processing. First they were subjected to four hours of classes on the military situation in Korea and were then led to the armory where they were issued brand-new cosmoline-coated M-1 rifles and M-2 bayonets, a shorter version of the M-1 bayonet used in basic training. They spent the afternoon cleaning their weapons, then stood in line to have their shot records checked and then, moved on to another line to receive an advance payment of twenty dollars. When they retired to the beer bar after dinner, Luis worked the room in an effort to collect his poker winnings.

Monday morning they were summoned to the Finance Office for interviews regarding allotments to be sent home, the preparation of wills and the designation of G.I insurance beneficiaries. Ben filled out an application to have $50 a month deducted from his pay and sent to his father. That would leave him with $32 a month walking-around money. His goal was to have at least $600 sitting in the Bank of America in Folsom when his tour in Korea was ended. In the afternoon, the replacements went out to the zero-fire range and fired their new weapons in order to adjust the elevation and windage settings.

That evening, in the clothing warehouse, they stacked the forty pounds of duds that they had been issued at Fort Ord on a long table and drew eighteen pounds of clothing that was more appropriate for winter in Korea. There would be no need for their wool and cotton Class-A uniforms, low quarter shoes, raincoats, heavy overcoats and garrison caps. These were collected and replaced with winter underwear, wool shirts and trousers, an olive-drab sweater, a wool muffler and a pile jacket to wear under their poplin field jacket. Each man was issued a pile field cap made of poplin and lined with alpaca. They retained their herringbone twill fatigues, cotton field caps and summer underwear. Their discarded uniforms would be laundered, checked for wear and issued to men who were going home or, temporarily, to men who would be coming to Kyushu, Camp Drake or Osaka for rest and recuperation. Other items of clothing and equipment would be theirs when they reported to their units.

On Tuesday morning Ben and his three friends from Fort Ord received their orders. The foursome became part of a one hundred and fifteen-man levy that was being assigned to the Fifth Regimental Combat Team. Ben and Rudy were destined for one of the rifle battalions and Luis was assigned to the 72nd Combat Engineer Company. All four men would travel initially to the 40th Division Replacement Depot in Ch'unch'on, since the Fifth RCT was currently attached to the Fortieth.

Jerry Holmes was surprised that he was being sent to the 555th Field Artillery Battalion. His MOS, like that of his colleagues, was "light weapons infantry." When he questioned the personnel specialist, the fellow shrugged and offered the explanation that there had been times when artillery outfits had been ambushed or assaulted requiring the artillerymen to fight as infantry. The 555th may well have requested some replacements with sixteen weeks of infantry training. That news didn't make Jerry feel better about his assignment.

On the evening of November 28th, the group of two thousand replacements set sail for Inchon, Korea. Early on the morning of December 1, they were awakened by the noise of the ship in the process of dropping anchor. When they assembled on the deck, the weather was clear and cold. Ben was thrilled by the sight of the rugged snow-capped mountains to the north and to the east.

Another antiquated Japanese train awaited the men bound for the Ch'unch'on "Rep'l Depot." It was unheated and furnished with hardwood benches. The smell was certainly no improvement over the troops quarters on the *D.H. Hill* although its source was a mystery. There was no toilet in sight.

Ben's spirits were not at all dampened by the wintry day. He was fascinated by the view of the frozen rice paddies and the little thatch-roofed farm villages with charcoal smoke curling from the chimneys.

At mid-morning, the train stopped for an extended period near Uijongbu. Soldiers from another replacement depot came aboard and took the remaining seats in the car. By now Ben was starting to notice the discomfort of the cramped wooden benches. His tailbone and his bladder had just about reached their limits when they reached the next town and he was able to get off and stretch a bit and relieve himself.

After that, the train, rolling along at twenty miles an hour, seemed to stop every five minutes. Whenever it did, crowds of hungry, shivering kids would come alongside and beg or hawk their wares. They flashed bottles bearing *Echo Springs* and *Southern Comfort* labels but had few takers. Most of the replacements were short of funds and had been warned that the local booze was either tan-colored anti-freeze or bourbon cut with water.

The plight of the children was distressing to Ben. He had considered himself somewhat financially strapped during his family's recent financial struggle. These starving little kids with dried mucous on their faces certainly put that perception in proper perspective.

Finally, after fourteen hours of cold, cramped misery, the train arrived at Wonju. From there they journeyed by truck to Ch'unch'on. The road from Wonju to Ch'unch'on was a muddy, narrow trail that wound up and down and around. Oxcarts filled with hay or household goods apparently had the right of way. The small convoy of deuce-and-a-half trucks stopped frequently to keep from running the carts off the road. There was barely enough room for two vehicles to pass without rubbing fenders. The sight of the town reminded Ben of pictures that he had seen of war-torn Europe.

Ch'unch'on, once a thriving small industrial and farming town on the highway northeast of Seoul, had been reduced to a pile of rubble. Several small factories had been gutted leaving shells of twisted steel. Bomb and artillery craters pocked the roads and streets and fields in and around the city. There were some signs, however, that the proud residents of Ch'unch'on were attempting to reconstruct parts of the town hoping that the armies wouldn't return and destroy it again.

On Wednesday morning, December 5, a convoy of seven trucks arrived to pick up the regiment's newest members. The trip north to the village of Tokkol-li, where the Fifth RCT was in reserve, took most of the day. The road wound through a string of cone-shaped rust-colored hills. In the troughs between the hills were dormant rice paddies. There was little vegetation other than some struggling scrub pines.

Because of the open ends of the trucks, the ride was "brass monkey" cold. There was some voluntary shifting of seats after each rest stop so that the same soldiers did not have to ride the entire distance at the back of the truck.

Ben noticed that the army had posted English-language signs at the outskirts of each small, nearly deserted village. They passed through Sugu-dong, Taegong-ni, and Tochon-ni before reaching their destination. Ben had an aptitude for languages and soon surmised that the suffix *dong* must mean *city* and *ni* must mean *hamlet* since Sugu was a much larger rubble pile than Taegong and Tochon where all that remained were the ruins of several small adobe huts.

The Fifth RCT had been at Tokkol-li for the entire month of November. Ben, Rudy and the others who had been assigned to the First Battalion were dropped off at battalion supply to draw down-filled sleeping bags, helmets, entrenching tools, field packs, cartridge belts and canteens.

Ben traded his leather combat boots for a pair of size 13 insulated rubber "thermo" or "Mickey Mouse" boots. Rudy Aguilar, foot size 8 ½, was out of luck. The supply sergeant was temporarily out of small sizes in the thermo boots so Rudy was issued a pair of shoe-pacs, leather boots with rubber soles and partial rubber uppers. The latter were more suitable for late fall or early spring. The sergeant was apologetic about it but explained that Rudy would just have to get by in shoe-pacs until the next shipment of thermo boots arrived from Japan. Rudy shrugged it off wondering what all the fuss was about. The supply sergeant handed him a couple of pairs of felt insoles and six pairs of ski socks to go with the shoe-pacs.

Laden with equipment, Ben and Rudy went in search of their new home. They had been assigned to Able Company. They wound through the maze of tents until they spied A Company's guide-on banner flapping in the breeze. Ben stood at the entrance to the headquarters tent and glanced around for a place to knock. Glancing up from his field desk and sensing the young soldier's confusion, Master Sergeant Frank Carroll growled, "What do you lads want?"

Struggling to remember whether there was some protocol for reporting in to first sergeants, Ben replied, somewhat tentatively, "We're Stewart and Aguilar, First Sergeant. We've been assigned to this company." They handed their orders to Carroll.

"You've gotta be the two replacements for First Platoon. Chogie on down about three tents and find Lieutenant Stebbins, your platoon leader. He'll assign you to a squad tent and then y'all come on back here this evening and check in with Cap'n Anderson. The company commander will want to have a chat with you two."

Second Lieutenant Andrew Stebbins had been a community college student in Macon, Georgia when the Korean Conflict began. Early in 1952, anticipating that he was about to be drafted, he enlisted for Officer Candidate School. He had been sent directly from Fort Benning to Korea in September to help ease the shortage of young company-grade officers. When Ben and Rudy reported to him, Stebbins looked like somebody had stepped in some doggie doodoo.

"Where're you boys from?" drawled a disdainful Stebbins.

Ben replied, "I'm from California, sir. From Orangevale, a little crossroads near Sacramento."

"What did you do there in the land of the fairies?" continued the lieutenant.

"Well, not much yet, really," said Ben with a forced smile. "I've been a student at Stanford for the past two years." Ben hoped that this would not turn into a long interrogation. He wanted to get settled and realize a little distance between himself and the platoon leader.

"We don't get many Stanford men here, Stewart. Here y'all are just another dipshit rifleman. And you, Agolar, or however you pronounce it, I'm afraid that the mess hall is fresh out of tortillas and beans."

"No sweat, Lieutenant," replied Rudy, covering up his irritation with an impassive face. "I've been able to survive on army chow for the past five months."

The two young men beat a hasty retreat from their first encounter with Mr. Stebbins after getting their tent assignment. When they found their squad tent, they were relieved to find that it had recently been winterized. Its plywood floor and charcoal heater were the army's response to the imminent Korean winter. Ben and Rudy found two bunks under which there was no one's gear and claimed them for their own.

The squad tent's other inhabitants had not yet returned from a day of training. Their day was being devoted to instruction on the setting and detection of anti-personnel mines and booby traps, the use of the 3.5-inch rocket launcher against enemy bunkers and the company in attack.

The Fifth RCT had received a great number of reinforcements in recent weeks and would soon go back up on the line. Colonel Alfred, the regimental commander, concerned about all the new men and also about veterans who might be a little rusty from manning positions on a stable front for a long period of time, wanted to restore his unit to maximum combat effectiveness.

"Well, Rudy, what do you think of the LT?" queried Ben.

Rudy hesitated a few second seconds and then replied, "Well he seems like a grade A asshole but I guess the army hires guys like him to keep us in the right mood to kill Gooks and Chinamen. Killing don't come naturally. Stebbins makes me feel like killing."

"Do you feel like killing Chinamen or Stebbins?" countered Ben.

"That's the part I haven't figured out yet," said Rudy. "So far I don't really have any beef with ol' Joe Chink. He hasn't done anything to bother me."

The chat was interrupted by a recording of a bugler playing chow call. Ben and Rudy grabbed their field jackets, pile caps and canteen cups and went in search of dinner.

The mess tent was nothing more than a tropical fly to protect the food from rain or light snow. The two newcomers waited in line until they could fill their mess kits with beef stew, their canteen cups with coffee and pick up some more of the large round crackers to which they had been treated on their first night in the army and many evenings since. When they finished eating they doused and brushed their mess kits, cups and silverware in a large, sudsy, gas-heated tub and then rinsed them in another tub of chemically-treated water.

Back at the squad tent, they encountered their tent mates for the first time. They were cooly welcomed by Corporal Rodger Kelly, a Southern Californian and Corporal Whitey Lockwood from Wilkes-Barre, Pennsylvania. Lockwood did ask what was currently on the hit parade at home. Ben and Rudy mentioned Rosie Clooney's *Half as Much,* Eddie Fisher's *Wish You Were Here,* and Tex Ritter's *Do Not Forsake Me* from the movie *High Noon.* Ben sang a few bars from each song, but Lockwood was unimpressed. The new songs weren't "country" enough for him.

PFC Gene Simms from Bend, Oregon and PFC Verne Taylor, a Canadian from Vancouver, expressed warmer greetings since they saw the newcomers as two more additions to the guard roster. The remaining members of the squad were KATUSA Privates Kim Won Pak and Kim Yup Sung.

More privates meant fewer cold evenings on guard mount for the individual soldier. There had already been one night when the temperature dropped to zero degrees Fahrenheit and nightly lows were expected to average about ten degrees throughout December. On the other hand, there was no KP duty. Kitchen police was happily handled by Korean nationals employed by the army.

"We haven't had a chance to shower since Camp Drake," said Rudy. What are the hours at the shower point?"

"Unfortunately there aren't any," responded Simms. "The shower point's fucked up and can't be fixed until Service Company gets the replacement parts they need. We haven't had a shower since Thanksgiving."

"Best you can do is get a helmet full of water from Sergeant Palmer in the morning and take a whore's bath," suggested Lockwood. "He usually has a five-gallon gas can of water sitting on his stove in the morning."

"Who's Sergeant Palmer?" asked Rudy.

"Palmer's our platoon sergeant."

"Is he anything like Lieutenant Stebbins?" asked Ben.

"Negatory," responded Corporal Kelly, "Palmer's a good man. Stebbins is a sorry son of a bitch."

Kim Won Pak nodded in agreement. "Yes, Sargie Palmer is good son of a bitch. He be in Korea rong time. He number one sojer."

"You tell 'em Kim One," said Kelly. "Before you know it your English will get so good they'll have to make you an officer. Turning to Ben and Charlie, he continued, "We call these two guys Kim One and Kim Two. It's easier than trying to remember their full names." Ben and Rudy shook hands with the two beaming KATUSA's.

Saturday morning the platoon attended a firing demonstration of North Korean and Chinese weapons. It was the first, but unfortunately not the last, time that Ben would hear the distinctive **r-r-r-rept** of the "Burp" gun. Attempts were made to demonstrate the firing of 61mm, 82mm, and 120mm mortars using U.S. ammunition but those trying to use the captured weapons were having an inordinate number of problems getting them to function. The weapons instructors apologized and said they hoped to try again with some better hardware. Sergeant First Class Rob Palmer considered the whole show a waste of a good morning. He told the hapless gunners that if they captured anymore weapons to "stick them up their ass" and turned and marched the platoon back to camp.

Rumor had it that Bob Hope and his troupe would entertain the regiment on Saturday afternoon but the comedian, singers and dancers that arrived were not of Hope's level of celebrity. Nevertheless, Ben enjoyed seeing well-groomed, well-fed, round-eyed young ladies for the first time in several weeks. He was reminded of Mary Ellen, so when he got back to camp, he rummaged around in his barracks bag for some stationery that he had picked up at a USO.

7 Dec 1952
Dear Ellie,
Well, I bet you've been wondering where I am and where I've been. Last Wednesday, a handful of us from Fort Ord arrived at our new home somewhere behind the lines in Eastern Korea. I've been assigned to Company A of the 5th Regimental Combat Team. The trip over was pretty cruddy. There was a

lot of seasickness and I spent most of my time on my bunk (the top one of six bunks) which I had to share with my barracks bag. When we got to Japan we turned in all the crap in our barracks bags and were issued clothing that was more appropriate for the cold climate here. How's that for Army intelligence?

There's not much going on here other than further training and occasional details painting rocks white to mark the paths through the mud in the company area. We did get to go to a USO show this afternoon. There was a great small instrumental combo and several really cute chicks. They reminded me of the one that I said good-bye to about a month ago at Camp Stoneman. I still feel really dumb when I think about that evening. Not too smooth, Stewart. I hope you have forgiven me.

I don't know exactly when we'll move up on the line and see some action. It is rumored that we'll leave here before New Years.

Please write me as soon as you can. My address and APO number are on the envelope.

Lots of love, Ben

After writing his letter, Ben realized that he didn't have any stamps and had no idea where he could find the nearest Post Exchange. His dilemma was soon solved when Whitey Lockwood explained that he just had to write *FREE* on the envelope in place of a stamp and write *Via Air Mail* and then take the letter over to the supply sergeant for mailing. It was one of the many benefits of soldiering in a combat area.

The next week sped by. Most of the training was done at night since nearly all contact with the enemy would take place after dark. The training focused on company-sized attacks, map-reading and patrolling. The experienced privates in Ben's squad were pulled from training on Thursday and assigned to a security detail for a nearby communications and tactical air direction installation. That left fewer men for Lieutenant Stebbins to badger so he focused most of his efforts on Ben and Rudy in an attempt to intimidate the two newest members of the platoon.

The men from Company A were relieved of guard duty by Company B on Friday. There was good news for all when it was announced that the shower point was back in operation.

Following showers on Saturday morning, Ben and the others donned clean underwear, fatigues and socks, cleaned and oiled their weapons and equipment and arranged everything neatly for a "junk on the bunk" inspection.

At 0900 Lieutenant Stebbins entered the tent with a smirk on his face and a little "chogie" stick in his right hand. He was accompanied by Sergeant Palmer. Stebbins stopped at Ben's bunk, hissed "Stewaht" and began examining Ben's mess kit and other items by flipping them with his little stick.

"Lieutenant Prick apparently doesn't want to touch anything belonging to a low life like me," thought Ben. "I don't know how much more I can take from this cracker-ass plowboy." But Ben remained outwardly unruffled so Stebbins moved on to see if he could bait Rudy Aguilar.

Just as the lieutenant was winding up his inspection, a tall black soldier, entered the tent and said, "Sir, I'm from Medical Company. Would this be a good time to talk to the platoon about cold injuries?"

It had been three months since Ben had heard that voice and seen that wide smile. He said, "Well, I'll be damned. Enter Grady Williams fresh off the boat from San Antone."

"You are still at attention, Stewaht!" snapped Stebbins. The lieutenant turned and nodded at Grady, stalled around for awhile, and when he felt that he had impressed the young medic with his importance, turned and exited the squad tent.

Grady turned to Ben, "Can I sit on your bunk, G.I?"

"No sweat. It's already failed inspection," replied Ben.

"Sorry about that," said Grady as he gestured to the other squad member to have a seat.

"Fellows, I'm Grady Williams, First Platoon, Medical Company. I've been assigned to help you guys stay healthy when we go back up on the line."

"Hey, Doc, you got some cough syrup with codeine?" interrupted Rudy. "I think I feel a little tickle coming on." Rudy winked at Ben.

"I've already got your number, Aguilar. I suggest you take a swig out of your canteen. Anyway, while we're up there, I'll be around to disinfect bunkers, poison the rats, check the chlorination of the water and, when the mosquitoes are thick, see that you folks take your chloroquine at least once a week."

"Is malaria much of a problem here?" asked Ben.

"That's what they tell me. But…most of all I'm going to ride you guys about your feet. You've got to wash your dogs daily and put on a dry pair of socks."

"How are you supposed to get your socks dry when you're up on the line?" asked Rudy.

Whitey Lockwood fielded the question. "You wash your dirty socks out after washing your feet. Then you ring them out and tuck them inside your shirt next to your skin. They'll be ready to wear the following day."

Grady noticed Rudy's shoepacs and shook his head. "If you don't get Mickey Mouse boots by the time we pull out, Rudy, you are going to have to be very careful about your feet. They'll sweat like hell in those shoepacs. See if you can get another set of insoles. You need to remove shoepacs frequently and switch to dry socks and insoles. Otherwise the skin on your feet will soften and drop off in chunks. Guys have spent as much as fifteen days in the hospital with shoepac foot."

After the squad meeting broke up, Ben and Grady had very little time for a reunion. The company was forming up in the company street. Following roll call, they marched to the parade ground for a regimental review. The music was provided by the 40th Division Band. At the end of the review, awards were presented. Three enlisted men received the Silver Star and nineteen officers and men received the Bronze Star, several with the V for valor. This was the first evidence that Ben had seen that suggested that the Fifth Regimental Combat Team had been through some scary times.

* * *

Monday morning, 15 December, the men in the rifle battalions boarded a convoy of deuce-and-a-half's and traveled a few miles north where they passed to the operational control of the 223rd Infantry Regiment. Company A was to relieve the 40th Recon Company on the line on the northern lip of the Punch Bowl, a broad valley formed by an ancient volcanic crater. It is some three and a half miles in diameter and rimmed by hills ranging from one to two thousand feet in elevation. The northern rim had been in UN hands since it had been captured by the First Marine Division on 3 September 1951.

When the convoy reached Inje, it turned due north on Highway 453 for the fifteen-mile trip to the Punchbowl. Entering the valley, they passed several rises in elevation in the middle of the bowl. Ben, from his vantage point at the rear of the truck could see dormant rice paddies and the ruins of several tiny villages or clusters of farm dwellings. There was an abandoned airstrip on the edge of the village of Songhwangdang.

Rudy was elated. "Fuckin-A, man. We're finally in four-point country and I'm gonna be able to use this baby." He patted his Browning automatic rifle fondly.

"Actually we won't get four points for this month," said Ben. "There aren't enough days left and you're gonna be sorry, Rudy. When they drop us off you'll have to hump that heavy mother the rest of the way up the hill." A BAR man had to carry his twenty pound weapon as well as twenty pounds of ammunition.

"That's right, Aguilar, you'll be wantin' to trade for a carbine or a grease gun," added Whitey Lockwood. "The facts of the case, though, the M1 and the BAR function better in this kind of weather. The gun oil turns into glue on the smaller weapons."

After a while the rutted pavement gave way to a one-lane gravel road. An MP stopped the convoy for about ten minutes to give the right of way to a group of returning trucks. When the road was clear they resumed their trip, encountering tighter and tighter turns as they ascended the mountain. Some of the World War II vintage 2 ½-ton trucks were not yet equipped with automatic transmissions and the drivers ground a lot of gears as they shifted up and down between first and fifth gears.

The convoy stopped a couple of miles south of the company's assigned sector. From this point on snow and ice made the road impassable for large vehicles. Besides, trucks were scarce and parts were hard to get. There was no sense bringing them within the range of enemy artillery. Men, however, were less difficult to acquire so they climbed over the tailgates and fell in on the sides of the dirt road and moved out to begin the long climb to their new position. After a couple of miles, the dirt road culminated in a narrow trail that rose five hundred vertical feet in the space of a quarter mile.

Ben watched as some supplies were being sent to the top on a tramway. "It would sure be nice to throw my gear on that thing," he sighed. His prayers were answered when Sergeant Palmer announced, "You men stack your packs over there by the tram. They'll come up on the next tramway trip."

Although relieved of their packs, the trip to the top was still difficult. Rob Palmer slung his carbine diagonally across his back and began the ascent. He instructed the others to follow him at five-yard intervals. There were times when he had to turn sideways and dig the sides of his boot soles into the muddy trail. The rest of the platoon took advantage of the small toeholds. By the time they reached the top, most of the men were carrying their helmets in order to give their necks a rest.

When they arrived in the sector assigned to A Company, members of the 40th Recon Company were already filing out of the communications and supply trench at the rear of the hill. They assured their replacements that their time on the line would be "cold and quiet." Ben was comforted by their report.

As they reached the crest of the hill, Ben was reminded of pictures that he had seen of World War I fortifications. Squad-sized fighting bunkers had been dug on the front of the hill. They were connected by a trench that varied in depth from five to eight feet. On the rear, or friendly, side of the hill there were a few sleeping bunkers which would house those men who were not on watch at the time. The trench on the front of the hill was indented with three fighting holes per nine-man rifle squad. These were short trenches that pointed toward the valley floor. That portion of Line Minnesota occupied by the Fifth RCT formed a shallow arc. It followed a clearly defined ridgeline with generally uniform, though precipitous slopes. Observation to the front of the positions was generally good except for a few close-in dead spaces caused by the steepness of the forward slopes. Fields of fire were short because of the steep slopes and deep draws.

The enemy, reportedly two regiments from the 15th Division, III North Korean Corps, occupied a series of hill masses opposite the regimental line (MLR) which formed a rough horseshoe with the open end facing south. Extending south from these prominent hills were numerous fingers leading gradually down into the valley floor to the front of the MLR.

These terrain features provided the North Koreans with an excellent defensive position. The principal hills were connected by wide, relatively level ridges which were believed to comprise his main line of defense. The many fingers leading south provided innumerable sites for his outpost positions. The high ground afforded the North Korean units excellent observation over their entire front and the Fifth RCT's main line of resistance. From the enemy's main line, he was in a position to support, by fire or reinforcement, any of his outpost positions with comparative ease and to command all avenues of approach.

Captain Anderson and Master Sergeant Carroll established the company command post in a small bunker off the communications trench, an entry trench that came forward from the friendly side of the hill. The fighting bunker on the extreme left became home for the company's 50-caliber machine gun. The middle bunker was assigned to the weapons squad so that they could quickly move the recoilless rifle from one end of the works to the other. The weapons squad was also responsible for any 60-mm mortar fire needed for perimeter defense or counter-battery fire. Mortar emplacements had been dug on the rear slope of the hill. Ben and Rudy and their fellow squad members were assigned to a fighting bunker between the machine gun emplacement and the weapons section.

The previous tenants had begun the winterization of the sleeping bunkers on the friendly side of the hill. As Ben drew aside the army blanket door, he noticed that rough planks and parts of wooden boxes covered the floor and that a small oil-burning Yukon stove, measuring 3'x 1'x 1', was doing a fair job of heating the space. It was fed by a five-gallon can of heating oil resting on top of the bunker. A small charcoal stove stood by in the event of an oil shortage. Heat had no way of escaping but out of the entrance. The heavily timbered roof covered with sandbags and earth was a good source of insulation. Stretchers, hung from the beams by discarded communications wire, served as bunks. An army of rats would discourage any sleepers from reclining on the ground.

Captain Anderson ordered the men to complete any winterization needed. He phoned in a request for Korean Labor Corps workers. He was uneasy about the shallow points of the trench, wishing all of it to be at least seven feet in depth. The loose dirt was used to reinforce bunker roofs that had been battered by recent mortar and artillery attacks. Throughout the next week, the men of Able Company worked on refurbishing the bunkers and seeing that the Korean laborers dug in all the right places.

The Koreans dug a new latrine hole on the rear slope, covered it with a wooden ammunition box seat and screened it with three ponchos. A couple of piss tubes were driven into the snow. Sergeant Palmer made quite a point of saying that he would "guaran-god dam-tee" harsh treatment for any man who didn't use the facilities. He didn't "want to see no yellow icicles" in the trench.

One evening after chow there was a squad meeting with Lieutenant Stebbins and Sergeant Palmer. Stebbins gave a brief map talk defining possible avenues of approach by the enemy and asked if there were any questions.

"Not about the lay of the land, Lieutenant," replied Ben, "but what do we know about the North Koreans across from us. What kind of fighters are they?"

Stebbins nodded at Rob Palmer and said, "You want to take that one, Sergeant? You probably ran into these guys early on."

"Not really," responded Palmer. "We're pretty sure that we're faced by the 45th and 48th Regiments of the 15th NKPA Division. During the early days of the war around the Pusan Perimeter, they tangled with the 2nd Division and a number of ROK units. Our regiment operated to the south and west of them. In September of '50, the ROK 1st Division surrounded them and beat the shit out of them. They didn't reappear until the following February. Since then they have concentrated on defense. They were pulled off the line last January and didn't return until July, so I would say they're probably pretty healthy and rested but have very little experience attacking. That suits me fine."

Lieutenant Stebbins took his leave but several members of the squad lingered to visit with Rob Palmer. Corporal Kelly asked, "Why are you here, Sarge." You paid your dues here a couple of years ago. You had a steady job at Fort Ord? I don't get it."

"I volunteered to come back. This is where I belong. I tried it Stateside for nearly a year and a half. I even tried marriage. But a wife and unpaid bills are too much stress. I'm better off here. I feel very lucky that my request to return to the Fifth RCT was granted."

"Never figured you for a family man," observed Whitey Lockwood.

"I didn't either until I met this gal at Mortimer's, a bar in Marina. Before I knew it, she hauled me up in front of the chaplain. It was okay at first but her two kids began to get to me. They were rotten as hell and I didn't know what to do with 'em. I'm happier here trying to raise you kids. She still gets my allotment check but I'm not going back there. I'll have to deal with that when I get home."

Rob continued as he glanced at Ben, Kelly and Lockwood. "I guess you college guys have a hard time understanding a man who just wants to soldier for twenty years. You probably think that's pretty stupid."

"I felt that way about career soldiers during basic," said Ben, "but not now. You're my college professor now. I need a crash course on everything you know, Sergeant Palmer. My goal is to earn my thirty-six points and make it home alive. You apparently know how to accomplish that."

"There are no guarantees, Stewart. But combat is no more dangerous than driving on Highway 101. Your staying alive on the highway depends on your driving skill and on your not being involved in an accident. Death in combat is just another accident; due sometimes to carelessness.

* * *

Around 1400 hours on Christmas Day, word came that the chow truck was waiting down the hill. It was three before Ben's squad was relieved to slip and slide down the trail for Christmas dinner. The squad members endeavored to keep their five yard interval as they descended. Christmas would be an opportune time for the North Koreans to drop some artillery rounds to the rear of Company A's position.

When they finally reached the truck they doused their mess kits in boiling water and then lined up by the large marmite cans to receive turkey, stuffing, green beans, mashed potatoes and gravy, and cranberry sauce. There were seconds. For the first time since leaving Japan, Ben felt full. After dinner, the Protestant and Catholic Chaplains conducted brief Christmas services.

In the middle of the night, Ben paid the price for his holiday feast. He awoke with stomach cramps, tried to ignore them for awhile, but finally accepted the fact that he'd better head for the latrine. He slid out of his warm mummy bag, pulled his boots on without tying them and stumbled down the trench, saying, "This is Stewart, I've gotta crap. I can't remember the fucking password. This is Stewart. I've gotta crap."

As he pulled back the poncho cover, Ben was relieved to see that the ammo box seat was unoccupied. He fought to drop his waterproof pants, wool pants, long johns and cotton undershorts and finally, with his bare butt exposed to a freezing blast of wind out of Manchuria, completed his mandatory assignment. As he returned to the bunker, he said repeatedly, "This is Stewart. I've just been out to take a crap." He didn't want some trigger-happy GI making it his last trip to the latrine.

The total snowfall in December had been only four and half inches but, as the year ended, the nights became even colder as deliveries of heating oil became fewer. Captain Anderson requested both oil and charcoal for heating but the division supply clerks seemed too concerned with their own shortage of ditto stencils, onion skin paper, and paper clips to pay much attention to his requisition.

On New Year's Eve, Able Company was relieved by the 40th Recon and was pulled off the line to join the rest of the First Battalion in a blocking position near the village of Chisong-ni. The troops rested, showered, donned clean fatigues and spent the next few days rehabilitating their equipment and winter clothing. Ben felt almost human again but was still somewhat frustrated by the fact that their sixteen freezing nights on the line had resulted in only three rotation points for December.

On Friday, 8 January, the Fifth RCT returned to its positions along Line Minnesota on the northern lip of the Punchbowl. Baker Company was deployed on the right flank of Company A in a section of the line known as Skyline Drive.

Around sunset, Sergeant Palmer pulled the platoon together for its usual after supper chit chat. He repeated a lot of information about likely avenues of approach by the enemy, where the regiment's artillery and mortars were registered, information on friendly patrols likely to cross their zone, what units were on the company's flanks and behind it. He would make a last check on ammunition, grenades and water and would ask if anybody had anything bugging them other than being in Korea. He announced that the password for the night was *Lily - Liver,* a significant linguistic challenge for any Gook that should overhear it being exchanged.

That night, Ben had early guard from 2000 hours until 2200. Afterward he removed his boots and climbed into his sleeping bag, fully clothed with the contented realization that he would get a whole night's sleep. He left the bag unzipped so that he could tumble out of it quickly in the event that they had some uninvited visitors. Then too, the mummy bag was really a little short for Ben's six-foot, two-inch frame and too pointed at the bottom for his size thirteen feet. Soon after falling asleep, he awoke to the sound of M-1's, burp guns and other automatic weapons over on the right. The firing went on for an extended period but no one disturbed the men in the sleeping bunkers so Ben rolled over and eventually went back to sleep.

The next morning they were told that Second Battalion had repulsed two company-sized attacks and a number of smaller probes. The assaults had been largely directed at Fox Company. Second Battalion had been cursed with a portion of the line that was lower in elevation than that assigned to the other two battalions. In addition, it was plagued by gullies to its front, which provided concealment and could not be probed by automatic weapons. Planting mines in them would have been a possibility but the battalion commander was reluctant to do so because the gullies might also be useful as ambush sites.

Sergeant Palmer, a proud alumnus of Second Battalion, explained that 2/5 had been the recipient of many tough challenges since its arrival in Korea in July, 1950. The sergeant expressed a lot of admiration for the officers and men of that unit. "If that's the case," thought Ben, "I would just as soon admire Second Battalion from afar."

Ben, Rudy, and Corporals Lockwood and Kelley were among the first shift that went down to the company mess point for breakfast. Ben thought about passing up the watery powdered egg mess but then thought better of it. It was already apparent that the waist in his fatigue pants had become at least an inch too large and he hadn't started out with surplus flesh. He downed some eggs and ate some Wheaties without milk. There were little cans of condensed milk but they had frozen slush in them. He observed Whitey mixing the frozen milk with a like amount of frozen jam and eating the concoction with great relish. Ben wondered if he would ever get hungry enough to do likewise. After they had washed and turned in their mess kits, the mess sergeant handed Whitey a six-man case of C-rations, canned fruit, cigarettes and toilet paper for lunch. His parting message was, "Now you fellas have a nice, safe day. I'll see you back here around 1730."

Ben and Rudy picked up some peanut butter and crackers to tote back up to the line. They would furnish a good snack before dinner time. The night before they had forgotten to partake of their peanut butter and crackers much to the delight of a gang of rats who found the tasty morsels after the troops had fallen asleep.

All was quiet until the following Wednesday and Thursday nights when patrols from King Company engaged enemy patrols. Ben was feeling a mix of relief and guilt that the enemy activity was being directed against the other two battalions. Rudy didn't share his feelings. He wished that Able Company would get its share of work.

On Friday morning ground fog blanketed the company area. After he completed his morning paperwork, Captain Anderson chose to take advantage of the fog and worked beside the men to improve the barbed wire obstacles in front of their position. Ben and Rudy worked together, each carrying several four-foot strands of barbed wire. Whenever Ben found a break, he would take the broken strand, thread it through the eye at one end of the repair strand and hand off the other end of the repair strand to Rudy. Rudy would then find the other end of the broken strand, thread it through the other end of the repair strand and pull it tight and wrap it back on itself to close the gap. They tied empty C-ration cans with pebbles in them to the wire so that the cans would rattle and clink if disturbed.

The wire detail withdrew to the trench when Luis Meyer and several other combat engineers arrived to set napalm mines. Ben and Rudy sat on top of the bunker and watched with interest as their basic training buddy and his comrades buried four five-gallon cans of jellied gasoline and fitted them with detonators. They attached the detonators to a trip-wire in front of the barbed wire apron and ran another wire to Lieutenant Stebbins' bunker. It would enable the platoon leader to detonate the napalm electronically. Each drum could spread deadly flames over fifty yards of frontage.

Luis came up for a quick chat before moving along to Baker Company to repeat the process. As he was leaving, he handed a small package to Ben. "Here, Stew, compliments of Uncle Sam."

"What the hell's this, Luis?"

"It's C4. It's a plastic explosive. It's great for heating C-rations. Just break off a little piece and light it. It burns just long enough to get you beans and wienies bubbling."

"Uh, thanks anyway, Luis. I don't mind cold C's." Ben returned the package.

"It's not gonna bite you for crissake, Stew. It's perfectly safe stuff," said Luis.

"Here, Luis, I'll take it," said Rudy. He snatched the small package and dropped it in a side pocket of his field jacket.

Once the engineers had moved on, the infantrymen re-set the machine guns to obtain better fields of fire. Then Captain Anderson spent much of the early afternoon roaming the company area and chatting with the men, partly to be sociable, but mostly to ascertain the state of morale.

A sack of mail arrived on the mess truck that afternoon. Ben received two letters from his mother. One of them contained a page written by his father, a rare occurrence. As he was reading the news from home, Rodger Kelley ducked into the bunker and asked, in a friendly tone, "Whatcha got, Stewart? A letter from some babe?"

"Nope. A couple of letters from home."

"Oh. How are things with your folks?"

"They're looking up. My dad landed a government contract for his machine shop so that's good news."

"What kind of contract?"

"Something to do with making spindles or axles for jeep trailers. It wasn't completely clear to me."

"Well, I'll bet he's happy there's a war on," observed Kelley.

"Sure, Kelley, he's filled with joy. His oldest kid is in Korea in a rifle company and all he thinks about is counting his money."

"Stew, every economist worth his salt says that the U.S. was heading for a depression and that this war has saved the asses of a bunch of corporate fat cats and Wall Street brokers. In fact those guys pushed Harry Truman into starting this mess. Sounds like your old dad just finally got his nose in the trough."

"Kelley, you're full of shit." Ben got up and headed out of the bunker. "I'm gonna go find a quiet place to read."

"Try the latrine, Stew, but be careful that your brains don't fall out."

* * *

On Friday night Rudy Aguilar was selected to be the BAR man on an ambush patrol that was led by Lieutenant Stebbins. Ben was appointed to the support squad. He and others would remain on alert while the ambush squad was out in the valley, reinforcing them if they ran into trouble.

After a briefing in the company command post by Captain Anderson, Rudy returned to the sleeping bunker, where he checked and double checked the working parts of his BAR. Sergeant Palmer had instructed him to pay particular attention to the gas port on his weapon. Carbon build-up could slow its rate of fire even to the point of freezing up during a fire fight.

Satisfied with the condition of the piece, Rudy tried, in vain, to get some rest. He was finally having second thoughts about the wisdom of an expectant father being in such a situation. He glanced over at Ben prostrate on his stretcher bunk.

"I was kinda hoping that Sergeant Palmer would lead my first patrol. I figure I'd have a better chance of making it back with him. He's a lot smarter than Stebbins."

"I hear you, señor," said Ben. "I've had about all the crap I can take from Stebbins."

"No you haven't, Stew. You and I are gonna continue to be shit-eaters until we get our thirty-six points. I'm not going to do anything that will keep me here in this asshole of the world one day long than necessary." Ben grunted his concurrence and went back to daydreaming on his bunk.

The patrol moved out at midnight. They were not quite in position when an enemy ambush patrol opened fire point blank. Two G.I.'s were killed in the first few seconds. One was carrying the PRC-10 radio. The hand set and antenna mount shattered as he fell, rendering the radio inoperative. After an exchange of fire that lasted more than a minute, Stebbins sent a runner to the rear for the support squad.

By the time Ben and the others arrived, all was quiet. Both patrols withdrew to the MLR carrying the bodies of the two dead squad members. As soon as they were safely within reach of the trench line, Captain Anderson requested artillery fire from the 555th FAB. It was not known whether there had been enemy casualties.

At daybreak, Ben was summoned by Captain Anderson. The commanding officer looked like he had been awake all night. He smiled faintly at Ben and said, "Stewart we need a big strapping lad like you to carry the radio whenever you go on patrol but we can't afford to release you to radio school. Have you had any experience with the "Prick 10"?

"We played around with it for a couple of hours during AIT, sir. That's all."

"Well, I'll ring you back when Sergeant Palmer wakes up. I want you to come back here and get some tutoring from him. Any questions?"

"Does that mean that I will be needed on every patrol, sir?"

"Not at all. You will still just do your share of patrols but we lost a damn fine radioman last night and we need to replace him."

That afternoon Sergeant Palmer sat down with Ben and a couple of other men from the platoon and delivered a quick orientation on the operation of the AN/PRC 10 army radio. The contraption weighed thirty-six pounds so he explained that they would be carrying side arms rather than their rifle on patrol. Palmer didn't have much good to say about the World War II relic. It had a relatively short range, poor battery reliability, could be easily jammed by the North Koreans but was often the only connection available between those under heavy enemy pressure and those in a position to help. He had them manipulate the controls and reviewed, with them, the language of army communications.

The following night it was Ben's turn to go on a combination recon/ambush patrol. This time Sergeant Palmer was in command. He instructed Ben to tuck an extra set of batteries inside his shirt to keep them warm. Low temperatures seemed to effect the chemical operation of the batteries and make them inoperative. Captain Anderson had requested low temperature batteries but they were on "back order."

As a matter of fact, a lot of requests were on back order. Probably much of it was due to the fact that the Fifth RCT was continually shifted from the operational control of one division to another. Anderson had suggested that it would simplify matters if the Regiment drew directly from the Eighth Army supply point in Yongdungpo, but this suggestion went unheeded or was dismissed with the explanation that it would lengthen the regimental supply lines. Sergeant Palmer put aside his carbine and drew a semi-automatic five-shot shotgun for the trip. Carbines had not been functioning very well in the zero degree weather.

At 1700 the patrol met in the CP. Captain Anderson picked up a clipboard containing the written patrol order from Headquarters First Battalion and went over the disposition of the enemy, sources of cover and concealment, the general route and the checkpoints. He then turned the meeting over to Rob Palmer who filled in the details. "Kelley, you'll take the point and I'll stay about fifteen yards behind you. Stewart, you'll walk about five yards behind me. You'll be a little safer there. This is your cherry voyage and I don't want to lose another good radio. Doc, you stay five yards behind Stewart and Whitey, you'll take rear guard with your BAR."

When Palmer dismissed the patrol, he asked Ben and Grady to stay. "This is the first patrol for you boys. Watch what we do. You've got to find that balance between stepping very carefully and keeping up with us and maintaining your interval. The ground is frozen and slippery. If you fall, you can bust your tail bone or, worse yet, damage the Prick 10."

Palmer demonstrated how to put the lead foot down weightlessly and feel for twigs and leaves. However, he added that was just for future reference as most noisy materials were now buried under several inches of snow and nothing could be done about he crunch of the snow.

"It's kind of like dancing the rhumba, isn't it, Sergeant?" chuckled Grady.

"If you say so," said Rob without cracking a smile. "Now, both of you, get your flak jackets on and get back here at 1800. Pile caps only. No piss pots on this trip."

Patrol members were issued the 1952 version of the flak jacket. Its two front panels and the back panel contained filler of 12-play basket-weave nylon. The filler was encased in plastic film and was inserted into an outer shell of oxford nylon cloth. It weighed eight and a half pounds and would stop shrapnel, a bayonet and a burp gun bullet. It would not ward off a machine gun or rifle slug. It didn't effect the movement of the hands and arms in any way. The advent of the flak jacket was readily accepted by the GI's. In a war with no clear military objectives and prolonged truce talks, personal survival was the soldier's objective.

After Sergeant Palmer left the CP, Ben paused to chat with Grady Williams who was checking the first aid supplies in his bag. "I don't know whether you heard about my "promotion" to radioman. You wouldn't like to trade jobs, would you? That medical bag has to weigh a lot less than thirty-six pounds. Besides I haven't seen you on guard or on any work details."

"I'll gladly pack your radio, Stew, and pull guard duty, string wire and burn the latrine. Anything you want. You can have this job. Every damn time First Platoon goes on patrol, I go with them. My chances of going home in one piece are worse than yours. Still want to trade?" Ben shook his head and headed for the sleeping bunker.

There was no opportunity this time to lie around half the night and get nervous. However, when the patrol left the line at 1843 hours, Ben was sure that the others could hear his heart beating and his gasps for breath. He had taken a leak twenty minutes before they departed by he felt like he had to go again. Sergeant Palmer whispered an order to take their weapons off safety.

Part of the mission was to determine whether there had been enemy casualties on the previous evening. Regardless of what they found they had been told to stay out until they made enemy contact or were in danger of running out of darkness.

When they reached the approximate location of the previous night's fire fight, a quick search revealed no casualties. Sergeant Palmer motioned to Ben to raise Lieutenant Stebbins on the radio.

Ben turned to the correct frequency and whispered into the mike. "One-six, this is one-two, over."

"Go ahead, one-two. This is one-six," responded Lieutenant Stebbins. Ben handed the mike to Sergeant Palmer.

"We're at the site of last night's party," said Palmer. "The area is squeaky clean, over." One-two was code for first platoon, second squad. One-six was the designation for the leader of first platoon.

"Well, keep your eyes open, one-two, over."

"Sir, given the temperature, I suggest that we Hank Snow at 0100 at the latest. Four hours should be plenty, over."

"Negative, one-two," responded Stebbins. "Battalion makes that decision. Y'all will come back when I call for you. Do you read, over?"

"Roger, wilco. One-two, out."

"One-six, out."

Ben appreciated that Sergeant Palmer had tried to negotiate a four-hour maximum, given the nighttime temperatures. As the night wore on, forty-four mortar rounds landed in the vicinity of Able and Baker Companies doing little more than tearing up some of the barbed wire emplacements. Ben, hoping that one of the rounds had Lieutenant Stebbins' name on it, was almost disappointed when the unwitting platoon leader's loud voice boomed through the radio handset at 0600 and ordered Palmer's patrol to come home. They were safely back by 0658 after spending a freezing but otherwise uneventful night.

When they passed through the gate between Companies A and B and entered the trench, Sergeant Palmer asked Ben if he had any questions about the patrol.

"Just one. When you tried to negotiate an early return for us you used the term "Hank Snow." Why did you do that?"

"Well, what's Hank Snow's big hit record?"

Ben's thoughts returned to Orangevale. He could hear the jukebox blasting at the Gateway Tavern. "It was *Movin' On,* I guess."

"Affirmative. You know that and I know that. But Luke the Gook, who's listening in on our conversation, probably doesn't know that. He's heard "haul ass" or "how able" so often that it has become part of his vocabulary. So we'll use something like "Hank Snow" until he figures that out."

Having missed morning chow, Ben rummaged through a couple of cases of C-rations looking for his favorite, ham and lima beans. He found pork and beans, beans and wienies, beans and beef, chicken and noodles, beef stew, and his least favorite, greasy hamburger patties. In addition to the entrée, each small box contained a couple of large round crackers, jam, powdered milk, powdered coffee, sugar, a chocolate bar, a cookie and a few cigarettes. Along with the food, there was a small can opener, called a P-40, some sterno tabs for heating the entrée and a few sheets of toilet paper for later. Ben wore a can opener on his dog tags chain just in case some factory worker had forgotten to pack one. He tucked the toilet paper into the webbing of his helmet liner.

He chose beans and franks, the company favorite. His comrades preferred anything with beans in it. Their least favorites were meat and spaghetti and meat and noodles. Such items tended to be too dry when eaten cold.

As Ben opened the little olive-drab can of cold beans, and stretched out on his bunk, he sang softly to himself,

> Big eight-wheeler moving down the track,
> Says my lovin' baby, I ain't comin' back.
> I'm movin' on. I'll soon be gone.
> You're flyin' too high for my little old sky,
> So I'm movin' on.

He was asleep before he emptied the can and slept fitfully until noon. He awoke, brushed his teeth, and thought how good a hot shower would feel. His last had been on New Year's Eve at Chisong-ni.

During the night, an Item Company outpost was attacked by a small group of North Koreans. GI's in the outpost employed small arms fire and several dozen grenades to ward off their attackers. After suffering two wounded and running dangerously low in ammunition, the outpost defenders withdrew before friendly artillery and mortar fire was directed on the outpost. When the barrage was lifted, a pursuit patrol was sent out but found nothing.

On 16 January an ambush patrol was sent out at 1843 hours. Ben and Rudy were on watch and were slated to respond in the event the patrol ran into trouble. Ben was resting in the fighting bunker when Company A's respite from an artillery attack came to an end. **W-O-O-O-OUMPH!** Rudy came rushing through the door seconds after the first 82-mm mortar round exploded on the barbed wire apron in front of him throwing snow, mud, and shrapnel in all directions. He and Ben rolled to the rear of the bunker and sat with heads bowed waiting for the next onslaught. Ben fought for breath and wet his pants while Rudy struggled to remember something comforting that he might have learned in catechism. Whenever they thought the barrage might have ended, they were battered by another aftershock. Forty-five rounds landed in the First Battalion area. The barrage succeeded in harassing and keeping everyone awake all night. The patrol didn't return until 0658, having surmised that they were safer out front than back at the MLR.

Shortly after midnight on 17 January, as the mercury dropped to minus twenty, Fox Company was subjected to intense artillery and mortar fire. An hour later they were hit by a company-sized attack that had moved up the draws on both sides of the company outpost. Fighting, sometimes hand to hand, continued for nearly an hour. A group of the North Koreans penetrated the MLR and a hand grenade fight ensued. A platoon leader led a counterattack and ejected the enemy from the works.

At 0350 hours, a patrol from George Company located the support platoon of the enemy assault troops and directed artillery and mortar fire on them. This resulted in an estimated ten enemy KIA and prevented the North Koreans from reinforcing their attack. Upon withdrawing, the enemy again subjected the MLR positions to an intense mortar and artillery barrage. Fox Company suffered three killed and twenty-one wounded. It was estimated that the North Koreans had lost forty-two killed and thirty-eight wounded.

Upon withdrawal, the enemy removed all of the dead with the exception of three corpses snarled in the barbed wire in front of the MLR. During the fight, enemy shelling had destroyed all wire communication with battalion and regimental headquarters. The 555th FAB fired 1375 rounds in support of the company during the action. The gullies in front of their line, which served to screen attacking enemy soldiers, were turning out to be quite a dangerous challenge for the men of Fox Company.

The following evening, Ben was sure that they were going to suffer the same fate as their brothers in the Second Battalion. Captain Anderson's brief report, the following morning, read, "Heavy incoming tonight, 73 rounds of 76's, 76 of 82-mm mortars, 5 of 60-mm mortar, 5 of 120-mm." When it was all over, Ben's pants were still dry. He had learned he could depend on the mildew-ridden ceiling over his head.   That night the thermometer registered twenty-four degrees below zero.   The next four nights were relatively quiet for Able Company. Apparently the North Koreans had decided to shift to diplomacy and began delivering loud speaker broadcasts every night between 2200 and 0100 hours.   The "brave soldiers of the First Battalion" were promised all sorts of comforts under the Geneva Convention if they would only throw down their arms and stop fighting for the "blood suckers on Wall Street."   The messages were a welcome source of amusement for the few tired GI's who were on guard and couldn't sleep through them.   Those not on duty were sound asleep in their bags at this time in the evening.   There were few night owls up on the line.   Chronic stress and outdoor living made everyone sleepy.

On the morning of the twenty-fourth, Rodger Kelley chose to take a short cut on his way to the ammo box latrine.   In doing so, he was fully exposed to the enemy line.   As he was part of the way up the hill, a rifle bullet went **sh-u-u-umft** into the snow six inches from his right foot. Kelly somersaulted back into the trench.

The rifle shot had been quite a surprise.   It was known that the NKPA had a few Russian carbines and some old 7.7-mm Japanese Army rifles but they had discarded most of them in favor of the burp gun.   Kelley received a good chewing-out from a relieved Sergeant Palmer.   The North Korean rifleman, apparently somewhere on Hill 1210, continued squeezing off shots in the direction of Company A for the rest of the day.

In mid-afternoon, Lieutenant Stebbins found Ben and Rudy in their sleeping bunker cleaning their weapons. He said, "The Old Man wants a patrol out after dark to try to locate that sniper.   Did I hear you boys volunteer?"

"Sure thing, Lieutenant," responded Rudy.   "But it's probably a waste of time.   I'll bet that old sniper goes home at night."

"Well, I'll see that your precious time isn't wasted, Aguhlar.   Be at the CP at 1700."   Ben and Rudy nodded and returned to their task.

At the briefing, Captain Anderson identified five check points between Able Company and the base of Hill 1210.   "Now, Lieutenant, I would prefer you go no further than checkpoint five, but you use your own judgment.   If there's any decent cover at checkpoint five you could at least hunker down there and wait for an ambush opportunity.   But we'd sure like to catch a muzzle flash from that sniper."

At 1800 hours the patrol filed out the supply trench, around the rear of the hill and through the gate between Able and Baker Companies. Lieutenant Stebbins had appointed Corporal Kelley to take the point, but the CO had countermanded that idea.   He didn't want someone who might want to settle a score in such a sensitive position, so another member of the

the patrol led off followed by Kelley. Stebbins and Ben, with the PRC-10, were in the center of the column and Grady with his medical bag and Rudy and his BAR brought up the rear.

The frozen snow crunched beneath their feet as they descended into the valley. Fortunately there was a slight breeze to help mask the sound. Occasionally someone would slip and fall. The rest of the column would then freeze and listen intently until Stebbins whispered for them to advance.

As they reached checkpoints one and two, Ben whispered their position into the radio and Captain Anderson marked their progress on an acetate-covered map. At checkpoint three there was a shallow gully running east and west. Stebbins motioned the patrol into the gully and signaled Ben to check in with the CP.

Twenty minutes passed and the lieutenant had not given the order to proceed. The men were freezing but were rather grateful for the long rest. The gully was some protection from the cold breeze. Finally Stebbins crawled over to Ben.

"Stewart, you tell the ol' man we are at checkpoint four."

"Say what?" whispered Ben with disbelief.

"You deaf? I said tell Able-6 that we have reached checkpoint four."

"That's not very smart, Lieutenant," whispered Ben. "If our guys detect some noise or movement down here and we're officially not here, we could get plastered with mortar and 50-caliber fire."

"If you were smart and had any guts, Stewart, you would be leadin' this patrol. You're nothin' but a buck-assed private. Now crank up the captain."

"If I had any smarts," thought Ben, "I wouldn't be here in the cesspool of the world trying to deal with some cracker asshole."

He clicked on the radio and hoped that the captain couldn't tell that he was nervous. Lying was always very hard for him. He feared that he might have difficulty looking the skipper in the eye during the debriefing. However, Anderson suspected nothing. He expressed his satisfaction with their progress and turned to mark his situation map.

The next forty minutes went very slowly as the men continued to crouch in the gully. Then Stebbins returned to Ben and said, "Tell the captain that we are finally at checkpoint five."

"I really wish you'd tell him yourself, Lieutenant. I've got a problem with this."

"You are gonna have a much worse problem unless you get on that radio and check in with Captain Anderson. There is nothing' wrong here, Stewart. The captain told me to use my own judgment. My judgment is to stay here and wait for an ambush opportunity. Now, you get the captain on the horn."

Ben flipped the switch, "Able six, this is One-two, over."

Captain Anderson responded immediately. "One-two, this is Able-six, go ahead."

"Able-six, we're at Charlie peter five. Sit rep normal. Over."

"Is the lieutenant right there? Over."

"Affirmative, sir. Here he is." Ben, fearing Anderson might be suspicious, gladly handed the mike to his platoon leader.

"Andy, you men made good time tonight. Any trouble out there?"

"Nothin' yet, sir. Haven't heard anything but a bunch of coughin' and spittin' from a batch of sick gooks up on the hillside."

"Well, hang on there until the appointed time. There's a patrol from Baker Company in your general area. I'll get word to them that you will be coming through around that time. Be sure that your point man remembers tonight's countersign."

"Roger that, sir. One-two, out."

"Able-six, out."

Victory/Garden was the countersign for the evening.

The trip back to the MLR was uneventful. Captain Anderson was there to greet them. He told them not to worry about the sniper because it was anticipated that the weather would clear on the next day and the Air Force was scheduled to clobber Hill 1210. Rudy had all the confirmation he needed to prove that the hike had been a waste of his time.

Sunday, January 24 presented a regular heat wave, hitting a high of forty-four degrees Fahrenheit by early afternoon. The pilots of several P-51 mustangs made repeated passes at Hill 1210. On the first pass they fired their 5-inch rockets at the North Korean artillery and mortar positions. After zooming quickly into the open sky, they returned and delivered canisters of napalm. Then, apparently spotting some enemy troops running to safety, they swooped in very low, with their fifty-caliber machine guns blazing.

Rudy and Ben watched the air show for as long as it lasted and then returned to their domestic chores. Rudy picked up a five-gallon can of gasoline at the rear of the supply trench and he and Ben trudged through the slush to the platoon latrine. They unhooked the tarp and removed the ammo box seat from over the pit. Rudy tossed a couple of canteen cups full of gas on the contents. Then he threw in a burning match and - whoosh- they had a rosy fire going. Meanwhile Ben wiped down the seat with an old wet T-shirt. When the fire was out, they tossed a little dirt over the residue, replaced the seat, tucked a new roll of toilet paper under the tarp and left, feeling like they had done their good deed for the day.

Early Monday morning, Rudy shook Ben gently as the former came off the midnight to 0200 watch.

"Hey, Stew. You awake?"

"It's two o'clock already?"

"Yeah. What's the password?" quizzed Rudy.

"Uh...*Leaping - Lizards.* I hope there aren't any Little Orphan Annie fans over in Gooneyland. They'll get that one in a minute. Of course if some dude says "reeping rizards," I'll go ahead and take him out. How's it goin' out there?"

"We lost another guy tonight. When the patrol from Second Platoon came back, they brought in Billy Hamilton, KIA."

"How did he get it?"

"Don't know. They didn't say. It don't matter. Dead is dead."

Ben remained quiet as he pulled on his boots, flak jacket and parka. Then he grabbed his rifle, web belt and helmet. As he got up to go, Rudy followed him outside. Handing him a slip of paper, Rudy said, "I'm kinda losing hope, man. If I should buy it, I want you to write to Raquel. I need her to know that I planned to take care of her no matter how it looks."

Ben tried to shrug it off. "Nothing will happen to you, hombre. You are an indestructible killer."

"I wish, but it can get plenty dangerous around here. And the baby is due any day. You will do it for me, won't you, Stew?"

"Of course I will. I gotta go. You hit the sack."

"Thanks, man. You're a good gringo."

"And you're a good beaner, señor. Get some sleep."

Ben found his way in the dark to the fighting hole and peered north at Hill 1210. He glanced back and forth and up and down trying to keep his eyes from fixing on one particular point for too long. He had learned earlier that when he fixed his gaze too long at the same point that he invariably saw things moving around out there. His mind was on his conversation with Rudy. He really envied the guy. Rudy would have two people to love and take care of when he went home. Ben, on the other hand, had at least six more years of school on his plate before he could even think about the comforts of a family.

The night was silent, there being no breeze. Suddenly Ben thought that he heard the rustling of trousers to his front. "Hey," he thought, "that did look like someone moving down there."

A few seconds later he thought he heard wire being cut. Ben tapped on the phone receiver and when Sergeant Palmer came on he said, "I think there's somebody down there, Sarge. Somebody's trying to get through our wire." He was right. Three squads of North Koreans had slipped by the company outpost without being detected.

A couple of seconds later a ten yard by thirty yard ball of flame turned the January night into a summer day. One of the enemy soldiers had tripped the napalm mine and a squad of North Koreans had disappeared in a three thousand degree inferno. For several seconds, the other two squads were illuminated.

Ben's M-1 was one of the first weapons to speak as he fired down the slope. Immediately other small arms, automatic weapons, and grenades were directed at the burp gun muzzle flashes. Fire from the Able Company outpost poured into the enemy soldiers from their flank. When the Triple Nickel joined the fray, the North Koreans withdrew quickly, taking an estimated fifteen wounded with them. They left behind the charred remains of the third squad. They also left scraps of carpeting that they had thrown over the barbed wire to ease access to the trench. When a disappointed Rudy arrived with his BAR, there was no one left to shoot.

At daybreak, the morning fog hugged the ground. Captain Anderson ordered everyone to clean up the previous night's mess while they could still take advantage of the fog. Sergeant Palmer beckoned to Ben and Rudy, "You two come with me and bring your entrenching tools and your gloves. We've got to get those roasted gooks off the wire and into the ground."

"Aw shit, Sarge," Ben whined. "Can't we get the Korean Service Corps guys to do that."

"'Fraid not, Tiger. They say that it's against their religion to handle dead enemies. Releases their spirits into the night air or something. Come on, let's get it over with. The engineers will be here soon to re-set the napalm mines."

Rob directed the two privates to dig a shallow ditch in front of the barbed wire while he began to pull the remains of bare orange and black arms and legs, small pieces of viscera and charcoal colored skulls with yellowed teeth off the wire and dump them in front of Ben and Rudy.

Rudy bent over and grabbed an ankle and started to drag the leg to the ditch, but the remains of the flesh just slid off the greasy bone. "Jesus, Joseph and Mary. This is one thing I will never be able to tell my kids. What did you do in the war, Pop? I wouldn't want them to know about this. Nasty, crappy business. Jesus."

Finally by dragging, carrying and using their entrenching tools the three soldiers committed the human remains to the earth. Purple blow flies were already circling the small pieces of flesh that remained on the wire.

"Nothing much we can do about those little bits," said Sergeant Palmer. We'll leave them to the flies and the rain. C'mon let's go use the Fels-Naptha." He winked at his two co-workers. "I'm ready for some lunch."

Rudy and Ben looked on with disinterest as Rob Palmer enjoyed a can of beef stew. "While, I've got you guys..." the sergeant began.

"What now, Sergeant Palmer, for God's sake?" said Rudy.

"The battalion commander is afraid there might be a follow-up to last night's probe. Captain Anderson wants patrols out far enough to give us more warning than we got last night."

"You gonna be taking us out, Sarge?" asked Rudy.

"No, the Captain has another job for me. You'll be goin' out with Lieutenant Stebbins." He knew how the young men felt about that information but his face didn't reveal any feelings. Theirs did.

"You gotta problem, Stewart? Got other plans for the evening or something?"

"No, Sarge, no other plans but Stebbins is an asshole and has a gift for making a patrol more dangerous than necessary." Ben gave Palmer a brief rundown of his previous patrol. The sergeant became visibly angry but said nothing. He would discuss it with the First Sergeant.

"Did you ever run into an asshole in civilian life, Stewart?"

"Sure, all the time. But generally I could avoid them. You can't do that here."

"I want a full report tomorrow from both of you on tonight's patrol. I can't swear that I can do anything about it. The only thing I can assure you is, that, in my experience, lieutenants come and go. Stebbins will probably receive a silver bar soon and they'll move him out of here. The next son of bitch could be worse."

That evening as the patrol moved north toward Hill 1210, all was quiet. Since the route was becoming familiar to the men there was less slipping and falling. Ben checked in with Captain Anderson when they stopped at the gully at checkpoint three.

When they reached the small clump of trees at checkpoint four, Stebbins spread them out and assigned fields of fire. There was no cover other than the bare, burned trees. The men knelt or squatted in the snow and listened. Ben checked in with the company commander.

After an hour had transpired, Lieutenant Stebbins became impatient. He slid over next to Rudy and whispered, "Aguhlar, I do believe those dinks are waitin' for us about half way up that finger of the hill about two hundred yards. Fire a few bursts up there. Let's see if we can stir 'em up.

"Did you see somebody up there, sir?"

"No, but they're up there. I can smell garlic."

"Why don't you request a mortar flare right over that part of the hill."

"Stop bein' a chickenshit, Aguhlar. Either fire or give me that BAR."

Rudy fired two four-round bursts at the side of the Hill 1210. The squad members froze. For over a minute there was complete silence but then the first mortar round exploded about forty yards to their front. A couple of seconds later, rounds exploded to the left and right.

"Haul ass. Back to the gully," shouted Stebbins.

As the column of men scrambled, Corporal Kelley, formerly the point man, brought up the rear. Lieutenant Stebbins assumed the point. Suddenly a mortar round exploded very close to the rear of the column. Kelley fell, shrieking more from surprise than from pain. A chunk of shrapnel had buried itself in his right buttock.

Whitey Lockwood and Grady Williams went back for him. The two pulled Kelley's pants down far enough so Grady could apply a large pressure bandage over the wound and strap it with two-inch adhesive tape. Then Grady snapped the protective point off a morphine ampule, stabbed Kelley in the butt, and squeezed the ampule until it was empty.

The two men hoisted the corporal between them and moved as fast as they could. Kelley could do less and less to help them as the morphine took effect. In twenty minutes his moaning had stopped and he felt like he could float back to the MLR.

Meanwhile Stebbins and the others had reached the gully at checkpoint three. As soon as Ben had Captain Anderson on the net, Stebbins reached for the mike and gasped for breath as he addressed his commander. "Able-six, we had a little problem. Took some mortar rounds. Aguhlar got spooked. Thought he had a clear target. Guess his muzzle flash gave us away. Over."

"Anybody down?"

"Believe Kelley is, sir. Yeah, here they come with him now. Looks like he's walking."

"Well, you might as well come on in. I'll alert medical to evacuate Kelley and let the outpost know that you'll be coming by ahead of schedule."

When they reached the point where the trail wound up a sixty-degree slope, it took four men to carry Kelley. The young corporal was drifting in and out of consciousness. When they reached the communications trench at the rear of the company, they placed Kelley on a stretcher and carefully descended the trail to the supply point. When they arrived, two battalion medical evacuation folks were there to relieve them of their burden.

Before relinquishing his patient, Grady filled out Kelley's evacuation tag and tied it to a button hole on his field jacket. The DOD Form 8-26 asked for the soldier's name and serial number, location of wound, date and time of wounding, name of nearest town, and time of last morphine injection. Grady scribbled the information and then signed his own name and serial number.

Corporal Kelley was loaded on to a litter jeep, a saline IV was initiated and he began a rough and painful journey to the battalion aid station. But as far as Rodger Kelley was concerned, he was heading in the right direction.

Once the patrol was dismissed, Ben and Rudy went back to their sleeping bunker. Their bitching about the screwed-up patrol didn't last very long. They were soon fast asleep.

Three nights later, while under heavy artillery fire, a rifle squad was hunkered down in the Baker Company outpost, when they spotted a North Korean platoon heading toward their company's portion of the line. There was a quick response to their request for artillery support. The rounds came in right on target, killing six enemy and wounding all others. The few enemy soldiers who could walk, withdrew. Patrols sent out the following evening found blood and tracks but made no contact.

For the remainder of January, a program of harassing and interdictory fire from light machine guns and automatic rifles was directed down the draws leading into friendly positions. Falling snow had made observation of the draws almost impossible during the hours of darkness and permitted the North Koreans, clothed in white parkas, to use the draws instead of the ridges as access routes into the Fifth RCT's positions. Periodic short bursts of automatic weapons into the draws prevented the enemy from making full use of them. Tragically, a stray bullet from this effort killed a young private manning Able Company's outpost.

The North Koreans made one more fanatical attempt in January to breech the regimental MLR. At 0245 on 28 January, after a ten-minute heavy mortar barrage, they attacked with an entire company along a twenty-yard front. They headed straight for George Company's fifty-caliber machine gun bunker. The gunner fired his weapon until it was knocked out by a grenade. He then defended his position with rifle fire until he was killed. Approximately thirty enemy soldiers penetrated the MLR but were finally beaten back in a thirty-minute bayonet and grenade fight.

A George Company patrol returning to the MLR, deployed near the company's combat outpost. As the North Koreans retreated past them, they came under surprise fire from the patrol and the outpost. Many enemy soldiers dropped their weapons and ran. The ambush resulted in an additional twenty-five enemy casualties. Only one patrol member was hit. Screening patrols picked up weapons and documents from twenty enemy dead.

On the evening of 29 January, Rudy pulled his canteen out of its carrying case and said, "Do you know what day this is, amigo?"

"The anniversary of some Mexican revolution or something," said Ben.

"Probably, but it also our twenty-first day on the line for January."

"That's right, man," said Ben. "We finally finished a four-point month. Twenty-one exciting days in the Orient. Twenty-one days closer to going home. I'll drink to that."

"A tu salud, young trooper," said Rudy as they clinked canteens.

"Y a tu, mi General," responded Ben.

For the next few days, it appeared that Luke the Gook was quietly licking his wounds. The relative inactivity on the part of the enemy and sub-zero nighttime temperatures led the regimental commander to order patrols relieved every two hours. Ironically, now that the weather was getting warmer, supplies of stove oil increased.

When Ben arrived at the chow truck on the morning of 2 February, he picked up a letter from Mary Ellen. He pocketed his mail. He was in a hurry to eat breakfast and get back to the sleeping bunker to pack. They were being relieved. Packing was a simple matter at this stage of the war. It meant rolling his change of underwear and socks up with his down-filled sleeping bag. There was no need to carry an extra set of fatigues. Clean clothes would be provided at the shower point.

Once he had assembled his gear, Ben had a chance to open the letter. The stationery was scented, a pleasing scent that couldn't be drowned out by the usual G.I odors of sweat, gun oil and mildew. Mary Ellen wrote:

January 22, 1952
Ben Dearest,
What a winter we're having!! It has been snowing non-stop in the Sierras. My parents took us skiing at Alpine Meadows a couple of weeks ago and we got snowed in. Nothing could get in or out of the South Tahoe area for over a week. The weather rarely cleared enough to go skiing. Fortunately, there were some very nice Cal students there so the time went by quickly. We had long debates in the bar and snowball fights on the slopes.
Well, alas, spring semester starts Monday and it's back to the old grind. Do you miss school? I'll bet you do. I think about you all the time and will always wonder what you're doing there and why you didn't leave the army to people who like that sort of thing or don't have your potential.
The fellows from Cal that I met are all in ROTC so they'll be officers when they graduate. They hope the war will be over by then. I wish it were over now. I miss you.
Write when you get a chance.
Love, Ellie

Since there was nothing to do but sit around and wait for the Filipino 19th Battalion Combat Team to relieve them, Ben responded to her letter.

2 February 1952
Dear Ellie,
 I got your letter today and enjoyed hearing about your trip to Alpine Meadows. This place where we are, on the northern lip of the Punch Bowl, is kind of like the Tahoe Area. We've had some pretty good snows lately. We've also had some fights on the slopes but I didn't enjoy that part of it.
 I'm pleased to report that there are no Cal students here. Well Grady Williams, our platoon medic, completed two years at Cal, but he's different. You may remember him. He was the Negro buddy that I introduced you to at our graduation from basic training. God, that seems like a thousand years ago.
 Anyway, Grady miraculously turned up here after completing combat medic training. It's good to have him here. My closest friend, Rudy Aguilar, is a high-school dropout from Nogales, Arizona. He reads Luke Short novels and doesn't know Rousseau from Caruso but he is a valuable pal on whom I know I can depend.
 I can tell you straight out that I haven't found anyone that enjoys soldiering in this bucket of shit called Korea and I haven't found anyone who doesn't feel that he has the potential for a successful life. We spend a lot of time in bull sessions so I think I know my buddies.
 Sure I miss school. I miss the stimulation of class discussions. I miss flushing a toilet in a nice warm bathroom, and digging my toes into a rug when I wake up in the morning. But most of all I miss you. If all goes well and we get enough time up here on the line, I could be home sometime in September.
       Loads of love,
       Ben

 Ben took his letter to the mailbag at the company CP. He found Captain Anderson completing some notes that would be useful to the relieving commanding officer of the Filipino unit. Anderson smiled and said, "Evening, Stewart. You about ready for a hot shower and some home cooking?"
 "Yes, sir. That I am. By the way, have you heard anything new from headquarters about the peace talks."
 "They're still bogged down. You already know that the communists have agreed to a prospective truce line. We're basically sitting on it right now."
 "So what's holding things up?"

"They're bickering over the POW situation. The commies are insisting that all North Korean and Chinese prisoners be returned and our people are being just as stubborn about offering asylum to those folks who want to defect."

"So what are they doing about the impasse?"

"Well, Ike has threatened to use an atomic cannon to light a fire under them if they don't get off the pot."

"Do you think the NoKos and the Chinese are gonna buy that bit of bullshit, sir?"

"Well, it might not be bullshit. You never know. Anyway, it looks like General Van Fleet won't have to make that decision. They say he's on his way out."

"Gee, sir, maybe a new Eighth Army commander would just tell us to pack up and go home."

"I'll vote for that but I'm not sure that it would make any difference in your life or mine who runs the Eighth Army...oh, here he is now. Go grab your gear, Stewart."

The conversation ended as Lieutenant Fernandez of the Philippines 19th Battalion Combat Team entered the bunker. Anderson greeted him and then took him on a tour of A Company's outpost and its sector of the line.

It was around two in the morning when the First Battalion reached its designated campsite on the floor of the Punchbowl. It was rumored that they would be in division reserve for at least two months. Depending upon the progress of the truce talks at Panmunjom, they might never have to go back up on the line.

SPRING 1953

WHEN THE Changsha Company arrived at its destination in the Chorwan Valley, other elements of the 220th Regiment, 74th Division, 24th Group Army were already in place. The regimental area was approximately ten miles north of the front line which their American enemies called Line Minnesota. They were told that the regiment's mission for the next few weeks would be that of digging a line of trenches, bunkers and tunnels that would serve as a secondary main line of resistance, a fall-back position, in the unlikely event that the Americans, specifically the U.S. Third Infantry Division, were to launch a strong offensive.

The regimental commander was anxious to get the work done before the position was discovered by U.S. observation planes. So far the enemy's aircraft were limiting their frightful work to the Chinese positions facing Line Minnesota.

Xing was grateful for the stay of execution. He could hear the rumble of artillery at night, somewhere off to the south, and was in no hurry to witness it up close. Besides, he was learning a new skill. His company had the job of cutting timber to serve as beams for bunkers. He, who had never been around horses before in his life, was learning to drive a team and wagon delivering the timbers to those working on the fortifications.

Each morning at 0500, the bugler would blow reveille. This was followed by a two-and-a-half hour study period. Although Political Officer Chao and Company Commander Chen continued to quibble over the content of the studies, Captain Chen was beginning to get the upper hand. The proximity of combat dictated that the priority should go to military topics.

Chen devoted many of his lectures to the tactical ideas of Lin Piao, Commander of the Chinese Fourth Field Army. It was particularly important, now that the battle for Korea was static rather than fluid, that his men understand the tactics of the "short attack," the type of assault that they would be implementing against the enemy's outposts and front line positions.

"The one-point, or short attack," said Chen, "is like sticking a long sharp-pointed knife into the enemy's weak spot. Continuous attacks must be carried out until the enemy breaks. If it appears that the enemy cannot be quickly exterminated, approach his strong point on three sides leaving what appears to be a loophole of escape, then fall upon him on four sides when he endeavors to escape."

Chen assured the men that they would not be called on to attack unless they outnumbered the enemy soldiers by a ratio of five to one and would not be ordered to attack unless there was a seventy percent chance of victory. Xing wondered who did the risk calculations but wasn't about to ask.

There were few times, during the long busy day, that Xing was able to suppress thoughts of his loved ones. He had written a few letters to Mei and to his parents but their content had been rather lean since he couldn't discuss where he was and what he was feeling. All letters from Mei had been intercepted and destroyed by Political Officer Chao, who surmised that they would have a deleterious effect on Xing's morale.

There had been some turnover of personnel in the company during the winter due to an outbreak of tuberculosis. Xing was overjoyed when one of the replacements brought him a letter from Mei with a recent photo of her and little Xing. However, it pained him to see that his son had changed from a baby to a little boy in several months time. How regrettable it was that he was not home to enjoy watching his child develop. Xing put the envelope in the inside pocket of his jacket, next to his heart, and decided to write a proper response to Mei and send it home with the first ill or wounded soldier that he could trust. He wrote:

My Dearest Wife,

It was with great joy that I received your precious letter and photograph. You will be saddened to hear that I never received any of your previous letters. It is army policy that we cut all emotional ties with those we love in order to devote all waking moments to the tasks of a soldier. You can rest assured that my devotion to you and little Xing is unwavering and the pain of our separation is constant.

Our company is deployed in the Chorwan Valley in western Korea. The Americans refer to this area as the Iron Triangle, because a triangle of railroad tracks connects the cities of Chorwan, Kumhwa and Pyonggang. We are engaged in the task of building some secondary fortifications and I am actually enjoying the hard work. I am working as a teamster and I haul logs to use as beams for the bunkers.

The food here is adequate. We have two meals a day, a serving of rice and vegetables around 7:30 and some rice, meat and more vegetables at four in the afternoon. However I haven't seen a drop of tea for several weeks. In the army, we boil water and call it "white tea."

After breakfast I hitch my mules to the wagon and work until the four o'clock meal. We are supposed to have the evenings free but the officers have usurped that time for classes and meetings. Occasionally, we are entertained by a troupe of actors, tough-talking, muscular women soldiers. They are dressed, unattractively in army uniforms. However, last week we were sincerely amused with their melodramatic play about the life and woes of being Peking prostitutes before they were liberated by the People's Liberation Army from the clutches of the Kuomintang government. All of their plays have a pronounced political message but are certainly more enjoyable than spending the evening with our esteemed political officer.

On the first of February, we received pay for the first time since we left Manchuria. I have no earthly need for the money. All of my food is provided, I receive free haircuts from the company barber and I don't use tobacco. I'll save the money since I may have to pay someone to deliver this letter to you.

My dear one, I hope that some day you will see this letter. You are always in my thoughts and in my heart.

> *Your husband,*
> *Xing*

In March as the days became warm and sunny, the 220th Regiment was alerted that it would be moving forward, about ten miles, to the main line of resistance. They would be placed on a portion of the line opposite the U.S. Third Infantry Division. Elements of the regiment that they would be relieving were already beginning to arrive back at the secondary line established by the men of Changsha.

On the morning of the fifteenth of March, during an unseasonable storm that dropped fifteen inches of snow, the company marched south reaching their assigned sector in time for "white tea" and their evening meal. Their predecessors filed out of bunkers and trenches that were in a sorry state of disrepair, revealing the devastation rendered by recent Allied air strikes. Long tunnels dug deeply into the rear of the hills would be their only source of shelter until they could fix the fighting bunkers and trenches.

As the battered veterans evacuated the area, Xing spotted Lu Fuchun, a former customer of his father's. "Mr. Lu, is that really you? How long have you been here?"

"Nearly two years, young comrade. We came in with the Fifteenth Army in the spring of 1951 and have been off and on this miserable dung heap for the past two years. You look very well, Hua Xing. Is this your first trip to the front?"

"Yes, comrade," said Xing, cautiously. "I enlisted last summer to try to do my small part."

"That was unfortunate, young friend. I suppose they have filled your ears with bullshit about the invincibility of the Peoples Liberation Army," said Lu, sarcastically, "and how we're going to break through to Pusan and destroy the blood-sucking, big-nosed Americans when the Russian planes and artillery arrive."

Xing looked around hoping that they hadn't been overheard. "Careful, old friend, I wouldn't want a cadre member to overhear us. I take it you are no longer a staunch member of the Party?"

"The Party can kiss my ass, Xing," said Corporal Lu. "I believed their lies until we got here and found out how outgunned we are, tasted the flaming death from the skies and the unceasing artillery attacks and experienced terrible hunger and freezing cold. My company has suffered sixty-percent casualties, in the past two years, just implementing patrols and small probes. They're finally taking us out of here. We'll be going home just long enough to fill our ranks with more fresh-faced babies. May you have good fortune, young Mr. Hua. I must go."

"Mr. Lu may I ask a favor?"

"You want to send a message to your family, don't you, young friend?"

"Yes, would you please take this letter to my wife. And you can keep this 48,000 JMP that I received on pay day. It will help with your expenses."

Lu grasped the letter and quickly filed it in his pocket. "You keep the script, Xing. I don't charge friends for favors. Besides I doubt that I will be able to exchange it for yuan when I get there."

Xing sadly watched the old soldier limp over to the area where his company was assembling for the return march to China.

Two days later, Xing did receive some information from his father. The envelope had been opened and there was obviously a page missing but the remaining page contained the following: "You will recall that financial problem that prompted your offer to help me. Despite your help, the problem has tripled in size. You must not be distressed because we will be able to manage."

Apparently the father's reassuring statement had persuaded Captain Chao to allow Xing to have that one page of the letter. To Xing, however, it was just further evidence that he had been betrayed by his government. His enlistment had gained nothing for his family.

* * *

Service Company had constructed a shower point of three large tents strung together on a wooden platform. The first tent was for stripping off one's dirty clothes. Water pipes with showerheads extended the length of the middle tent and clean clothes were issued in the third tent. Colonel Fisher's decree that all companies were to report as scheduled to the shower point, as part of preparation for a command inspection, was totally unnecessary.

Ben and his buddies ecstatically shed their clothes for the first time in many days. Fatigue shirts and pants went into one pile, long underwear went into a second, and t-shirts and brown-and-yellow stained boxer shorts went into a disgusting third. Ben expressed pity for the poor Korean civilians that would have to wash something so repulsive. He favored just burning the horrible stuff or, better yet, draping it on the barbed wire apron to keep the Gooks away.

Rudy volunteered to remain in the first tent to guard their wallets, boots and belts. He would shower when the others had finished. During the past couple of days he had sought solitude frequently after receiving word from Miss Raquel Valencia of Nogales, Arizona that he was the father of a seven pound, two ounce baby girl. Raquel named the little girl Alicia after her mother. She hoped that Rudy wouldn't mind not being consulted.

Rudy didn't mind. He was too happy, too relieved, too filled with dread, and too angry about being nine thousand miles away from home to worry about the baby's name. He had a lot of things to sort out.

Armed with bars of Fels-Naptha, the other squad members stepped under the shower nozzles and let out a collective sign when the hot water touched their skin. They lathered their shaggy manes and their bruised and pimply bodies with the strong soap. After toweling dry, they were issued clean underwear, fatigues and socks. The fresh clothes reeked of strong soap and bleach.

There was a feeble attempt by the shower attendants to find the right sized fatigues for the clean soldiers. Ben's fatigue shirt fit fine but the pants had a thirty-inch inseam. They were a bit short for long legs. The shirt had large combat PFC stripes on the sleeves. He'd have to remove them as soon as he could get to his bayonet. That seemed a shame though since he was about due for a promotion. In a recent letter his dad had asked him why he was still a buck private and wondered why the army hadn't noticed that his son was "first class."

As he sat on a bench to dress, Ben was surprised to spot a familiar face next to him. He said, "You're Bill Luttrell, aren't you? Played halfback for Stanford in 50-51."

"How did you know that?" responded the surprised corporal.

"That was my freshman year on the Farm," responded Ben. "It was the year we played Illinois in the Rose Bowl. Exciting first quarter. We won't talk about the final score. Oh... I'm Ben Stewart, Able Company."

Luttrell stopped lacing his boots, extended his hand and smiled. "Yeah, well, it wasn't long after that that my grades slipped. I became ineligible for football and lost my scholarship. So I volunteered for the draft in the hope that I would get to see Europe. That didn't happen obviously. I got here in July of last year. I should have enough points by the end of May to rotate home.... Well, good luck, Ben."

"And good luck to you, short timer," said Ben. "Maybe I'll see you back in Palo Alto, some day."

"Maybe," muttered Luttrell doubtfully as he turned and headed for the tent entrance.

Those men that hadn't bothered to shave for the past month were told to do so. The keeping of a neat mustache was permissible, so Ben did so. The shock of seeing his rather meager but matted beard, dotted with small pieces of rotting food, had led to his shaving as soon as they were off the hill and he could get a helmet of hot water. He devoted the rest of the day to washing and trying to dry his field jacket and pile jacket liner. He wasn't able to do much about the food grease and gun oil stains.

On Tuesday, the battalion packed up and moved to a larger assembly area; one that would accommodate the Second and Third Battalions, as well, when they came off the line. Two hundred nineteen members of First Battalion, senior to Ben and his Fort Ord buddies, boarded two and half ton trucks to begin the drive to Kimpo Air Base where they left for a week of rest and recuperation (R & R) in Japan.

The majority, those who weren't going on R & R, were heartened by the arrival of the PX supplies. There were free candies, candles, cigarettes, toothpaste, writing pads, and envelopes. The truck also contained items that had been ordered in advance like wallets, radios, watches and cameras.

Two days later, the Third Battalion minus King Company, arrived at the campsite. The battalion had been relieved by the 62nd Regiment, ROK Army. King Company had been shifted to reinforce Second Battalion. The Second Battalion, having seen a disproportionate amount of action during January, was rewarded by being left on Line Minnesota to inspire and instruct the South Korean troops.

At this point in the war, the South Korean troops were confident, seasoned, well trained, but still equipped with obsolete World War II equipment. They didn't need coddling. The assignment didn't sit well with a lot of the men in Second Battalion who felt that they had more than served their time in the bucket.

That weekend the enemy observed the Korean New Year. On Saturday, suspecting that the celebrating might get out of hand, all UN line units were put on 100% alert. Shortly before midnight, the North Koreans began a series of announcements over their loudspeaker system. The basic message was, "We are going to attack the Punchbowl and Heartbreak Ridge tonight. We have three hundred mortars and three hundred artillery pieces. We took the hill before and we will do so again." Despite the broadcasts, the night was relatively quiet, but few of the GI's got any sleep.

A week later, on 21 February, a supply truck on its way to make a delivery to the First Battalion was ambushed, apparently by guerrillas, just outside the Punchbowl area. Another truck, bearing replacements, reached the ambush site a short time later. They found a dead driver and a wounded passenger.

Screening patrols from First Battalion went on a "skunk hunt" searching Line Kansas, the secondary or fall-back MLR, all day on the 23rd, for the perpetrators. They returned at 1945 hours having found no sign of guerrillas.

Further guerrilla activity was reported on the twenty-fifth. This time the Third Battalion was sent after the bad guys. Their luck was no better than that of First Battalion.

Following the landing at Inchon in September, 1950, the Allied forces moved north so quickly that many North Korean soldiers were cut off from their fleeing units. A number of these men evaded capture and joined forces with groups of communist guerrillas in the south. Throughout the war these guerrilla bands remained a pain in the ass for the United Nations forces.

On 28 February, General Maxwell Taylor, new Eighth Army Commander, General White, X Corps Commander and General Ruffner, 45th Division Commander visited the Fifth RCT. After lunch and a briefing at Regimental Headquarters, General Taylor and his party went up on the line to visit the Second Battalion CP and an observation post of the 555th FAB.

March began with a storm warning and west winds at 30-35 knots. Companys G, F and K were the only elements of the regiment that were still on the line. While the bulk of the regiment trained on the Punchbowl floor, King Company continued to send out patrols.

On 3 March, visibility was intermittently obscured by a thick ground fog. At one point the fog lifted revealing a column of twenty North Koreans approaching the right flank of King Company. Another twenty were spotted moving from Hill 772 straight toward the company's portion of the MLR and a third group was heading toward the left flank of the company, that sector assigned to First Platoon. Apparently, like their Chinese counterparts, the North Koreans had been studying Lin Piao's attack strategies. Immediate artillery, mortar and small arms fire halted the attack about one hundred and fifty yards in front of the MLR. The North Koreans withdrew, leaving four dead. There were no American casualties. When night fell, Company K was relieved by South Korean troops and was ordered to return to its parent unit, the Third Battalion, on the floor of the Punchbowl.

Early March was sunny and pleasant for the reunited Fifth RCT. The men of First Battalion spent the mornings of the first week training at the squad level. They covered squad defense, overlapping fields of fire, and bayonet fighting. This was done without the growling and shouting of gory slogans. Either the experiencing of real gore had diminished the instructor's appetite for such behavior or it was realized that ferocious noises would come instinctively during hand-to-hand fighting.

During the afternoons there was a lot to do to improve the campsite and repair the roads that were beginning to thaw and get sloppy. Ben and Rudy spent several afternoons lining the paths with rocks and then painting them white. On Saturday the 8th, a single shell exploded in Company B's area. It was officially listed as 122-mm but probably came from a Soviet-made 152mm gun to have traversed such a long range. No one was hurt but some of the pathways and roadwork had to be redone.

On 11 March, the men awoke to snowy skies. By nightfall, fifteen inches had fallen. The good news was that training was suspended. The bad news was that the storm had rendered the roads impassable. All units were put to work clearing the roads. By evening, emergency traffic could get through. The following morning four more enemy artillery rounds fell in the battalion area.

The skies cleared on 20 March and the rest of the month would remain sunny. The muddy roads began to dry. Daytime highs were in the mid-sixties while nighttime lows averaged thirty-three degrees.

A special company formation was called that afternoon to commemorate the history of the Fifth U.S. Infantry. While the men stood at parade rest, Captain Anderson said, "The day after tomorrow we'll be going back up on the line. I regret to say that we will be short one fine soldier. Second Lieutenant Andrew Stebbins has been promoted to first lieutenant and now that he has that silver bar, he'll be needed elsewhere as a company executive officer. Before he goes I have ordered First Lieutenant Stebbins to perform one last duty. I have asked him to talk to us about the origin of the regimental motto. Lieutenant Stebbins, front and center!"

Stebbins strode forward, cutting square corners as he marched, and snapped a sharp salute at his commanding officer. Then turning to face the company, he said, "Good afternoon, men. Let me first say that I will miss my associates here. Like myself, most of you are citizen soldiers. You'd rather not be here, you're constantly griping, asking questions, making suggestions and, if permitted, would go around looking like a bunch of beatniks. You're a royal pain in the ass, but I'm proud to have served with you. You're typical of the men who have fought and won all of America's wars. And that brings me to this afternoon's topic."

"The story goes that on the night of 25 July 1814, Colonel James Miller, CO of the Fifth U.S. Infantry, was summoned by Major General Jacob Brown. American regulars had been trying throughout the day to capture British artillery positions above Lundy's Lane near Niagara Falls. Their bodies were scattered all over the hill. When Miller was asked if the Fifth Infantry could capture the guns, he said, "I'll try, Sir" and his regiment of citizen soldiers then stormed the heights and captured the cannons. From that day forward, the motto "I'll Try, Sir" has inspired the men of the Fifth Infantry as they stormed Chapultapec Castle, put down Indian up-risings in Minnesota, whipped General Sibley's Confederates in New Mexico, fought the Moros in the Philippines, and slugged their way across Europe in World War II. There are seven little cannons on the regimental crest to symbolize our victory at Lundy's Lane."

After the formation was dismissed, Ben and Rudy decided to head for the PX tent to pick up some things they would not have access to once they returned to the MLR.

"Well, that was sure good news about the lieutenant, Stew. He'll be a problem for some other poor doggies, now."

"As an XO he won't be leading any more patrols, though," responded Ben. It's a good day for the army."

"But what did you think of his speech?" asked Rudy. "Didn't it make you want to hump up those hills out there and clean out the Gooks?"

"Not really. I hate to admit it, but he's not a bad public speaker. I kept thinking though about that colonel who said, "I'll try, sir" rather than "We'll try, sir." He apparently intended to assault the guns by himself. Then at the last minute he decided to take his dogfaces along. Too bad for them. I'll bet their bodies were scattered all over that hill. The colonel probably got promoted to brigadier."

"I'll bet he didn't even go up that hill," said Rudy. "He probably hunkered down behind the trees and squawked at his platoon leaders over his prick-one. What do you bet?"

"Prick-one, Rudy?" chuckled Ben. "Of course, and PFC Guglielmo Marconi was his RTO. You know you've got a hell of an imagination."

* * *

After dinner on 22 March, the First Battalion departed the reserve area and began their three-hour trek back to Line Minnesota. Ben noticed small pine seedlings, miniature iris, some forsythia adorned with yellow blossoms and wild plum trees just beginning to bud. He wondered if such delicate creatures would get a chance to mature or would just be blasted off the face of the earth.

Ben was brooding about the poor timing of their deployment. There was too little of March left to garner four points for the month. Why couldn't the army have some compassion and schedule unit reliefs on or near the first of the month? This seemed to be nothing more than a plot to keep them from going home.

Reaching their old positions, the First Battalion, Fifth Infantry relieved the 19th Battalion Combat Team and assumed responsibility for the western rim of the Punchbowl. A water buffalo (tank trailer) had been hauled up by the tram since the existing water point was no longer adequate to support the battalion.

There was a surprise daytime appearance of the enemy on Hill 1200. Fifteen North Koreans, in dijon mustard-colored uniforms, were observed erecting and working around a large red flag, apparently in preparation for their coming May Day celebration. Patrols were sent out in the evening but made no contact. There were thirteen rounds of "welcome home" mortar fire incoming during the evening.

At 0600 on 26 March, an enemy patrol was spotted crossing the valley below. Weapons Platoon unleashed mortar and 75-mm recoilless rifle fire killing one and wounding two. Captain Anderson's request for artillery support from Company B, 245th Tank Battalion yielded good results. The enemy bunker from which the company had previously been receiving sniper fire was destroyed. Although there was some incoming mortar fire, the tank fire effectively kept the enemy from employing direct fire artillery against friendly positions and provided excellent supporting fire for a patrol that was trying to get back during the fracas. For the last few days of the month the enemy's efforts were focused on that sector of the line controlled by Charlie Company.

During the first week of April, patrols were shortened to "security detachments" by order of the 45th Division Commander. There were nightly reminders that the 111th North Korean Corps hadn't gone home, including enemy 51-caliber machine gun fire, red and green flares fired from Hill 1211, and sporadic barrages of incoming mortar and artillery rounds. On 6 April, shortly after midnight, Ben reported noises coming from finger #8, an extension of Hill 1211. Rudy, having relieved Ben on watch, heard the sound of wire being cut. There were no further developments. The next night a "security detachment" returned with the body of one of the company's newest privates. The war on the ridges continued to slowly gnaw away at Able Company.

The following Tuesday morning, the First Battalion moved on down to the assembly area at Tokkol-li. By Wednesday morning, the entire RCT had reached the assembly area, having been relieved by the 224th Infantry Regiment. The 555th FAB left the Punchbowl for the first time since arriving there in June, 1952.

* * *

On Saturday, 18 April, the Fifth RCT and the Triple Nickel FAB formed a convoy and headed southwest across the Korean Peninsula. The troops were needed to reinforce the line in the Chorwan Valley. That portion of the MLR ran through country that was warmer and lower in elevation than the terrain around the Punchbowl. It would very likely be the avenue of attack if the Chinese were to attempt a sixth offensive. The Fifth RCT left the control of the 45th Division and became attached to the Third Infantry Division.

The rice paddies at the lower elevations were beginning to thaw. As he caught his first whiff, Ben was reminded of the smell of the restrooms off the lobby of a little hotel that his grandparents had owned and managed in Walnut Creek. The hotel had been built in the 1880's. The restrooms had neither fans nor outside windows. When Ben and his brother were small, they would climb under the door in the men's toilet stalls, lock them and crawl back out. Finally, after several complaints from distressed travelers, his grandparents threatened to cut off the boys' ice cream ration if they didn't shape up. That put a stop to the toilet stall prank. There would be many times during the next few months when a whiff of the air would remind Ben of the toilets at the Colonial Inn.

The convoy climbed for a couple of hours until it reached a pass. At this elevation there were still patches of snow beside the road and blanketing the ground in the thick pine forests. Every time Ben dozed off, the truck would hit a rut.

As they made their descent to the west, the road wound through cone-shape hills that were steep and spiny with little natural vegetation other than scrub oaks, stunted pines and occasional ming trees.

The reddish earth made Ben think of the gold-country soil that he had seen beside Highway 80 on the way to Lake Tahoe. Beyond every few ridges was a river or creek bed. He wondered if this land had also been gold mining country before it became a place of destruction and death.

By early afternoon they were rolling through small villages, peopled mainly by women and children. Soldiers from the Third U.S. Infantry Division strolled the dirt streets. Some turned their backs to avoid eating the dust kicked up by the trucks but others couldn't pass up an opportunity to taunt as the trucks slowed to a crawl.

"What outfit are you girls from?" yelled a bystander.

"The Fifth RCT, jerk off," replied Whitey Lockwood."

"You look like you're reporting to sick call."

"You ought to know, horse shit, you've been on the road," responded Rudy.

"Present arms," ordered Rodger Kelley, and the twenty-four passengers flipped the bird to their tormentors. The men from the Third Division returned the salute.

When they reached their destination, an assembly area in Chipo-ri, they were one hundred and twenty miles west and about thirty miles south of that morning's point of departure. The remainder of the afternoon was devoted to setting up tents, digging latrines and cleaning weapons.

After the chores were done, Ben and Rudy had a few minutes to cruise the area before evening chow. They came upon a small group of soldiers with brown hair and moustaches. Each man had a loaf of french bread and a bottle of wine sticking out of his field jacket pockets.

Rudy, feeling that he had come upon some Latino brethren, said, "Buenas tardes, amigos." The men stopped and stared at him.

"Hablan español?"

"No," responded a young corporal. "*Milateh elinika?* You speak the Greek?"

"Fraid not," said Ben. "What outfit are you guys with?"

"Outfit?" echoed the young Greek. "Oh, let me to you introduce myself. I am Corporal Iannis Karsatos, 3rd Company, Greek Expeditionary Force. We now fight with the Third Battalion, Fifteenth U.S. Infantry and these are my comrades." The two young Americans introduced themselves and shook hands with their allies.

Ben had always thought that people from the Mediterranean were short in stature but these men were all well built six-footers. They were dressed in U.S. Army uniforms. Several had cut holes in the sides of their combat boots to accommodate their wide feet.

"What are you doing here?" asked Rudy.

"We are come to lead your battalion up to the line," said Corporal Karsatos. "Each of these men speaks some of the English."

"You speak it very well, Iannis. What we mean is why have you folks come all the way from Greece to Korea?" interjected Ben.

"We are here to kill *komunisti notos*...how you say it...communist bastards," said an older man who had been introduced as Sergeant Plessas. "No more *komunisti* in Greece. We wipe them all out five year ago. Have to come here to kill *komunisti.*"

"Yes, Sergeant Pressas speaks for the rest of us," said Corporal Karsatos. "We came here to fight the communists. We have seen what communists do to innocent people in Greece and to innocent children. We are volunteers. Some in our ranks are former communists who have come here rather than go to prison. When I join the Greek Army in 1946, we were trained by American General Van Fleet and his non-coms. We were equipped with American weapons. We know American military strategy. We like fighting beside our American friends. Why are you men here?"

"We were drafted," replied Ben. "We're conscripts. I guess we're here to take care of each other until we can earn our thirty-six points and go home. I almost envy folks like you who have a real reason for being here."

"Well, Privates Ben and Rudy, I hope you do get home to your people. Maybe we see you in five days when we go back up to the line."

"Yeah, hope so," said Rudy. "How do you say 'see you later' in Greek?"

"Probably closest thing is *sto kalo*. It means 'so long.'"

As Ben and Rudy turned to leave, Rudy said, "Sto kalo, hombres. We've gotta Hank Snow."

"Hombres? Hank Snow?" muttered the young corporal reaching for his English phrase book.

Ben had one other conversation with Iannis while the Fifth RCT was still in reserve and he was able to learn more about the record of the Greek forces in the Korean Conflict. On December 9, 1950, an eight hundred forty-man infantry battalion, known as the Royal Hellenic Expeditionary Force arrived at Pusan. After a short period of training, the Greeks were assigned to the Seventh Cavalry Regiment of the First Cavalry Division. They served as a fourth battalion for the division.

The Greeks found Korea to be much like their native land so they quickly acclimated to the mountainous terrain and bitter weather. A few, like Iannis Karsatos, were fluent in English but the others quickly learned the basic English vocabulary needed to describe terrain, equipment and military maneuvers.

On the night of 29 January 1951, approximately three thousand Chinese soldiers attacked the eight hundred Greeks on Hill 381 near Chongju. In their first major action in Korea, the GEF repelled the Chinese by using grenades, bayonets, rifle butts and, when their ammunition was exhausted, bare hands and entrenching tools to hold the hill and prevent the CCF from surrounding nearby troops.

Iannis said that when he arrived as a replacement in May of 1952, the Greek Expeditionary Force was in reserve. They soon shifted south to the prisoner of war camp on Koje-do to help quell the rioting prisoners. After that problem was resolved the Greeks moved north again and were attached to the Third Infantry Division in the Chorwan-Kumwha area.

*   *   *

After dark, on 24 April 1953, the First Battalion of the Fifth Regimental
Combat Team moved into its new position, twenty miles north of Chipo-ri,
on Line Missouri.   They relieved the Greek Battalion that had been
attached to the 15th Infantry Regiment.   Tragically, one Greek officer was
killed by enemy mortar fire during the relief, otherwise the sector of
responsibility was assumed by the First Battalion without incident.
Company A paused as the long column of Greeks filed out through the
supply trenches.   The tired soldiers carried their M1 rifles over one soldier
and a short-handled shovel over the other.

When daylight came, Ben surveyed the new neighborhood.   Clouds
were gathering in the sky in anticipation of the coming summer rainy
season.   The First Battalion's portion of Line Missouri ran along a low
ridge, rising in the valley to the west and gradually lowering into the valley
in the east.   The enemy positions were approximately fifteen hundred
meters to the front on a dominating ridge, Hill 533.   There were two
fingers emanating south from the hills and draws on both sides of the
battalion area that could serve as good approach routes for enemy attacks.
It was believed that the enemy works were populated by two battalions
from the 24th CCF Army.

On Friday night, 25 April, a battalion of Chinese assaulted a combat
outpost that was code-named Harry.   Heavy Weapons Company dropped
six hundred and seventy rounds of high explosive on the attacking force.
They were joined by repeated salvoes of high explosive and white
phosphorous from the Triple Nickel.   The Chinese artillery responded in
kind, taking the life of another PFC from Able Company.   The Chinese
withdrew taking all of their casualties with them.   They were very security
conscious and didn't want UN patrols searching their dead or bringing in
their wounded for questioning.

On Saturday morning, Lieutenant Stebbins' replacement arrived.   Paul
Clanahan was a brand new second lieutenant from the University of Notre
Dame via ROTC and Fort Benning.   That afternoon he held brief squad
meetings outside the bunker that he would be sharing with Sergeant
Palmer.   He told the squad that his training at Benning was quite current,
having been reshaped by Korean veterans, and that he would be sharing
what he had learned with all of them.

As the meeting broke up, he stopped Ben and said, "PFC Stewart, I
understand you're a Stanford man.   Play any football there?"

"Not really, sir.   Just intramural stuff.   Went out for track in my
freshman year."

Clanahan leaned forward and in a subdued voice said, "Well, I'm glad to have you in my platoon, Stewart. They tell me you are a good RTO. You know, the only difference between you and me is this little gold bar on my collar." He fingered the insignia of his rank.

"There's one other difference, sir," said Ben quietly. "I've been here since the first of December."

"Well, Stewart, I understand your concern, but don't worry," said the lieutenant, somewhat stunned. "I intend to depend a lot on Sergeant Palmer until I get up to speed."

Ben smiled and nodded, resisted a slight urge to salute, and turned away from Clanahan and left. The new guy seems pleasant, thought Ben, but the chummy little tête-à-tête had given him an uncomfortable feeling. Having to deal with a likeable platoon leader might be difficult.

On 28 April it began raining and didn't stop for a couple of days. When the rain let up, an enemy squad probed the wire in front of Baker Company. Twenty minutes later they were joined by a second squad. The Chinese soldiers threw potato-masher grenades in response to the G.I.'s use of machines guns, mortars and artillery. It was estimated that there were six enemy wounded. There were no friendly casualties.

On the first of May, Ben received two letters from his family and one from Mary Ellen. He opened hers first. It was just one page.

April 23, 1953
Dear Ben,

In your last letter you wrote about the possibility of your returning to school next fall and our picking things up where they left off. Several weeks ago that was my hope, too, but now I guess it's not going to happen. I just got pinned to a fellow from Cal, one of the boys that I met skiing. He's a Delta Tau Delta and we have a lot of the same interests. And let's face it. He's here and you aren't.

I wish that I didn't have to give you this news in a cold old letter. I know that your life is miserable enough as it is. But I can't very well fly over there and explain this situation to you.

Well this is about all I have to say. Given the way things are do you still want to hear from me from time to time? Mom and Dad send their love.

Be safe,
Ellie

Ben crammed the letter in his breast pocket and took a stroll on the friendly side of the hill. His blue funk lasted about thirty minutes. When he felt better, he wrote his response.

Dearest Ellie,

Well, I guess that wasn't too much of a surprise. I'm out here on a different planet nine thousand miles away from you. Your life goes on at home and I can't do anything about that. I would like to hear from you whenever you get a chance to write. Letters from you and my folks have been my only reminders that there is still a better world somewhere.

I'm due to go to Japan soon for a week of R&R. I was going to buy you something nice while I'm there but now I guess I'll just save my dough.

Lots of love to you and your folks,
Ben

P.S.   Did I really have to lose out to some schmuck from <u>*Cal?*</u>

* * *

On 15 May, the Fifth RCT was relieved by the 65th Infantry Regiment. The combat team withdrew to an assembly area beside the Han-Tan-Chon River, one of two main streams flowing south through the Chorwon Valley.

As they set up camp, Ben cornered Sergeant Palmer. "Have you heard how long we are going to be off the line, Sarge?"

"Probably two weeks to a month," said Rob. "You aren't going to get your four points this month, are you, buddy?"

"No, looks like we're going to be about six days short. The damn army knows just when to move me so that they can keep me here until I'm eligible for Social Security. At the rate we're going, I'll have only twenty points by the end of the month."

"Well, you're more than half way there. Frankly, Stewart, I thank God for every day I'm off the line."

The late spring weather was fair and unseasonably warm. A training program was initiated to keep the men out of mischief. It included a long overdue review of military courtesy, field sanitation, supply economy (the thou shalt not use more than ten sheets of toilet paper a day course), interior guard duty, assembly and disassembly of weapons and scouting and patrolling.

As the days dragged on, Ben realized that he really hadn't been able to dismiss from his mind the hurt of losing Mary Ellen's affection. He wasn't sure whether it was the loss of her that bothered him so much or just feelings of envy for the young civilian men who had so many opportunities to get their arms around someone sweet and warm. Could he have steered his life differently? Had he chosen a course of study more in line with his aptitudes, it was very likely that his grade point average would not have suffered. Then, too, he hadn't even investigated student loans at the bank or through the university to ease the financial problem. He probably could have avoided this year on this pile of shit. He really had had options that were seemingly closed to most of the poor slobs in the army. Well, so be it! He would just have to go get his "tough shit card" punched, earn his elusive thirty-six points and head for home.

* * *

In mid-May the names of PFC's Benjamin Stewart, Rudy Aguilar and Luis Meyer appeared on the lists of those eligible for five days of rest and recuperation in Japan. On the 23rd of the month, the three men met with others going on R & R, to listen to a forty-five minute lecture from the chaplain on how to behave in Japan. He implored them to forsake "whoring and drunkenness" and focus on the good shopping bargains and the excellent museums and other cultural pleasures. There were a lot of grinning faces but most everyone was able to keep from chuckling. Soon a convoy of trucks arrived and the three excited comrades climbed in a "deuce and a half" bound for Kimpo Airfield.

"The chaplain was right," said Luis. "I'm going to keep my eyes peeled for some good shopping bargains. Not goin' to pay five dollars for pussy, if I can get in for three."

"As a matter of fact, Luis," observed Ben. You look so damn sexy in those over-sized fatigues and your hair hanging over your ears that the girls will probably want to pay you."

"Not long now," said Rudy, as he gave Ben a playful punch on the shoulder. "Old Stew won't be a sorry-assed cherry for long." There was a chorus of chuckling and whistles.

"Shut up, Rudy!" Ben was visibly embarrassed by the mention of his virginal status and didn't want the entire Eighth Army to know about it. "As if you aren't anxious to get your ashes hauled."

And so the banter continued as the convoy moved southwest to Seoul. Luis suggested a little game of blackjack but he had no takers. Everyone had better plans for their money. Finally they dozed as the convoy passed through the outskirts of Seoul, waking momentarily each time their truck hit a pothole.

When they reached Kimpo Field, the young soldiers shook out their stiff muscles, de-trucked, crossed the tarmac and boarded an old twin-engine C-119. They found room to sit on the long benches that ran the length of the fuselage.

Shortly after take-off, the plane touched down at Itami Air Force Base near Osaka, Japan. They were herded to a large warehouse where they presented their leave orders to a non-com at the R & R Processing Office. They then showered and were issued clean underwear, socks, and a class-A uniform with a necktie. Everything was class-A, that is, but their battered combat boots. Nevertheless, Ben felt pretty spiffy. He joined the line to exchange his military script for Japanese yen.

Showered, shaved and solvent, the trio picked up their passes and set out in search of dinner, etc. They were besieged by a legion of cab drivers as soon as they exited the gate. One of the drivers caught their attention because of his flawless English. Taro Seki introduced himself as a starving university student majoring in English, and offered to be their driver and guide for their five-day stay in the Nara-Osaka area. They agreed on a price and climbed into the cab.

"Beer and chow, James," demanded Luis and the driver pulled out into the traffic and headed for downtown Osaka.

"Not yet," said Ben. "Take us to one of the Army's hotels. We need to get a room before the rest of those eight-balls get into town."

"Military hotels very expensive," said Taro. "I can take you to a little family hotel for nine dollars a night."

"Does it have American toilets and showers?" asked Ben.

"No, it has what you G.I's call "squatty potties.""

"Take us to the military hotel, Taro."

He took them to one of the hotels that had been leased by the Army and the three of them were able to find a room for thirty dollars a night. That was affordable since they would be splitting the cost three ways. The hotel had a nice restaurant with American fare. Ben was looking forward to five days of showers, clean sheets and minced ham and eggs for breakfast and steak for dinner. He couldn't get over the wonder of electric lights and carpets. He'd been living like an animal for a long time.

As he drove, Taro carried on a narrative about the city of Osaka. He explained that much of it had been destroyed by Allied bombing raids during the war but that the Osakans had been quick to rebuild the important industrial and commercial center and that the city's population had doubled in five years, making it the third largest in Japan, after Tokyo and Yokohama. The neighborhoods of small wooden houses, incinerated during bombing raids, had been replaced by large, modern apartment buildings to house the burgeoning population. Many well-to-do Osakans had moved to the suburbs to escape the city's crowded conditions, high prices, and pollution.

Downtown Osaka lies on the delta of the Yodo River, where the river pours into Osaka Bay. As they passed the many tributaries and canals, Luis said, "When I was in high school, I took a trip with my folks to Italy. This place is a lot like Venice."

"As a matter of fact," said Taro, "Japanese tourists call Venice the Osaka of Italy. A major difference is that Venice has been an international trading port for centuries while Osaka has been engaged in international trade for no more than ninety years. It took my people a long time to overcome their suspicion and lack of tolerance for foreigners."

Taro pulled to a stop in an older part of the city. "I'll bet this place is crawling with M.P's when the sun goes down," observed Rudy.

"Yes, but we'll just be here for the dinner hour," promised Taro. "I would hope that you would enjoy a real Japanese dinner on your first night in Osaka." Ben had his taste buds primed for filet mignon, medium rare, but decided against registering an objection. As they entered the restaurant, the young guide was warmly greeted by the hostess.

Taro continued his narrative on the geography and history of Osaka while the young men downed a couple of rounds of *Kirin* beer. They were sure that Taro would be getting a commission from the dinner check but were feeling mellow and readily accepted his offer to order for them.

The waitress brought a combination of seafood including eel, shrimp, turtle and *kaminabe,* a fish stew cooked in a paper pot. It was accompanied by rice and sweet potatoes. Ben enjoyed almost everything, but was reluctant to sample the eel. He had encountered too many of the slimy creatures, at home, while swimming beneath the Folsom Bridge. After a couple of glasses of *sake,* he was able to down one bite; but that was all. Rudy and Luis had no problem ingesting their share of the delicacy and registering their satisfaction with polite oriental belches.

Once dinner was over, Taro said, in a half whisper, "Well, are you ready for your cultural exchange with the ladies?"

"You better believe it.," said Luis. "Our chaplain advised us to enjoy the cultural pleasures of your fair city and I think we should follow his lead. Let's go."

"Are the girls in this neighborhood?" asked Ben. "Chances look pretty good around here for landing in the stockade or getting a dose of clap or both."

"No, we won't be staying here," responded Taro. "We are going to a place where the girls look like they're from Hollywood. And as for venereal disease, all of the women are checked weekly by the health department."

Taro drove until they came to an old but well-kept residential neighborhood. The homes were two-story structures enclosed in walled gardens. They had been built before World War II by prosperous merchants and professionals but had been eventually sold by heirs who were fleeing to the suburbs. Finally they stopped in front of one of the gates. Rudy jumped out and said, "C'mon, Stew, this is your big moment. Pussy, pussy have-a yes, G.I."

Taro winked and said, "There is no hurry. We can just have a drink here if you like. Whatever happens." He rang the doorbell and they were soon met by an elderly Japanese man dressed in western suit and tie. Once more, Taro was greeted as if he were family. The man ushered them into a living room containing a bevy of young women, a bartender, and a couple of noisy Canadian soldiers, members of Princess Pat's Light Infantry. Three of the women approached Ben, Rudy and Luis and took their drink order. Ben felt full from two beers and dinner so he opted for a scotch on the rocks.

The elderly gentleman put a Glenn Miller single on a small table-top record-player and Ben's "waitress" asked him to dance. Ben had never danced with such a tiny partner, but she was amazingly graceful and responsive to his lead, taking long smooth strides to the beat of *Moonlight Serenade*.

Luis was quite taken with his dancing partner and somewhat reluctant to go when Taro suggested that they might like to go try another house but he acquiesced and joined the rest as they returned to Taro's sedan. As they drove away, Taro said that he would bring Luis back to the first house if he didn't find a girl that he liked better.

At the second house, there was another round of drinks all around. While they were exchanging pleasantries with the madam, a taller than usual Japanese woman with Eurasian features approached the group and said, "Taro-san, please introduce me to your tall American friend."

"Mr. Stewart, may I introduce my lovely friend, Keiko MacKenzie."

"Hi, Keiko. It's nice to meet a fellow Scotsman. Who was MacKenzie?"

"My father was a Marine assigned to the American Embassy in Tokyo during the early 30's. He left my mother when he was transferred to the Philippines and we never heard from him again. He may have died on Bataan. My mother never married him but she insisted that I carry the MacKenzie name. She didn't foresee how much pain my Scots name and occidental features would cause me during my years in school. The other children made me feel very ugly. Japanese people think they are the master race and they generally look down on someone of mixed parentage."

"Well, as a matter of fact," said Ben, "the Scots feel that they are God's chosen people. So you are the product of two proud peoples."

They began to dance to Artie Shaw's arrangement of *Stardust* and Keiko pressed close to Ben. "I can't believe that you were ever seen as being ugly," Ben whispered.

Keiko chuckled, "That was long ago. As a teen-ager I grew taller than most of the boys at school and no one dared tease me anymore."

"I know," said Ben. "After I grew nine inches in my eighth grade year, school yard tough guys stayed out of my way. Until now, I was able to avoid fighting."

"That must be horrible and hateful over there. What do you hate most about it?" the girl asked.

"Going to the bathroom at twenty degrees below zero," Ben responded with a smile on his face.

Keiko giggled and taking Ben's hand said, "Shall we go upstairs, or am I rushing things? Would you like another drink?"

"Just a minute," he said. "I've got to check in with my boys." He walked over to where Luis and Rudy were chatting with Taro. "You guys see anyone you like?"

"Nah, we were just talking to Taro about heading back to the first place," said Rudy.

"I'm staying," Ben stated.

Luis and Rudy looked at each other and burst out laughing. "Okay, Lone Ranger," said Luis. "We'll come back for you later. Hope we can recognize you in your deflowered state."

Ben grinned and returned to Keiko. "They'll be back later. I don't think I need another drink, what were you saying about going upstairs?" Keiko took his hand and led him up the staircase and down the hall to her room. Once inside, she stood on her tiptoes and kissed him on the lips. Then she stepped back, removed her kimono, threw it on a chair and turning her back to Ben, gestured for him to unhook her bra. After tossing her bra on the chair he reached around, grabbed her breasts and said, "Guess, who." Keiko giggled nervously, not really understanding Ben's attempt at humor. Then she slipped off her panties and turned to face him.

"Rudy was so right," thought Ben. "This is my big moment." But then he realized that he had conflicting needs. The evening's beer and scotch and tea had reached critical mass.

"Are you all right, Ben?" said Keiko, observing his worried look.

"I'm fine. I just have to pee."

"It's right across the hall," she said. Hurry back and…take off your tie while you're at it."

When Ben returned he tossed his tie over the back of the chair. Keiko kissed his neck as she unbuttoned his shirt. Then she slipped his t-shirt over his head and planted kisses on his chest. He was amazed how quickly she slipped the clasp on his web belt and dropped his trousers. Then she gestured for him to lie on the bed and she slid over to him.

Much to Ben's mortification, as Keiko was gently guiding him into place with her hand, he reached climax. "Oh, God, I'm sorry," he moaned. "This is so embarrassing."

Keiko kissed him on his forehead. "Don't worry Ben-san. You will be fine in a few minutes."

"Fine for what? I'm through for the evening, aren't I?"

"Of course not. Don't worry about it." Keiko held him close. She asked him about his home in the Sacramento Valley and expressed a desire to see her father's home in Montana some day and perhaps find someone from his family. The two chatted like a couple of California teen-agers.

Soon, with very little effort, she had him aroused again and this time her pupil successfully rewarded her for her kindness. Then he kissed her tenderly on the forehead and said, "Miss MacKenzie, that was great! I guess you probably know that I'm just a beginner."

Keiko shook her head. "No, I didn't. You're such a handsome, sweet guy. You can't fool me. You've had a lot of women. I can tell."

"When we go out on patrol, I'm a radio operator," explained Ben. "And whenever I hear something like that, I say, 'Bullshit One. This is Bullshit Two, Over.' But thank you anyway."

Keiko knew intuitively that Ben was through for the night so she suggested that they take a bath. She helped him into a robe and they walked down the hall to a room that contained three large tubs. As she bathed him he started to become aroused again but she giggled and suggested that he save it for another night. He was becoming too sleepy to object.

When they descended the stairs, Taro and the madam were waiting for them. The older lady handed Ben a small slip of paper. He glanced at it briefly, paid her five hundred yen (about two dollars) and turned to bid Keiko good night.

"Will I see you again?" she asked.

"How about tomorrow night?" he replied.

"Yes, please come after nine thirty," she said.

Ben saw Keiko the next night and they agreed to meet in downtown Osaka on the following day for lunch. Afterwards they visited Osaka Castle, built in 1584, and Keiko explained the historical exhibits. Then she helped him shop for gifts for his family. Ben benefited considerably from her bargaining ability. When he asked about being with her that evening, she explained that she would be unable to see him because she had to go to a party given by a bunch of local businessmen for some American clients.

"Keiko, I have only two more evenings in Japan," responded Ben to the unwelcome news. "Can't you get out of that thing tonight."

"No, Ben. I've been scheduled for tonight's party for some time."

"Please, Keiko. You've quickly become very special to me. I want to be with you."

"I'm sorry, Ben. I have a commitment."

"Yeah. I know about your commitments," he added with sarcasm.

"Ben, it's what I do. We can be together tomorrow evening. Now please get me a cab. I'm afraid I'm going to be late."

* * *

On the following evening, Ben's last night in Japan, Taro dropped him at Keiko's place of employment with a promise to return at 11:00. When the madam came to the door, she was surprised to see the young soldier and informed him that Keiko wasn't there.

"Where is she?" asked Ben, his heart sinking.

"She went on holiday. She no tell you? Poor boy, you come in. I show you to other nice girls."

"No thanks, ma'am. But could you call me a cab? I'll just head back to the hotel."

"I'll try to reach Taro-san," she replied and proceeded to call around. Having no success, she called for another cab.

While Ben was waiting for his cab, the woman handed him a business card written in English. "This way you can write to your sweetheart. She will be sorry she not see you."

The following morning at breakfast, Rudy and Luis noticed Ben's gloomy countenance but attributed it to his having to return to work. Then they returned to the R & R Center, turned in the class-A uniforms and regained their freshly laundered fatigues. They boarded their return flight to Kimpo shortly after ten o'clock.

As Luis was buckling himself in, he turned to Ben, "You missed a great party last night, old timer. I don't remember much about it but judging by my headache and the taste in my mouth, we must have had a great time. When we came in you were out like a light. What happened?"

"Nothing happened. Keiko stood me up. She took off on her own R & R without telling me."

"So, big deal, you had to settle for one of the other chicks."

"Actually I didn't. I just wanted to see Keiko."

"Ben, old buddy, pussy is pussy," said Rudy. There's just two kinds, good and better. Are you telling us that you wasted your last night on R & R."

"Uh oh, young Private Stewart is in love and his heart is broken and he's lost his virginity," said Luis teasingly. "What a mess! I don't think you're going to be ready to go back up on the line, trooper. We'd better chopper you to the psycho ward."

"C'mon, man. She's just a puta for crissake," said Rudy.

"Yeah, I know it" agreed Ben. "Let's drop it. I'll be okay in a day or two."

Ben's funk continued throughout the return trip. He had mild fantasies of marrying Keiko and taking her home to California. She was a smart girl and would have no difficulty finding a legitimate job in San Francisco in international commerce or something that would help them make ends meet while he finished Stanford and went on to medical school. Then he'd stop in the middle of his reverie and think, "This is crazy."

Nevertheless, as soon as he was back in his bunk in the squad tent, he wrote a letter to Keiko, revealing his feelings. The process of writing helped clear his head. He didn't send the letter. He just needed to try it on for size. He took out another sheet of stationery and wrote:

Hi MacKenzie,
How's my bonnie lassie? I'm sorry that we were unable to get together
for my last night in Osaka. I want you to know much I enjoyed my
few days in your fair city. You made it wonderful.
I hope that you will be able to come to the U.S someday and search
for your relatives. I will help you in any way that I can. You can
always reach me through my parents at 8994 Greenback Lane,
Orangevale, California.
Meanwhile, things are fine here. We're still in reserve so nobody is
shooting at me and I don't have to shoot at anybody. That's apt to
change soon. If you get a chance, please write me in care of the APO
address on the envelope.   Love, Ben-san

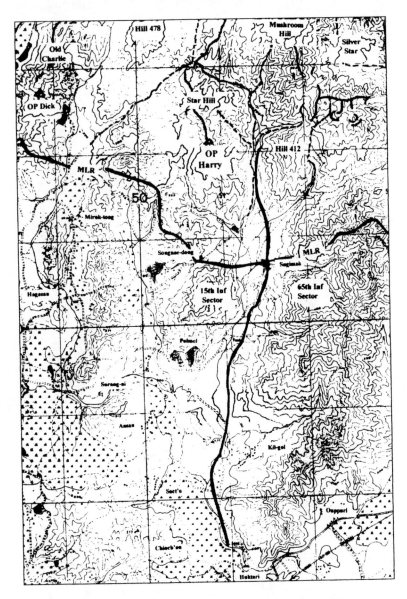

Topographical map showing location of Outpost Harry,
northeast of Chorwan (*National Archives*)

JUNE 1953

ON 4 JUNE the Communist negotiators agreed to all Allied proposals. Unfortunately, South Korean President Syngman Rhee found that he could not, emotionally nor politically, accept the armistice terms.   He complained that acceptance of the truce would doom the Korean people to continued division and that South Korea would be permanently incapable of supporting itself economically.

Washington dispatched Assistant Secretary of State Walter Robertson to Seoul to negotiate with Rhee. The communists were so enraged with the South Korean leader that they continued vicious attacks on the UN line inflicting an average of nine hundred casualties a day. The G.I's were equally as angry and they fought off the attacks, resulting in an even greater number of North Korean and Chinese casualties.

On the eleventh of June, the First Battalion, Fifth Regimental Combat Team moved to a blocking position, in the vicinity of Surang-ni, behind the 15th Infantry Regiment, 3rd Infantry Division, the unit that currently occupied a sector of Line Missouri. Four hundred meters northeast of the MLR lay Outpost Harry, a company-sized installation. It was situated on a hill that was approximately 1280 feet high and about three hundred meters south of a much larger mass, Star Hill, occupied by the enemy. As it lay in the main avenue of approach to the entrance to the Chorwan Valley, Outpost Harry had been subjected to many strong enemy attacks.

* * *

From his vantage point at the rear of what the Americans had dubbed Star Hill, Xing had noticed a lot of activity, on the part of his division, beginning in late May and running through the first two weeks in June. During the hours of darkness, there was a significant increase in the number of supply trucks coming in from Manchuria. He observed the construction of many new artillery and anti-aircraft positions near the rear toe of the hill. Conscript laborers worked around the clock improving roads and bridges on the main supply route; diving for cover whenever they heard the drone of an enemy observation plane. It was obvious that something big was brewing.

The additional eighteen Soviet-made artillery pieces added their weight to the regular nightly din. They helped increase the amount of fire directed toward the U.S. Third Division Artillery emplacements from 270 to 650 rounds per day. For a few days, less fire was directed toward outpost, main line positions, and supply roads in an effort to concentrate on the neutralization of the U.N. forces' artillery support.

During company meetings, Xing and his comrades had learned that the friendly units in their sector were his battalion along with two other battalions from the 220th Regiment as well as the 221st and 222nd Regiments of the Seventy-fourth Division of the Twenty-fourth Army of the Peoples Liberation Army. Political Officer Chao assured them that they greatly outnumbered the opposing UN forces.

On the afternoon of 11 June, Captain Chen spoke to the company in a flat, no-nonsense voice. "You are all aware of the small American outpost some three hundred meters to our front. It is very important that we wrest the hill from the enemy. Once we have secured the outpost, we will be able to see into their rear area. Second Battalion fought bravely last night, terrified the handful of enemy soldiers manning the outpost but did not succeed in capturing it. We will finish the job for them." Captain Chen fixed his eyes on each of he company members as he spoke. Xing lowered his eyes, endeavoring to portray respect and mask his feelings.

"Shortly before midnight," continued Chen, "our artillery and mortar battalions will shell the outpost. We will move out as soon as the barrage begins so that we will be in striking distance when it lifts. Our company, led by Lieutenant Hsiao, will attack the east side of the outpost, near the rear. Other companies will get into position so that, when the whistles blow, the attack will come from all sides. We do not want any of the Americans to escape. We will destroy them all. Are there any questions?

"Yes, Company Commander," said Chu. "What is the enemy's strength?"

"There is room for no more than a reinforced company on the outpost. We have been told by members of the Third Battalion to expect them to be armed with two light machine guns and a half dozen automatic rifles. The rest will be using their M-1s. Many will have been killed by the artillery barrage by the time we get there."

"Company Commander Chen, what will happen when the objective is ours?"

"Very good question, Comrade. One of the other companies has been designated to occupy the outpost. We and the remainder of the battalion will pull back midway between Hill 412, right here, and the outpost," said Chen pointing to the map. We'll wait to see if the Americans counterattack. When they do we will hit them on the flank and destroy them. Any other questions? Do you all agree to the wisdom of the attack?"

There being no objections, Captain Chao, the political officer, took over the meeting. "Good. You have agreed to a plan that is guaranteed to be successful. Remember all of you that the people in our homeland expect us to fight bravely and win the battle. If we do so, we can finish the war shortly and our glorious service will shine on our heads and our families will be recognized as honorable soldier's families when the news is reported to our native villages and towns. Our loved ones will receive additional rations of rice and meat and they will be very pleased with us."

"Will you be joining us in the attack, Political Officer?" said Xing from the rear of the group.

Chao smiled at Xing's impertinence but was able to control his response. "No, Comrade. The leaders have insisted that I remain at the company command post to relay messages from battalion. I am also needed here to comfort any wounded of which, I hope, there will be few....Squad leaders, please take over and have the men sign the oath."

Xing, Chu and Ho huddled with the other five men in their squad while Squad Leader Sung went over last-minute details. Then he produced a form entitled *A Solemn Pledge to Kill the Enemy* and proceeded to read aloud.

We eight members of the squad hereby solemnly promise to be determined to kill the enemy by helping the leader in this combat and achieve merits to our most glorious honor.

1. We will fight bravely without being afraid of enemy fire and make our firearms effective to the greatest extent.

2. We will overcome every difficulty. We will fight bravely even when we become tired and hungry.

3. We will be united and help one another, so that we may not retreat even a step.

4. We eight members of our squad, without fail, will kill and wound more than three enemies for the people of China and Korea and for our leaders.

5. Should we fail to do these things, we wish to be punished.

Upon reading the fifth point, Sergeant Sung signed and dated the pledge form, rolled his thumb on the oily barrel of his weapon and affixed his thumb print to the paper. Then he passed the document to Vice Squad Leader Teng for his ratification. Xing was the last to sign. He felt the words were empty. He had no idea how he was going to react to close combat but he was not going to kick off a philosophical debate over a worthless piece of paper.

At 2300, Baker Company of the 15th U.S. Infantry moved into position on OP Harry. As they did so, Squad Leader Sung's little group moved down a finger of Star Hill to its line of departure.

Shortly before midnight, Outpost Harry began receiving a barrage of mortar and artillery fire. Xing, Ho and Chu stepped out together across the valley floor. Xing and Chu carried burp guns but Ho carried no weapon other than wearing a vest crammed with thirty concussion grenades. In a few minutes, they stopped and huddled together in the dark within two hundred yards of the objective.

An hour later a red flare rose from Star Hill, signaling the attack. The platoons in the vanguard rushed up the slope and had soon overrun the trenches on the right and right rear of the outpost. As planned, the Chinese hit from all directions. Lieutenant Tsiao's platoon waited in the dark for orders to join the attack.

Xing had a sudden urge to urinate and gestured to Sergeant Sung for permission to step back away from the squad and relieve himself. Sung shook his head so Xing just relaxed and gave his pants a good soaking.

Within minutes, a square of fire from Third Division Artillery ringed the outpost. An Air Force flare ship arrived and its crew promised to drop flares until daylight. Xing was beginning to regret the fact that they had not gone in with the first wave of assault troops. The situation was becoming ever more dangerous. In the light of the shell bursts he could see men falling as they continued trying to reach the trenches above the eastern slope.

Shortly before 0100, a green flare rose from the hilltop ordering the surviving Chinese to withdraw to prepare for another attempt. The men currently engaged in the attack would be left without support. They would have to fend for themselves. Xing was so relieved that he forgot about the discomfort of his wet pants. As they moved back to Star Hill, artillery and machine gun fire went overhead, directed at OP Harry.

At ten minutes to three, Baker Company of the Fifth RCT crossed the MLR and headed for OP Harry. Charlie Company had relieved them on Hill 361. They could see artillery fire dropping on the outpost from enemy emplacements on Mushroom and Star Hills. Heavy Mortar Company of the Fifth RCT replied to the Chinese barrage.

At 0400 the reinforcements from the Fifth RCT joined the survivors of B/15 on Harry and, after catching their breath from the climb, went on the attack, pushing the remnants of the Chinese forward. Captain Tarts, CO of Baker of the 15th, reported from his bunker in the center of the outpost that he had phone communication with those to the rear of the outpost but no contact with those in the front. Incoming fire had his CP zeroed in and he couldn't get out of the bunker. Tarts said that he was slightly wounded and that he had one able-bodied man with him and eight others who were seriously wounded. He was told that a Major Connors would be coming out to relieve him of command and would be there soon to coordinate the efforts of the two Baker companies.

Around 0530, a helicopter and a half-track arrived at the supply point. The latter delivered Major Connors and some new radios and the evacuation of the wounded began. At 0619 Connors reported that Harry was fully in the possession of friendly hands. He requested all counter fire possible be directed on the Chinese positions to cover the evacuation of the wounded and the consolidation of the friendly forces.

* * *

At 0743 on 12 June, First and Third Platoons of Company A of the Fifth RCT set out to traverse the short but demanding distance from the MLR to OP Harry. Heavily laden with their weapons, ammunition and packs, they picked their way down the slope to the valley floor.

Ben found breathing difficult. He felt like somebody was sitting on his chest. Surely, he thought, every Chinaman on Star Hill is watching us. When would the relative quiet be shattered by incoming artillery and mortar rounds?

There was a small stream at the bottom of the hill and a copse of scrub oaks. The area served as the supply point for OP Harry. They halted in the cover of the trees to wait for First and Third Platoons of Love Company, 15th Infantry. As they rested, the outpost above began receiving heavy artillery fire. The defenders requested that counter-battery fire be focused on the OP's right flank. It was then shifted to the north to catch the withdrawing Chinese troops. The incoming fire decreased when the Chinese reached Star Hill.

In a few minutes the four relieving platoons formed in a long file and began ascending the steep hill by way of a long communications trench. Ben was very grateful that it wasn't his turn to pack the radio. In addition to his usual gear, he was packing a litter that would be used to transport dead or wounded boys from B Company down to the supply point.

The two Baker Companies were waiting at the top of the hill when their reinforcements arrived. Ben overheard a medic tell Grady that Baker of the Fifth RCT had suffered one hundred and twenty-six casualties on its watch. The four platoons had held the outpost against a reinforced regiment of enemy troops.

An hour later, two platoons from Charlie Company of the Fifth RCT arrived on the outpost. The place was getting crowded. The relieving soldiers spent the rest of the morning helping with the evacuation of the dead and wounded Americans. By noon all wounded had been evacuated but Ben could still smell the sweet, putrid odor of rotting body parts rising from the torn-up earth around the position.

During the evacuation of the casualties, an M-39 half-track had dropped a load of 2 X 10 planks and empty sand bags at the supply point. As soon as their litter-carrying task was completed, Sergeant Palmer ordered the platoon members to help a small detachment of engineers carry the planks and sand bags to the top of the hill. Only four of the bunkers on the outpost were intact. The others would have to be rebuilt in haste before the next Chinese artillery barrage.

There were so many new and salvageable planks that the engineers and riflemen were able to place them on edge over supporting beams forming wooden ceilings that were ten inches thick. The bunkers on the rear of the hill and the outpost CP in the center were reparable during the daylight hours. Those on the front of hill, facing the Star Mass, were visible to the enemy. Their refurbishing would have to wait until nightfall.

Shortly after 10:00 P.M., Ben and Rudy were taking a breather at the bottom of the trench when the first incoming barrage of the evening arrived. They scrambled into the nearest bunker to escape the wrath of the 76mm white phosphorous shells. Then answering fire from the 3rd Division Artillery began hitting too close to the outpost. The OP commander, the CO of Love of the 15th, requested illumination and insisted that supporting fire either be lifted completely or redirected well to the right and left of Harry.

Either enemy or friendly fire had taken out his land phone line so that he would have to communicate by radio until the following day when signalmen could find the break. Third Battalion, 15th Infantry, aimed both of its searchlights at the outpost.

When Ben and Rudy started their watch at 0100 everything was quiet. They entered two firing holes at the left rear of the outpost, spread M-1 and BAR clips on the sandbags in front of them and conversed quietly. Sergeant Palmer came by to check on them and advised them to save the chitchat until morning.

"You don't suppose the Chinamen will take tonight off, do you Sergeant?" asked Rudy.

"I'm sure they'd like to but I seriously doubt it. The Chinks won't quit attacking until they run out of foot sloggers and that won't happen soon. But you guys are going to do fine. Now, pay attention. Heavy Mortar's going to start dropping illumination flares every five minutes or so. Let me know if you see anything. And watch for red flares over Star Hill. Oh, and lay out some grenades on those sand bags." Rob turned and moved on in order to check on Whitey Lockwood.

At 0223 a rattle of small arms fire from the front of the outpost brought Rob Palmer and the remainder of the platoon on the run. "Things are still

OK here, Sergeant Palmer. Are we going up front to help those guys?" asked Rudy.

"No way. You stay put. The forward platoons can handle that. Chinese probe the front of an objective first with a small group and then hit the flanks with their main body. They're out there somewhere."

As a parachute flare descended at 0255, it revealed the Changsha Company approaching the toe of the slope. The silence was immediately shattered by the coughing sound of the BAR's, the pop of the M-1's, and the clinking sound of expended clips. Small arms fire poured into Harry from the hillsides to the north and mortar rounds coming from the vicinity of Star Hill began straddling the fence.

Sergeant Palmer moved quickly from one end of the line to the other, stopping frequently to fire a burst from his carbine. "WATCH IT. WATCH IT, AGUILAR. POUR SOME FIRE INTO THAT BUNCH COMIN' ON THE LEFT... STEWART, DON'T LOOK AT ME, GODDAMMIT! KEEP YOUR EYES ON THE CHINKS... LOCKWOOD, GET THAT SONOFABITCH ABOUT READY TO THROW... YOU THERE, NEW GUY, THOSE CHINKS ARE CLOSE ENOUGH FOR GRENADES. USE 'EM. Hell, I'll do it myself. WATCH IT, YOU GUYS. KEEP POURIN' INTO THEM! ...MEDIC! ...WILLIAMS. WHERE IN THE HELL ARE YOU? ...AGUILAR'S DOWN. GET OVER HERE ON THE DOUBLE..."

* * *

Xing's mind raced as he moved forward with Chu and Ho. He felt that one way or the other this was going to be his last night of misery in the People's Liberation Army. Suddenly he realized that he was alone. Something had happened to his two companions. That settled it. If he could just make it to the trench alive, he would surrender. He didn't believe the party bullshit about Americans mistreating their prisoners. The South Koreans would, but these men ahead were Americans. Gripping his weapon tightly, Xing dropped to the ground and crawled toward the deadly fusillade pouring from the trenches of Outpost Harry.

Ben could no longer hear the "bum-bum-bum" of Rudy's BAR. Glancing to his right he could see Grady's back as the medic knelt beside someone on the ground. Grady was trying to resuscitate the wounded man.

Ben was startled as Rob Palmer yelled, "STEWART, LOOK BEHIND YOU." Ben turned just in time to see a Chinese soldier drop into the trench about eight feet behind him. The young soldier looked stunned as if surprised to see Ben. Ben was shocked, too, but his paralysis was of shorter duration. As the intruder began to raise his sub-machine gun and his other arm, Ben rammed his bayonet into the man's chest, withdrew it, and rammed another clip into his M-1.

As he lay at Ben's feet, Xing made snoring sounds as he fought for his last few precious breaths. He was soon released from the People's Liberation Army.

Ben returned to the firing hole and resumed shooting at the dark figures on the slope that were being illuminated by lurid orange artillery explosions. His hands were shaking and the stench of the cordite and the horror of the experience began to produce waves of nausea. He was just going to have to accept the fact that Grady was working on a badly wounded man right at Rudy's position but certainly not Rudy. That's impossible. Rudy's indestructible. Besides, he's got family responsibilities. Ben rammed another clip into his rifle.

"STEWART...GET OVER HERE. As Ben squeezed by Grady to report to Sergeant Palmer, he looked down and saw that Rudy was lying on his stomach. Blood covered his neck and back.

"Looks like a chunk of shrapnel slipped right between his helmet rim and the top of his flak jacket, Stew," said Grady. "Rudy was gone before I got here."

"Stewart," said Palmer. "Do you know where the CP is?"

"Yeah, I worked on it this afternoon."

"Well get over there right away. They need an RTO. The captain's radio guy was wounded."

When Ben reached the CP the officer was trying to operate the PRC-10 himself. "Are you the RTO? I can't get anything but a bunch of static and an occasional Chinaman on this thing. Can you fix it?"

Ben put the receiver up to his ear. "Sounds like the Chinese are jamming the frequency, sir. Let me try another one."

Ben finally made contact with 3rd Battalion CP enabling the captain to report that the outpost was in complete darkness, that there was a severe ammunition shortage and that they were continuing to receive automatic weapons fire from the left rear. He was assured that ammunition and reinforcements were on the way.

An hour later, Sergeant Palmer, stuck his head in the CP bunker and announced that fourth platoon of Able Company had arrived at the top of the hill and that the Chinese were withdrawing north-northeast toward Star Hill and Star Ridge. He was told to have the new platoon pass through to the front of the outpost and help with the wounded. When Ben renewed contact with 3rd Battalion, the outpost commander happily reported that the Chinese were gone, that an additional platoon from "Rotary Red" (1st Battalion, 5th Infantry) had arrived but that they would still need more men, medical supplies, litters and litter bearers, and half-tracks and helicopters to evacuate the wounded. He made it abundantly clear that the current defenders of Outpost Harry needed to be relieved. All of their weapons were in bad shape.

Ben and Whitey Lockwood carried Rudy's body down to the supply point, placed it in the waiting half-track and covered it with his poncho. Once Rudy's handsome face was concealed, Ben found it a little easier to realize that his friend was gone. He glanced once more at the pair of thermo boots sticking out from under the poncho and turned to retrace his steps up through the supply trench, muttering, "Jesus, Rudy, you never even got your summer boots. Well, those rear-echelon assholes could never get it right for you. They can cancel your order now...Why you, Rudolfo Aguilar? I knew you as a good buddy but your government didn't. They thought you were just a piece of shit, so they sent you to this asshole of the world."

"Hurry up, Stew," said Whitey. "The sergeant wants us to haul ass out of here as soon as Charlie Company arrives. We've got to pack up."

When they reached the top, Sergeant Palmer had just finished searching Xing's body. "Nothin' on him but, what looks like, a couple of letters from home and this photograph. There's nothing here that S-2 would want to see." He handed the documents to Ben, who glanced at the snapshot of a young woman holding an infant.

"What do you want us to do with this dead Chink, Sarge?" said Whitey.

"Just get him out of the way. Pitch him down the slope for now. There'll be a bunch of Gook laborers comin' along pretty soon to bury the dead and repair the bunkers."

"I thought that the South Koreans were refusing to pull burial detail," said Ben.

"Not over here on the west side," said the sergeant. "A good number of them are Christians so they don't have any religious hang-ups and they are poorer than hell and glad for the work. Now get him out of here."

Ben bent over and returned the picture of the young family to the inside pocket of Xing's jacket. Then he and Whitey lifted the body to the lip of the trench and gave it shove.

"Scrawny little guy, fortunately," said Whitey. "Has sort of a smile on his face. Do you suppose he finally found out what he was doing here?"

"I doubt it," grumbled Ben. "I think he was just happy to see his ancestors. But neither he nor Rudy knew what he was doing here."

"Join the club," said Whitey.

"Roger that, cowboy." Ben picked up his pack and rifle and he and Whitey joined the rest of First Platoon. At Sergeant Palmer's command to "saddle up," they turned south and headed down the communications trench toward the supply point. Twenty-four hours of horror and no sleep had wrought a lot of change in Ben. The fear of being zeroed in by a

Chinese mortar man was no longer there. "Who gives a rat's ass?" he thought.

When they reached relative safety at the rear of the MLR, the platoon members collapsed and Sergeant Palmer went in search of First Sergeant Carroll and information regarding an assembly area. Ben was startled when a voice said, "Hey, podner, you carve any notches on yer shootin' iron last night?" Ben glanced up and recognized his Greek acquaintance, Corporal Karsatos.

"I'm afraid so, Iannis. Don't tell me you guys watch cowboy movies in Greece."

"Oh, yes, and we get "Gunsmoke" on the radio every Thursday evening…. Where is your friend, Rudy?"

"Rudy's gone, Iannis. They brought his body in on the half-track. He took a freak hit to the back of the neck. Shrapnel, I guess."

"I'm sorry, Ben. I know. I lose many friends. Boys from my village. It's not easy."

"That's just it. Rudy wasn't from my village. If it hadn't been for the Army, I would never have known him, never would have been his friend and depended on him. I would never have had to feel what I'm feeling now."

"Yes, you are a fortunate man, Ben. You had a friend like Rudy."

"Oh, is that it?" At this point, Ben was able to pull himself away from his own misery long enough to notice that Iannis, too, looked like someone who had just come off outpost duty. His face was flushed and the white of his left eye was angry and red.

"You don't look well, Iannis. How are you feeling?"

"I feel like I'm getting a little of the *grippe,* the flu. Just feel shitty all over. In a day or two, I'll be fine."

"If I were you, I'd check with your medic. Take a couple of APC's or something. Oh, looks like we're falling in to pull out. *Sto kalo,* Iannis. Talk to your medic. That's an order."

When Able Company reached the assembly area behind the MLR the men turned in their grimy down-filled sleeping bags for lightweight summer bags. They were dismissed and told to initiate their new bedding.

The following morning, at mail call, Ben was handed a couple of letters from his mother and another one with some Japanese lettering stamped on it. His heart began to beat rapidly as he thought it might be a reply from Keiko. Then, upon reexamination, he realized that it was the letter that he had mailed. The Japanese words must have been the equivalent of "Return to Sender."

"God, get me the hell out of this part of the world," he prayed.

PART III

MIDSUMMER 1953

FOR THE REMAINDER of June and on into early July, attacks and counterattacks ebbed and flowed along the entire length of the MLR. The approaching cease-fire provided the adversaries a strong motive to be in a superior position when the shooting stopped.

At Panmunjom the negotiations were as belligerent as ever. They continued to be slowed by the failure of the two sides to reach an agreement over the issue of involuntary repatriation of prisoners of war. The western members of the UN Command were growing weary as their constituents clamored for peace and agreement.

President Syngman Rhee insisted on negotiating a deal that would leave his nation able to defend itself when his allies went home. After twelve days of bargaining with The Assistant Secretary of Defense, Walter Robinson, Rhee finally accepted the financial terms of a US-ROK Mutual Security Treaty and agreed to end his obstruction of the truce agreement.

The Chinese launched their final major offensive on July 13. This action, known as the battle of the Kumsong River salient, was directed in part against the 3rd, 40th, and 45th Infantry Divisions of the U.S. IX Corps. Six Chinese divisions took part in this desperate effort to get in the last word.

* * *

When the men of First Battalion, Fifth Regimental Combat Team were relieved from Outpost Harry they anticipated that they would be going to a reserve area for a rest. However, their convoy turned west and stopped, a short time later, delivering them to the left flank of the Third Division. They were ushered into a blocking position on a secondary MLR and commanded to provide security for Outpost Tom, a two-platoon OP that served to guard against surprise attacks from the dominating hills to the northeast.

It was still dark when Sergeant Palmer shook Ben awake. "Wake up, Stewart. They want to see you at regimental headquarters. They're sending a jeep. He'll be down by the supply point at 0530."

"Where?" Ben responded drowsily.

"You are to report to the regimental S-3. His name is Major Jones."

"What the hell for, Sarge? Did I screw up or something?"

"Not that I know of. But you can't go down to regiment looking like that, soldier. There isn't time for a haircut but I've got some water heating in my bunker. At least you can shave."

"Thanks, Sarge. That'll help wake me up."

"And I'll see if I can't rustle up some fatigues sportin' a few less oil and food stains," added Palmer. Observing the moist, salt-stained armpits on Ben's fatigue jacket, he said, "Hopefully the major don't have an acute sense of smell." Ben smiled and made a mental note to remember Rob Palmer every Father's Day or...maybe Mother's Day would be more appropriate.

The sun was just rising as he hurried down the communications trail and found the jeep. The driver sat in the front seat and a KATUSA soldier rode shotgun in the rear.

"You PFC Stewart?" inquired the driver.

"Yeah. What's this all about?"

"How in the hell would I know? I'm just supposed to fetch you down to S-3, dead or alive." Ben climbed into the front passenger seat and dropped his rifle between his knees.

As the jeep bounced and splashed its way along the road to the rear, Ben's anxiety heightened. What's happening at regiment? Has something terrible happened at home? He knew that the S-3 office had something to do with the planning and review of operations. Were they upset with somebody's performance on OP Harry and had picked Ben at random for a briefing? Nah, why the hell would they be interested in what a PFC has to say?

Ben entered the S-3 tent at the stroke of 0700 and identified himself to the sergeant at the entrance, who nodded in the direction of a stocky, ruddy-complexioned major. He walked over to Jones, saluted and said, "PFC Stewart reporting as ordered, sir." Major Jones rose, returned the salute and offered his hand to the young soldier.

"Good morning, Stewart," said the major. "Were you with your company on Harry?"

"Yes, sir," responded Ben, quietly. "So," he thought, "that was why I was summoned to headquarters."

"We were very worried about you men, especially when we couldn't get through on either the ground wire or radio." Ben started to share how he felt about the experience and then decided not to do so. The major returned to his seat and motioned to him to sit down.

"When are you due for a second stripe, Stewart," queried the major as he looked at Ben's sleeve.

"Probably not until September, sir, unless we take a lot more casualties or have corporals E.T.S-ing home early."

"Well I need a man who can speak, read, write and pound a typewriter without making a bunch of mistakes. We're short as hell on typing paper and onion skin and we have *tokusan* work to get out. I've checked you out with Personnel. The job is slotted for an E-4 or higher. The job and the stripes are yours if you want them...Do you have any questions?"

"Typing what sort of documents, sir?"

"We crank out a daily journal, almost minute by minute, of the regiment's operations. Much of it is from the recordings of radio traffic that comes to us from the battalions each morning and then there's other correspondence. You'll be kept pretty busy."

"Well, Major if you're OK with a typing speed of twenty-six words per minute, I'm your man. I'm sure I can do the job for you." Ben didn't have to think twice about agreeing to become a "rear-echelon MF." He would miss Sergeant Palmer a little, but had formed no really close ties with any of the other survivors in First Platoon. Clean clothes, regular showers and hot Class-A and B rations would be a welcome change. The only downside would be that of leaving a four-point zone. That would probably delay his trip home by a couple of months, but, on the other hand, working at headquarters would give him a much better chance of going home in one piece.

"Good!" said Jones. "Sergeant Hendricks, cut a memo on Stewart and get it over to Personnel. Or rather...Stewart, hang around until the sergeant is finished and then run that memo over and wait for your orders. Then go back to your battalion and pick up your gear. Flash your orders around, see the armorer and trade in your M-1 for a carbine, draw some corporal's stripes from Head and Head Company supply, sew them on and be here tomorrow morning at 0730."

Major Jones rose, grabbed his helmet and his chogie stick, and brushed by Ben as he left the tent. Suddenly he turned, saying, "and Stewart, treat yourself to a shower and some clean duds while you're here."

Ben spent the rest of the day at regimental headquarters waiting for uninspired personnel clerks and supply sergeants to give him what he needed. He also had plenty of time to become more presentable. Before discarding his filthy field jacket, he emptied the pockets and found that he still had the two letters belonging to the dead Chinese soldier. A morbid curiosity had prompted him to keep the letters. Someday he would find somebody to translate them and perhaps they would disclose something about the young man who came so close to being his executioner.

It was dusk when Ben returned to the sector of the secondary MLR that had been held by Able Company that morning. He was greeted by a bunch of unfamiliar faces. He went to the company command post and was confronted by a Master Sergeant Regules.

"You lost, young trooper?"

"I hope not, Sergeant. Could you tell me what happened to Able Company of the Fifth. They were here when I left this morning."

"You must be Stewart. That's your pack and fart sack over there in the corner. We relieved Company A so that they could provide infantry support for a raid by the 64th Tank Battalion on Chink positions near an area called Jackson Heights. Sergeant Palmer dropped your gear off here. Said you would probably be around to pick it up."

Ben unfolded a note that had been wedged in the webbing of his pack. He moved closer to the candlelight to read it.

> *Corporal Stewart,*
> *Congratulations on your promotion. You and I can now hoist a beer together in the NCO Club if we both live to see garrison duty again. I know that you will do well on your new job. You may like it so much that you will decide to re-enlist when your two years are up.*
>
> > *Best of luck,*
> > *Robert Palmer*
> > *SFC   Infantry*

Ben smiled, put the folded note in his shirt pocket and thanked Sergeant Regules for his help. When he reached the supply point, there was no one around. Ben's transportation had disappeared into the night.

He thought about going back and asking Sergeant Regules if he had any ideas about where he might find a ride back to Headquarters and Headquarters Company. Then he shrugged, slung the pack over his shoulders and set out on foot. What the hell, it couldn't be more than a three-hour hike.

A half hour later a south bound 2 1/2-ton truck pulled alongside. The driver leaned out the window. "Hey you, dogface, where are you goin'?"

"Head and Head of the Fifth. You going my way?"

"Yeah, I'm heading to the regimental motor pool right near there. Hop in. Actually, do you think you can drive this mother? Come on and get behind the wheel."

"Well, I don't know. I've never driven one of these things before."

"Nothing to it. It's fluid drive. Just put it in drive and step on the gas."

Ben slid in behind the wheel, slipped the truck into gear and gave it some gas. The vehicle jerked forward and they were on their way. The driver pulled a pint bottle of bourbon out of his field jacket pocket and took a big swig. Then he offered Ben a drink.

"Here, buddy, I really appreciate gettin' a chance to relax," sighed the grateful driver. I've been all the way down to Yongdongpo today, then up to the line with a load of rations and my ass is draggin'. Have a drink."

"No, thanks said Ben. "Maybe some other time when I've had more driving experience. But you're right there's really not much to driving a deuce and a half." Ben kept the speedometer around thirty MPH and took directions from his relaxed companion. When they were about a half mile from the motor pool the driver shifted back behind the wheel and took them to the motor pool.

When Ben reported to work in the morning, Sergeant Hendricks said that Major Jones was over at regimental S-2 tracking the progress of Operation Ranger, the tank-infantry attack. Ben was told to stick around in case he was needed. He decided that he would while the time away by typing a letter home. He wanted to be warmed up in case he was needed to type an after-action report on Operation Ranger or to make entries in the S-3 daily journal.

Then he remembered his pledge to write to Rudy's Raquel in Nogales. He glanced around looking for some paper to slide into the Royal portable typewriter.

"Sergeant Hendricks, where do you keep the typing paper?"

"What are you gonna do with it?"

"I promised my buddy that I would write his girl friend if he got killed, and he did, so I need to get going on a letter."

"That's personal mail, Stewart. You've got to use your own stationery for that. We're mighty short on supplies around here."

Ben shrugged. "War is hell, ain't it, Sarge?" He fished some USO stationery out of his pack and struggled with the letter for most of the morning. He wrote:

Dear Miss Valencia,

By now you have most likely received word that your Rudy was killed in action on June 12. I was beside him when it happened. I am certain that he died instantly and suffered no pain. I am also certain that he was thinking of you and your little girl shortly before his death because the two of you were always on his mind.

He was so excited about being a father and he spoke of you so lovingly that I envied him. He was counting the days until he

*would be going home, marrying and taking care of the two of
you.*

    *Rudy had been my friend since basic training at Fort Ord.
He was wise and brave and a good and loyal buddy. I'm
grateful for having known him.*

    *I would be happy to write more about Rudy's life here in
Korea. If you would like more information, you can reach me at
the APO address on the envelope. I hope to leave for home by
November and can always be reached there by writing to me at
8994 Greenback Lane, Orangevale, CA.*

I share your sorrow,
Cpl. Ben Stewart
Hq & Hq Co, 5th RCT

    That done, Ben began a letter to his folks but had to put that on hold
when Major Jones strode into the tent and boomed, "Stewart, you're going
for an airplane ride."

    "Would that be for Mather Air Force Base near Sacramento, sir?" said
Ben wistfully.

    "Afraid not," responded Jones. "This will just be an easy little hop to
spot some Chink mortar emplacements. Your folks in Company A and the
tankers have run into a lot of mortar fire and we have no way of knowing
where its coming from unless we get an L-19 into the air. Our guys can't
move forward and they're having trouble hooking up to the disabled tanks
and towing them out of there. The S-2 is short handed, his I & R Platoon
is out on a hike, and we really need somebody up there that can handle a
radio, spot those emplacements and read coordinates on a map. You'll be
flying at twenty-five hundred feet to stay out of range of small arms fire.
You'll find the landing strip about a quarter of a mile up the side of that
hill. Better hustle. Report to Lieutenant Viafore. We need to silence those
mortars."

    Ben jogged up the dirt road until he located the landing strip. He was
not impressed by its length. It was no more than a city block long. Two
Piper aircraft were parked beside the strip while a third sat ready to roll at
the end of the runway. Ben found Viafore and a couple of ground crew
members in the tarpaper shack that served as Aviation Company's
headquarters.

    The crew members helped Ben with his parachute and strapped him
into the rear seat. Lieutenant Viafore climbed into the front seat and told
Ben to keep his hands and feet off of everything but the radio. Viafore
kicked over the engine, which sputtered and shook and rattled the tiny
aircraft. When he was satisfied with the sound, he released the brakes and

taxied down the steel mesh runway, seemingly using every inch of it before the plane was airborne.

When they had flown less than three thousand yards north of the MLR, Ben spotted the stalled tank column. Then he easily discerned the Chinese MLR, a wide reddish scar that wound through the green foliage. Months of artillery and napalm bombardments had reduced the area to bare earth. Finally he spotted a group of Chinese working their 60-mm mortars on the northern, or defilade, slope of Hill 391.

He turned the radio to the correct frequency and, with some excitement in his voice, said, "Rotary 3, this is Stewart, over." When Major Jones came on, Ben gave him the six-digit coordinates of the mortar emplacements. Jones repeated the location. In several minutes artillery and heavy mortar fire sent the few Chinese survivors scurrying.

Lieutenant Viafore dipped his wings in salute to the men of Operation Ranger and headed back to the airstrip. When he spotted it, he opened full flaps and put the Piper Cub into a forty-five degree descent, aiming for the north end of the landing strip. Ben closed his eyes and whispered, "So this is what it's like to be safely off the line. God help me."

Viafore stopped the plane a few feet before the end of the runway by standing on the brakes. After being helped out of the plane, Ben doffed his chute, slipped on his field cap and began to depart.

"Where are you going, Stewart?" said the lieutenant. "You're going to be needed here until we hear differently."

"Do you mean permanently, sir? That wasn't the understanding I had," said Ben.

"No, we're probably talking until those tank platoons get back to the MLR. The hills are still full of Chink mortarmen."

Thirty minutes later Lieutenant Viafore and Corporal Stewart were back in the air. Mortar rounds were falling on the tank column from a different position. As they flew north over the tanks and infantry, Ben used some field glasses to scan the gullies and hillsides for the mortar emplacements. He saw nothing but muddy earth and tree stumps.

"I can't see a damn thing down there, Lieutenant."

"Let's get a little closer," said Viafore as he began to descend.

"Hey, aren't we pretty close to small arms range?" asked Ben.

"That's the idea," said the pilot as he continued his slow descent. Soon Ben could see tracers whizzing by the Piper. "Oh Lord, take me back to Able Company," he prayed. By now he could see gun flashes and then could make out the Chinese trenches and gun emplacements. The mortar sites must be close behind. Then he spotted them, almost imperceptible flashes coming from tiny holes in the red earth. He soon had Major Jones on the radio.

"Sir, they're firing from spider holes about thirty yards north of Chink trenches at, let's see...that would make it about coordinates 5-5-6-4-1-1. Guess they're registered in on the road. That's where the rounds are hitting."

"Coordinates 5-5-6-4-1-1," repeated the major. "Keep that bird in the air until we're sure we've got 'em this time."

Lt. Viafore ascended once more to twenty-five hundred feet while Ben kept the target in sight. A short time later, several eight-inch "bunker buster" rounds arrived from Ninth Corps Artillery. Their trajectory was a bit long and too far to the left of the spider holes. Ben raised Major Jones again.

"Rotary 3. I'd guess...drop five zero, right eight zero. Fire for effect."

The next barrage from Ninth Corps and supporting fire from Third Division Artillery was right on the nose. By the time that the Piper Cub was lined up to land on the postage stamp-sized landing strip, the two artillery units had prepared another sizeable chunk of Korean earth for planting and the Chinese mortarmen were out of business.

There were no more calls for help from Operation Ranger but Viafore suggested that Ben stick around while it was still daylight. Surveillance flights could continue until nightfall and Ben might be needed.

The following morning when Ben arrived at the S-3 tent, Sergeant Hendricks greeted him with a smirk. "The major was happy with the piece of work you did yesterday, Stewart."

"Is that so? You suppose he'll put me in for the bronze star with a dingle berry cluster."

"I doubt that. What he wants you to do is to chogie over to the motor pool, get yourself a jeep license, check out a vehicle and be back by 1000. You're the new driver for this section. I've been relieved. Thank you." Ben shrugged and headed for the motor pool.

Getting a license was a rather casual affair. He produced his California driver's license and then was given a road test in a jeep, ¾-ton truck and a deuce-and-a-half. He was given a license for all three vehicles.

Ben tinkered with his new jeep for a while and pulled up at the regimental headquarters shortly after ten. Before he could get from behind the wheel, Major Jones spotted him, hurried over and climbed into the passenger seat.

"Let's go, Stewart. I want to be up at the Triple Nickel before noon."

"Where are they, sir?"

"I'll show you, but first go get your carbine...and helmet, Stewart. Stow that fatigue cap and get your helmet. You're supposed to wear your helmet around here. You could be hit with a fifty dollar fine for running around in your field cap. There's a goddam war going on, Stewart. By the way, where's the windshield for this vehicle?"

"It's at the motor pool, sir. It's better not to have glass around if we should come under fire. I don't want any glass splinters in my face. I left the canopy and the doors there as well so we can bail out of this thing if we run into any incoming."

"So, what do we do if it rains?" Major Jones smiled and winked.

"You pull on your poncho, wrap your towel around your neck and you probably get wet. There's a goddam war going on, sir."

Ben was back at the jeep in a couple of minutes, properly equipped. He nervously ground the gears a little trying to find reverse gear but soon they were on the way to the 555th Field Artillery Battalion. Climbing hills on dirt roads was rather challenging for a beginning jeep driver but they succeeded in finding Headquarters Battery of the Triple Nickel around noon chow time. Major Jones sought out the battalion commander and Ben went in search of Battery A and Jerry Holmes.

When Ben found Jerry, the lanky youngster was just crawling out of the sack. He had been on the midnight to 0600 shift the previous night. Gerry looked Ben over through bleary eyes.

"What is it with the spit-shined boots and clean fatigues? Did your old man get elected to Congress?" cracked Gerry.

"No, I got a new job. Somebody in the Fairy Godmother Department found out that I could type. I'm with Regimental S-3 and my boss is up here for a visit. He's over with your colonel talking about whatever it is that officers talk about."

"Well, I'm glad for you, Stew. Maybe now that you're a big wheel you can tell us what's going on with the war?"

"The latest news," said Ben, "is that President Shit-man Rhee has ruined the peace talks. Apparently he freed fifty thousand Gook POW's who said that they didn't want to go back to the north. That screwed up the talks at Panmunjom."

"Well," said Jerry, "as long as they keep talking, I keep earning four points a month. But I know it's been hell for you guys in the rifle companies. Do you ever hear anything from Rudy Aguilar, by the way."

"Rudy died on OP Harry, Jerry. I guess you didn't hear." Jerry just shook his head.

"Do you have time for lunch, Stew?"

"Thought you'd never ask."

Lunch was more of the shredded pot roast that they had experienced on their first night at Fort Ord. Ben insisted that Jerry had planned it just for him. He had to admit though that the beef wasn't bad and he enjoyed the canned tomatoes and peaches as well.

As they ate, Jerry described his duties with the Triple Nickel. His howitzer crew was currently on the 2400 to 0600 shift. Many of their recent fire missions had been in support of OP Harry although they had served a number of other requests.

"I'm the gunner on that 105 right over there," explained Jerry. "It has a range of 12,500 yards and, if need be, we can drop fifteen to twenty rounds a minute on the Chinks."

"What does a gunner do?" asked Ben.

"Well I get the fire mission from the battery commander over the phone, relay it to my crew and we adjust for direction and range. Then I line up the cross hairs on the scope with the two aiming stakes out yonder. My number one man sets the elevation and then my number two guy loads the shell. Man number two rams the breech block closed and we're ready to boogie when the section chief yells, "fire." When the mission is completed we clean the gun until it's standin' tall." Then after pausing, he added, "I'm really sorry about Aguilar, Ben. I had no idea that you guys were on Harry."

"I'm sorry about him too," said Ben. "He really turned out to be a good friend. During basic training he seemed like some kind of pachuco gangster but he was really a fine and decent guy."

Major Jones broke up the conversation. It was time to head for home. The two young soldiers promised to find each other when the entire regimental combat team went into reserve.

* * *

While Able Company of the Fifth RCT was engaged in Operation Ranger, Peter Company of their Greek allies, back on OP Harry, was experiencing a brief respite. The Greek soldiers and a few men from the 10th Combat Engineer Battalion used the quiet nights of 15-16 June to strengthen the fortifications. The rest of the Hellenic Expeditionary Force was placed on Hill 312 on the MLR in the OP Harry sector to give the battered US battalions a chance to refit and rest.

By this time the stench of putrefying human tissue on the outpost was so bad that many of the men wore wet cloths over their noses. During daylight hours the 10th Engineers were bulldozing pits in the valley south of the OP to finally bury the Chinese dead.

On the afternoon of the 16th, Peter Kallas, a medical corpsman with Company P, entered the CP bunker and reported to Sergeant Thanos, ranking NCO on the outpost, that Corporal Karsatos wasn't getting any better.

"Sergeant, Karsatos is still running a fever. It won't come down with analgesics. Now both eyes are red and starting to get puffy. He doesn't want to leave but don't you think we ought to evacuate him?"

"Let's wait a little. We may have another quiet night and if he's not better in the morning, we'll put his ass on the next half-track back to town. Just keep him in that small bunker by himself. I don't want any more sick men."

"No problem there. He doesn't feel like moving around. I'm worried about the rats though. I've warned Karsatos to try to stay awake and protect himself from them. They've been eating very well out here and they're quite huge. They're probably full of disease."

"Well, keep me informed of his condition and the rat situation, Corporal."

"Will do, Sergeant."

* * *

It started out as if it were going to be another quiet night but shortly after ten o'clock, incoming artillery and mortar fire began kicking up the dirt around the command post and the forward observer bunker. A few minutes after midnight, those on watch reported that a large number, an estimated two battalions of CCF, we moving south from Star Mass toward Harry. Sergeant Thanos got on the phone and requested supporting fire and continuous illumination.

As they watched the enemy approach, one soldier began to sing the Greek national anthem and soon the entire company had joined him. Some of them would never again see their beloved homeland.

Iannis Karsatos couldn't sleep through the racket. He pulled his boots on without buckling them, donned his helmet, grabbed his M-1 and cartridge belt and staggered out of the bunker. He felt weak and terribly tired.

"What's all the racket?"

"Chinamen are attacking up the right slope. Go back to bed, Karsatos," growled Sergeant Thamos. "We can handle it."

"I can do it, Sergeant. I can't sleep anyway. You guys are making too much noise."

Iannis realized just how weak he was when he tried to ram a clip into his rifle. Ordinarily the operation required a quick push with his thumb. Now he was forced to use the whole heel of his hand.

The Chinese soldiers were periodically illuminated by the flares and searchlight beams. Iannis was very woozy. He was experiencing blurred vision, but he could tell from the tracers that his shots were properly overlapping those of the men beside him. After twenty minutes of mayhem, the whistles and bugles sounded and the enemy soldiers pulled back. After a few minutes of quiet, a couple of the Greek defenders became too curious and were downed by small arms fire somewhere in the darkness.

"You goddam people keep your heads down and remain alert. They're out there no more than a hundred and fifty meters or so...Karsatos, how are you feeling?"

"I feel like *scatá*, Sergeant. I feel like puking and have a headache. But I can still do my part."

"You're leaving here in the morning. You belong in hospital."

"Yes, Sergeant. If you can promise me there will be a tomorrow morning, then I'll promise you that I'll go to hospital."

Sergeant Thanos grunted with annoyance and turned to return to the CP. He didn't have time for such nonsense. There were Chinese battalions out there and lots of work to do.

At 0230 the CCF battalions attacked again. By this time, an armored platoon from Tank Company of the 15th Infantry and a platoon of infantry from N Company, Hellenic Expeditionary Force, had reinforced OP Harry on the right, in the valley. They would serve to help protect the outpost's more vulnerable flank.

Sergeant Thanos yelled as he came running back down the trench. "We're being hit from the north and northwest and they're close enough to toss grenades. Second Platoon come with me. First Platoon stay here and lay down oblique fire if you see a good target. And watch straight ahead and to the rear while you're at it."

Lieutenant Pappas scooted along the trench line to check on each position and offer encouragement, "This is a critical time, men. If we can repel them once more they won't have time to organize another attack under cover of darkness. Kill the bastards...Come on, daylight."

Corpsman Kallas found Iannis slumped down against the sides of his fighting hole. A quick check revealed that he wasn't wounded although he seemed to be going into shock. Kallas dragged him into a nearby bunker and checked his breathing and pulse. He found the pulse to be less than sixty beats per minute but didn't know what to make of it. Kallas shrugged and said, "Keep your butt in here, Iannis, it sounds like I'm needed at the north end. If you see a rat, bayonet the bastard." Iannis didn't respond.

By 0313 the Chinese were in the trenches on the north nose of the outpost and engaged in hand-to-hand fighting with the Greek defenders. The Chinese artillery barrage had actually increased as their soldiers reached OP Harry. The Greek Battalion commander dispatched two platoons from Company N to reinforce the outpost. At 0400 the Chinese began to withdraw and firing became sporadic.

A half-track arrived with the first daylight and Corporal Karsatos was evacuated with the wounded. When he arrived at a 15th Infantry clearing station, the doctor took one look at Iannis' flushed face, bloodshot eyes and noted some apparent hemorrhaging in his soft palate. "Put this young man on the next available chopper," he ordered. "He needs to get to the 8228th MASH. It looks a hell of a lot like hemorrhagic fever to me and we're getting a late start. Don't give him any more fluids." In twenty minutes Iannis was tagged, slipped into an insulated casualty bag, placed in the chopper basket, and was on his way to Songu-ri, northeast of Seoul.

The night of June 17-18 turned out to be the CCF's last hurrah in regard to Outpost Harry. Estimated Chinese casualties, on that night, were one hundred and twenty killed in action and four hundred and eighty wounded. The Greek defenders suffered four KIA and twenty-five WIA.

Mid-afternoon on 18 June, the remainder of N Company marched out to Harry and relieved the men of Company P. They, in turn, were relieved by Company O on 21 June. During a quiet period on 24 June, the men of Company O completed the burial of fifty dead Chinese that had been decomposing since the action of the 18th. Companies O and N alternated responsibility for OP Harry for the remainder of the month, a period of inactivity on the part of the enemy.

The radio code name for the Greek Battalion was "Spartan." Like those magnificent Spartans of old, they had fought skillfully and courageously and were a credit to their homeland. From September 1950 until December 1955, ten thousand one hundred and eighty-four Greek soldiers served in Korea. During that period, they suffered casualties amounting to one hundred eighty-four killed, five hundred forty-three wounded and two captured. They were respected by friend and foe for their fighting prowess in Korea and received many citations for their actions.

JULY 1953

THE 8228TH Mobile Army Surgical Hospital in Songu-ri was approximately fifty miles southwest of the Third Division's sector of responsibility very close to Seoul and the port of Inchon. Following an unexpected epidemic of hemorrhagic fever in the late spring of 1951, this particular MASH unit was designated as the hospital for those U.N. troops afflicted by the deadly viral disease. The hospital did not become fully operational until April 1952.

During the early months of the epidemic, the mortality rate was 20%. After a training program for unit surgeons and medical corpsmen was instituted at the 8228th MASH, familiarizing them with symptoms and primary care, the mortality rate was cut to 5% of those who became ill. Those infected with the disease were given the same eligibility for helicopter evacuation as seriously wounded surgical patients.

The cause and carrier of Korean hemorrhagic fever were unknown at the time. It was apparent that more soldiers were stricken during the hot, dusty days of late spring and early fall and that cases of the disease were rarely encountered before the United Nations established a static battle line on the 38th Parallel. Although front-line medics were susceptible to the disease, it didn't appear to be transmittable to the staff at behind-the-lines facilities like MASH units.

* * *

Iannis Karsatos was semi-conscious when he arrived at the 8228th MASH. He awoke to the blur of a lovely young female face, framed by dark hair, looking down at him and saying, *"ti farmaka alerghika?"*

"I speak some English," whispered Iannis, "and I know I was allergic only to sulfa drugs. Made me delerious when I was little kid."

"Thank God, Corporal, you speak English," she said. "The little bit of Greek that I learned from my *papu* doesn't amount to much."

"Where am I? What happened to me? Who are you, pretty lady?" Iannis couldn't remember much more than the hike out to Outpost Harry with his company. He remembered feeling ill and not being of much help to his comrades.

"I'm Lieutenant Beth Sklivas. I'm a nurse in the U.S. Army. You're in the hospital with a viral infection. Captain McConnell will tell you more about it when he makes his rounds. Just try to rest and, if you need to pee, ask us for a urinal. We need to keep track of your output."

"I'm very thirsty," said Iannis.

"First I need to take your temp, then you can have a few ounces of juice and maybe some more later whenever you urinate. It's best that you not have too much fluid."

"But are not fluids good for the flu?"

"You probably don't have the flu, Corporal Karsatos. Captain McConnell will explain all that to you."

Lieutenant Sklivas made a few more entries in Iannis' file. She entered his temperature of 102.6. His systolic and diastolic blood pressures were low and his pulse rate was about twenty beats below normal. He had a very flushed face and eyelids and was experiencing shaking chills but he wasn't going to give up until he had an answer.

"What is the trouble with me? Is it serious?"

Beth put down Iannis's chart and responded, "Most men sent here have been diagnosed with hemorrhagic fever. The disease gets its name from the tiny hemorrhages in your eyes and throat, around your belt line and see, there, where you've been poked with needles. The little capillaries have burst. You'll feel lousy for about a week and then you should start to get better. The doctor will tell you all about that. How's your head?"

"It aches all the time. You have aspirin?"

"Here, we've got something better than that." She raised his head and helped him swallow the meperidine sulphate tablet. "It will help you get a little nap, too."

It was evening before Captain McConnell came by with Beth Sklivas to check on Karsatos. They noticed that he had ignored his beef broth and jello.

"Not hungry, Corporal?" asked the doctor. "You've barely touched your tasty rations."

"I sorry, Doctor. Everything I eat makes me feel like to vomit."

The doctor nodded as he fielded the familiar complaint. "I'm glad that you can speak English, Karsatos. My Greek is limited to a knowledge of the alphabet...Now, tell me. Before you came here to the hospital did you eat anything or drink anything that was prepared by the locals?"

"Locals?"

"Did you accept or buy any food or drink from the Korean people?"

"No, sir. We were on outpost. Had C-rations and water from petrol cans. Before that just ate food from company kitchen; Greek bread, rice, vegetables, lamb stew and things. Am I poisoned by food?"

"No, Corporal, at least we don't think so. You seem to have hemorrhagic fever and we're not really sure what causes it. Furthermore, we don't know of a medicine that will cure the disease. We can only relieve the symptoms and it's up to your body to do the work."

"Can I die from this fever?"

Captain McConnell hesitated a little before responding, "It can happen but death is rare now. We've learned a lot about treating your illness in the past year. How's his urine, Beth?"

"There were only 750cc today."

"Albumin?"

"Yes, sir. It's present."

"Albumin is bad?" asked Iannis.

"It means that your kidneys are fighting the illness, Corporal," explained McConnell. "That's why we have to carefully watch your fluid intake and measure your urine. We don't want kidney failure. Even when you're well enough to get up and use the latrine, you must measure your urine. We base the fluids that we give you on the previous day's output."

Turning back to the nurse, Captain McConnell said, "Let's get 1000 cc of 5% dextrose going here. Karsatos, I'm afraid that you are going to get stuck with needles a lot while you're here. We have to test your blood everyday. That's one of the ways that we will know when you are getting well. Now let me have a look at you."

McConnell pulled back Iannis' top sheet and poked and prodded. The corporal's spleen and liver seemed to be of normal size; no sign of enlargement. However his lymph nodes were swollen and his blood pressure and pulse were still on the low side. The doctor redraped the sheet over the young soldier, patted him on the shoulder and wished him a good night.

When Beth Sklivas returned to start the IV, she asked, "Do you have family in Greece?"

"My father is living but my mother and my two sisters were taken away by the communists and murdered. I was away at university when it happened."

"Oh, God, I'm awfully sorry." When she regained her composure, she asked, "Would you like to write to your papakas? If you feel up to it, that is. I can't help you unless he can read Greek words in English letters. My papu didn't teach me to write."

"No. Maybe I feel like writing letter in morning. Right now, too weak."

"Sure. You get some sleep. Good night."

"Oh, Nurse Beth. What about my unit? Does Lieutenant Pappas know where I am?"

"Captain McConnell will keep the Third Division medics posted about your condition. They will get word to your commander."

"Thank you. Good night, Lieutenant Sklivas."

"Good night, Iannis Karsatos."

Despite being completely exhausted, Iannis slept very little that night. Pains in his calves and thighs in conjunction with his headache made him very uncomfortable. He was given another dose of meperidine.

Around midnight he awoke and splattered his sheets with vomit before he could cry for help. A night nurse and an orderly cleaned him up and he was given a shot of atropine to settle his nausea. The retching caused more hemorrhaging in his eyes. By morning the last dose of meperidine had worn off and his headache had returned.

On his fifth day in the hospital, Iannis' headache disappeared and he began to sleep for several hours at a time. He was not so flushed. But, for the following week, he continued to uncomplainingly struggle with back and leg pains accompanied by fever and shakes. His temperature ranged between 101 and 103.

Beth Sklivas checked on him frequently, helped him walk to the latrine, urinal in hand, measured his urine, stuck needles in him and changed his IV's. Iannis would have been delighted to have met her under other circumstances.

As his strength increased, Iannis was more willing to talk to Beth about his life during the Italian and German occupation and the ensuing civil war. She learned that he had grown up in the town of Sparta on the Peloponnesus, a large peninsula in the southwest of Greece. Her own grandparents had migrated to San Francisco from the same area, countryside of small valleys and rugged mountains and coastline.

"Do you want to talk about your mother and sisters, Ianni? What happened? I don't know much about the Greek Civil War."

"I don't mind. I can talk about them. I think about them all the time. I do hope to find their remains someday and bring them back to my village. I was told that their bodies were found in the mountains by some shepherds who buried them."

Iannis was struggling to sit up in bed so Beth helped him. His sense of smell was returning and he enjoyed her Camay soap scent as she moved closer to him.

"My father owned a *kapheneion* on the outskirts of Sparta," he continued. "Do you know what that is?"

"Must be like a coffee shop in our country."

"Yes, I imagine so. He sold mainly wine, beer and light food. He worked very hard, six days a week, to support our family. His patrons were largely villagers and travelers but he was courteous to the Italians and then to the Germans during the war. He was a very - how you say - pragmatic man. He would take honest money from anybody. During and following the war, he was careful not to be seen as sympathetic to the Nazis nor the partisans nor later as sympathetic to the communists or the royalists."

"Who are the royalists?"

"In 1946 elections were held in my country and the people voted to restore the monarchy. King George II returned to the throne. The ELAS, the Popular Liberation Army, many of whom had fought with the partisans during the world war, didn't accept the elections. They revolted. Some of the young men in our village left to join the ELAS. They falsely accused my father of having provided information to the security battalions during the war. The security battalions were local men who had been armed by the Germans and who collaborated with them.

Iannis continued, "In September of 1946, I left home and enrolled at the university in Athens. One week in December, when my father came to the city on a shopping trip, the ELAS, *andartes* we called them, roamed from town to town on the Peloponessus taking hostages. My mother and sisters were at home with no man to defend them. They were seized and our home and the kapheneion were burned to the ground. The Communists took them into the mountains, in the direction of Thebes, where four thousand innocents died. I don't know whether my family members were shot or froze to death and you can imagine how difficult it will be to find their remains."

The two sat in silence for awhile. It was evident that Iannis had had his say. Beth tucked him in for the night.

"What about your father? Did he return to Sparta?"

"There was nothing for him there. Father lives in Athens with my uncle and works as a bartender. There was nothing there for me either. I immediately enlisted in the army and was sent to a training camp in Tripolis in the central highlands. We were trained by American non-coms and assigned to the Ninth Hellenic Division. It took us three years to put down the rebellion. I'm getting a little tired just thinking about it. Goodnight, Lieutenant Beth."

"Good night, Corporal Karsatos."

On the fifteenth morning of his hospitalization, the young Greek awoke and felt a strange gnawing feeling in his stomach. He felt like he could handle any American food the staff could throw at him, the greasier the better. Captain McConnell, on early morning rounds, popped a thermometer in Yanni's mouth and beamed as he pulled it out and checked. The mercury was riding at 98.8 degrees.

You're doing great, Corporal Karsatos. Are you ready for some real chow?" Iannis smiled and nodded gratefully.

The smile disappeared, a few minutes later, when an orderly brought him a small bowl of cream of wheat and a piece of dry toast. He downed it quickly and then sipped his tea. He finally felt like communicating with his father. He would have given anything to hear the old man's voice on a phone. When the breakfast mess was clear, he sat on the edge of his bed and began to write.

> *Dear Papakas,*
>
> *This is just a brief note to inform you that I have been in hospital but will soon be leaving. Do not be alarmed. I was not wounded. I contracted a virus and felt terrible for a few days but am feeling much better now thanks to the ministrations of a lovely Greek-American girl named Lieutenant Beth Sklivas. She and a Dr. McConnell have cared for me in a hospital ward housed in a new kind of dustproof tent called a Jamesway, I believe. It is cooler than a canvas tent in the summer and warmer in the winter. So now you know that the United States government feels that your son is very important to the war effort and has given him nothing but the best of care.*
>
> *How are you and Uncle George getting along? I am surprised that the two of you have put up with each other for more than three years. Give him my best regards.*
>
> *Our job here in Korea will soon be accomplished and I will be coming home. There is no telling when that will happen. I'm so anxious to get completely well and return to the Battalion. Write to me there since I know I will be checking out of hospital soon.*
>
> > *Your loving son, Ianni*

As Iannis was addressing the envelope, he was quietly approached by a couple of visitors. He was pleased to see Corporal Peter Kallas, his company medic. Peter was accompanied by a tall, black American soldier that Iannis had never met.

"Well, Karsatos, you're looking better than when I last saw you," exclaimed the medic. "American food and pretty nurses have been good for you."

"Thank you for coming, Peti, but to tell you the truth I haven't been able to enjoy the food and nurses. I've been sicker than hell."

"I realize that now," admitted the medic. "We have been sent here to the hospital today for a class on hemorrhagic fever. I wish I had had this class a month ago. I would have kicked your butt off that hill and into the hospital much sooner. I regret that I was so ignorant, Iannis."

Then Peter began to speak in English. "Excuse, Grady. Iannis, this is Grady Williams. Grady is a medic with the Fifth RCT. Grady is also a friend of Ben, the young soldier from California."

Karsatos extended his hand. "Yes, how is Ben? Last time I see him he, as you say it, was down in the dumps."

"Ben is much better," responded Jim. "He landed a gentleman's job at regimental headquarters. Three hot meals a day, a soft bed and daily showers. He even smells a lot better than he used to."

"Please, when you see him, tell him that I am a lot better, too. I am glad for Ben. He is a nice young fellow. Ben doesn't belong in Korea. He is schoolboy, not soldier. He belongs in school gaining wisdom and chasing girls. I am glad that he has a safe job."

"I'm sure he would agree with you, Corporal," said Grady. "He'll be glad to know that you have recommended that he go home. I'll relay your greetings."

"We have to get back to our meeting, Ianni," said Corporal Kallas. "Sto kalo. We look forward to your return."

"Sto kalo, my friend."

Iannis was happy that the visit had been short. He enjoyed the break in routine but he felt like he had done a days work.

The young corporal improved each day. He was quite restless and didn't need much encouragement to ambulate. Free of IV tubes, he spent a lot of his time wandering the ward and getting acquainted with the four other patients. All had been involved in the Chorwan Valley fighting, three were riflemen and one was a medic. Beth Sklivas helped him get outside for a little morning sun before the afternoon breezes arrived to kick up the red dust.

On Monday evening, 27 July 1953, Iannis Karsatos was fast asleep when the guns went silent in Korea. Nurse Sklivas gave him the good news the following morning. He had been aware of the armistice negotiations but was very skeptical. He couldn't understand cutting a deal with communists, the masters of treachery. You made peace with communists by completely eradicating them. He told Beth that he wanted to be out of the hospital in plenty of time for the next communist offensive.

On a mid-August evening, Captain McConnell dropped by Iannis' bed during his rounds and said, "We're about to kick you out of here, Karsatos. What do you think about that?"

"I'm glad, Doctor. I'm happy to get back to my battalion and help with the training. I was told that a second battalion will arrive soon from Greece. I am very much needed."

"You're not going back to your battalion, soldier. If your urine tests continue as they have been, you'll be out of here by Monday afternoon...on your way to Kimpo where you'll catch a hop to Osaka and then board the next C-47 heading for Greece."

"But, sir. I'm strong again. You know that. Can't you tell my battalion commander that I am fit for duty?"

"Sorry, Corporal. I can't tell him that you are strong enough to hump your way up a sixty percent hill with pack and rifle and you know that. I did send word that you are probably strong enough to survive a trip home on a medevac. Your buddies will be home soon and I would imagine that your father needs you."

After Captain McConnell left, Ianni began to realize how very badly he wanted to see his father and his homeland. Besides, the Royal Hellenic Expeditionary Force was being brought up to regimental strength. With that doubling of firepower, they'd be able to keep the communist bastards on their side of the line until he was able to return.

* * *

During early morning darkness on 19 June, Ben and Sergeant Hendricks loaded the field furniture, typewriters and footlockers filled with files and supplies into a ¾-ton truck. They worked quickly because headquarters personnel from the 23rd Infantry Regiment, Second Infantry Division, had already arrived and were eager for the Fifth RCT to vacate.

Ben had picked up the mid-sized truck at the motor pool the previous evening. Once loaded, they pulled into line in the convoy. Sergeant Hendricks put a couple of cans of ham and limas on the engine block, nestling them among the spark plug wires. "These C's will be pipin' hot by dinner time."

"That long, huh, Sarge?" observed Ben. "So what's the plan for lunch?"

"On my side of town, we called it "dinner," drawled Hendricks. "Guess the army has the best idea, just callin' it noon chow. That we can all speak the same language."

"Roger that," said Ben, putting an end to his most stimulating conversation yet with his section chief.

As he turned on the engine, it began to rain. The summer rainy season was beginning. As the column began to move, the wheels of the vehicles kicked up an unlikely combination of red mud and dust.

The latest "latrinogram" was that the rifle battalions were going back up to the northern rim of the Punchbowl. In late afternoon they arrived at Chipo-ri, where the Fifth Infantry Regiment would spend the next ten days in reserve. Ben went looking for Luis and Jerry but discovered that the engineers and the 555th Field Artillery had remained with the Third Division. Heavy Mortar Company had also remained behind to support the Second Infantry Division.

The next few days of inactivity at Chipo-ri were made miserable by torrential rains. The downpour threatened general flooding and, in spots, necessitated wading to get from one part of camp to another.

There was some respite from the rain on 24 June. Sergeant Hendricks informed Ben that it was time for him to go down to the motor pool and pull maintenance on the jeep. That was the driver's responsibility but Ben wasn't wild about the idea of a muddy crawl under the vehicle with a grease gun. Major Jones interceded with the commanding officer of Service Company on Ben's behalf. He had too much work for Corporal Stewart to do in S-3. Captain Stillman could assign one of his grease monkeys to lube the jeep and the 3/4 ton truck.

On 1 July they moved to Inje, in the Soyang Gang Valley, just a few miles south of the Punchbowl. The short move over muddy roads began at 0255 in the morning and wasn't completed until 1630 that afternoon.

For the next two weeks the training program stressed platoon and company offensive tactics. This focus on the attack was a bit disconcerting to Ben. He hadn't been off the line long enough to see things through dispassionate rear-echelon eyes. Surely there were no plans to attempt to gain more ground before the armistice.

Sergeant Hendricks confirmed that the word going around was that the brass at army and corps level were of the opinion that the Allied bargaining position would be improved if the U.N. troops were to leave their defensive positions and grab some more real estate.

"That's crap, Sarge," said Ben. "Captain Anderson kept us up on what was happening at Panmunjom. The armistice line has been set for months as the line of current contact. Our guys are on the armistice line or, at the most, would pull back a couple of kilometers. We'd just have to give back any new ground and the lives lost in taking it would have been wasted."

"Well it appears that Ol' Joe Chink hasn't heard about that or he'd stay home of an evening," argued Hendricks. "It ain't gonna be over 'til it's over."

27 JULY 1953

DURING THE NIGHT and on the morning of 14 July, an estimated two divisions of Chinese Communist Forces crushed the ROK Capitol Division. A two battalion force headed straight for the 555th Field Artillery, overrunning their position. The battle for the Kumsong Bulge had been joined.

By 0230, enemy artillery and small arms fire was so intense that Charlie Battery could no longer fire its guns and had to engage the enemy with small arms. By 0410, Baker Battery was neutralized by artillery and so it had to fight as infantry. At that point the battalion commander issued the order to close station and move back. As Battery A was leaving, its perimeter of defense was broken and fire fights broke out. Battery A saved five of its artillery pieces. All other howitzers belonging to the battalion were lost.

Upon arriving at a new position, about two miles to the rear of the original line, all extra weapons and ammunition were distributed to all available troops and a perimenter defense was established. The five 105-mm howitzers that had been saved were laid and fire was directed on the positions previously vacated in order to destroy materials left behind. By this time the entire Third U.S. Infantry Division had arrived and had filled the gap.

On the morning of the same day, the Air Force bombed the vacated areas to add further destruction. The afternoon newspapers credited the South Korean bug-outs, rather than the Third Infantry Division, with stopping a big Chinese drive on the east central front.

On Monday, 27 July 1953, Lieutenant General William K. Harrison, of the U.N. Command and Nam Il, of North Korea, entered the wooden building at Panmunjom. At 1001 they signed the first of eighteen documents prepared by each side. It took them twelve minutes to sign them all. Then each man got up and left the building, without speaking. The cease fire would take effect twelve hours later.

For those twelve hours, the Chinese delivered a massive artillery barrage, especially between eight and ten in the evening. They apparently *wanted to dispose of their ordnance and all of their propaganda leaflets so they wouldn't have to carry them home. Twenty-seven enemy gun positions were plotted by the Counter-fire Platoon of the Fifth RCT and were subsequently destroyed by the 158th Field Artillery Battalion of the 45th Infantry Division.*

At 2040 hours a heavy mortar or artillery shell made a direct hit on a bunker in the sector of the line controlled by Third Battalion, Fifth RCT. The bunker promptly collapsed pinning six men inside the fallen debris. One of the wounded, SFC Harold Cross of K Company, died at 0200 hours on 28 July. He was the last American to die in the Korean War.

* * *

Corporal Stewart and Sergeant Hendricks were on duty in the S-3 tent, at 2200 hours on 27 July, when radio messages began pouring in from the battalions describing the cessation of hostilities. Easy Company reported that Chinese troops on the ridge opposite its position walked out in front of their of their fortifications and began singing. Then the adventurous platoon of enemy soldiers crossed the valley and laid gifts of Chinese candy in front of Easy Company's barbed wire apron..

"Well," said Hendricks. "That's all she wrote."

"That's it?" replied Ben angrily. "I can't believe it. We came here and blew the crap out of this country. The people are poorer than ever. Their president is a treacherous son of a bitch. Rudy Aguilar and a lot of other guys will never grow old and North Korea is right back where they were three years ago. Back in business. That's all there is?"

"It matters not, Stewart. You're going home."

"Not as fast as I want. I wonder what this is going to do to our point totals?"

"The scuttlebutt is that we'll get three points a month for the next three, even though we won't be shuttling back and forth to the MLR," said Hendricks. "But then I never know whether to believe that stuff."

When morning came, the Fifth RCT withdrew to Pol-Mol where it spent the next two weeks in equipment maintenance and training. The days were devoted to physical training, dismounted drill, troop information and education, and inspections.

Luis Meyer had one more unnerving experience before his tour of duty was up. At 2300 hours on 1 August, he was assigned to a night time mine clearing detail which was given the task to clear a path to some men reportedly injured in a minefield. The detail moved through 175 yards of the known minefield and recovered two men; one dead and one injured.

A week later, Luis and his 72nd Combat Engineers headed west again to prepare for the relocation of the Fifth RCT to Chipo-ri. The engineers were ordered to establish a semi-permanent campsite. They bulldozed and ditched twenty-one hundred yards of road and cleared a six thousand square yard parade ground. That done they were assigned to logging operations in order to clear an area for a rifle range.

On 10 August, the rest of the Fifth RCT joined them. Four days later, Jerry and the 555th FAB and the Heavy Mortar Company arrived. The whole family was back together again.

During July and August, seven hundred and forty-two new enlisted men and two hundred and four hospital returnees swelled the ranks of the regimental combat team. Given so many green and rusty troops, the regimental commander, Colonel Lester, decreed that all units would put into effect the prescribed twenty-six week training program. However, the weather was rather uncooperative. There were fourteen days of rain in July and a heat wave in August.

Ben was kept very busy dividing his time between S-3, the source of the training plans, and the rifle range where everyone was required to re-qualify with their individual weapon. There was physical training each morning before breakfast and classes throughout the day on map reading, mines, booby traps, crew-served weapons, Korean history and culture, and other matters related to the combat training of the individual soldier.

On the first of September, the badly hung-over trio of Luis, Jerry and Ben walked over to the motor pool where Ben said farewell to his comrades. Luis and Jerry were being transferred to the Sixth Army Training Command at Fort Ord. That was perfect for Luis, who could live at home and commute to work but Jerry had been hoping for an assignment in the northwest. Because of his June assignment to Headquarters and Headquarters Company, Ben would need at least another two months to earn his thirty-six rotation points.

Major Jones distributed a memo to all rifle and provisional companies announcing that his staff would be conducting a twenty-hour discussion leader's course. Each unit was required to send someone to the classes. Lieutenant Ryan, the Troop Information and Education Officer asked Jones to lend him Corporal Stewart for the duration of the program so that he would have some assistance with the teaching of the course. Ryan greeted the students and bluffed his way through one of the twenty hours, leaving Ben with the other nineteen.

In addition to the discussion leader's class, Ben went to Personnel and helped with the search for prospective teachers for on-duty classes in basic English and mathematics. Then he got involved in the administration of achievement tests and General Educational Development Tests to more than four hundred soldiers. Ben welcomed the heavy workload. The days flew by.

During September, the Army began preparations for cold weather. Cold weather clothing had been distributed by month's end. Materials began arriving for the first of ninety Quonset huts that had been set aside for the Fifth RCT. Ben and the other members of Headquarters Platoon hoped that there would be a Quonset for a platoon barracks but that was not to be the case. A dump truck dropped off a load of one-inch lumber so that they could begin the winterization of their sleeping tents.

By late October the rain and miserable weather had returned. The first snow of the season arrived on 12 November. It fell fairly light on the valley floor but the surrounding mountains wore a beautiful white blanket.

Ben's ticket for home arrived on the fifteenth. He received orders to report to the port of embarkation at Inchon on 2 December, precisely a year after his arrival in Korea. He was being transferred to the Second Division Replacement Depot at Ft. Lewis, Washington.

During the next two weeks he took time from the office to undergo a physical exam and to turn in his carbine and field equipment to the company armorer and the supply sergeant. November 30 was a very welcome payday. Ben had done a better job of saving money during his months with a rifle company. His assignment to headquarters had meant more haircuts and sundry expenses and accessibility to the post exchange.

DECEMBER 1953

ON 1 DECEMBER, Ben climbed into an empty truck headed for the supply depot at Ch'onch'on. From there he took the train to the harbor at Inchon. There were hundreds of troops milling around, rather anxious that they might miss an announcement and miss the next ship to Japan. Those who had come straight from line outfits were relieved of their weapons.

The men were directed to a large building. They entered a large room with benches along the side where they stripped completely and turned in their clothing and the contents of their duffle bags to a group of Korean workers who were behind a counter sorting clothing. From there they were herded into the shower. After bathing, they received half of a regular issue of "state-side" clothing; one wool uniform, one pair of combat boots, one set of herring-bone twill fatigues, one field jacket, one overcoat, etc. Ben's new clothing was brand-new and fit surprisingly well.

The following morning they boarded an LST for the three-day cruise to Yokohama. It was wet and miserable when they finally got to Camp Drake. Ben spent most of the next two days in the barracks. He browsed the PX and gathered up the decorations to which he was entitled: the Korean Service Medal, the National Defense Service Medal, the Good Conduct Medal, and the Presidential Unit Citation for his participation at Outpost Harry. He also bought a smart overseas cap with blue infantry braid and a sewing kit.

He tried reading but couldn't concentrate, so he walked a lot. He conversed briefly with other rotatees, but steered clear of the many poker games in progress. After dinner he read until he became drowsy and then climbed between the clean white sheets and was unaware of anything until awakened by piped-in music the next morning.

At morning formation, on December 8, Ben learned that his group would board a bus that afternoon bound for Tachikawa Air Base. He would not be taking the slow boat home. He would be flown to Ft. Lewis by the Military Air Transport Service. He had told his parents, in his last letter, that he would not be home in time for Christmas. Apparently Santa

Claus had other ideas. Following formation he went to the phone center and sent them a telegram.

As he settled into his seat on the MATS airliner, Ben finally felt like he was really going home. An end had finally come to his visit to a land of dirt, shit, terror, loss, mangled bodies, sweltering heat, freezing cold and long periods of loneliness and boredom. He was really going home!

They landed at McChord Air Force Base, south of Seattle, early on a Saturday morning, after flying from Japan to Okinawa and to Hawaii before coming on to the Seattle area. The tired but excited returnees deplaned and boarded a bus to nearby Ft. Lawton.

The rain fell just as it had been falling during their departure from Japan, but Ft. Lawton was no Camp Drake. Its World War I vintage barracks were heated by pot-bellied oil stoves rather than central heat. The plumbing was corroded and noisy. However, if all went well, Ben would see very little of the run-down port of embarkation.

He went to the clothing warehouse and received the other half of his uniform allocation. After that he was interviewed by finance clerks to review his pay status. Unfortunately, there was no evidence that he had been underpaid. It would have been nice to have a little extra for his trip home.

At the transportation office, Ben presented his orders to the clerk.

"I see you have a thirty-day delay enroute in Sacramento before you report to Ft. Lewis. How do you want to travel to Sacramento?" asked the harried PFC.

"Fly, I guess. Wouldn't that be the fastest way to get there?"

"There are several MATS flights from McChord to Travis Air Force Base, but not until Thursday," said the clerk. "Then you'd have to get from there to home."

"How about the train?" asked Ben.

The clerk dug through the papers on his desk and came up with the Southern Pacific schedule. "The Shasta Daylight heads south tomorrow at 1100 hours. You'd be in Davis, California by 0900 Monday morning."

"Let's do that then.... You know the last time I rode the Daylight, I was three years old and I wet the berth. I can still see the disappointment on my grandmother's face."

"Well, try and control yourself this trip," advised the bored clerk as he filled out Ben's travel request. "Don't drink anything after dinner."

Having taken care of that detail, Ben phoned home collect. Bill Stewart excitedly accepted the charges. Ben struggled to control his composure as he went over the train schedule with his father. His business completed, he said, "Just tell Mom that I can't talk very well right now. I'll see you Monday morning."

"OK. One more thing, Ben... Ben?"

"Yes, Dad?"

"Call your Uncle Joe and Aunt Ada while you are in Seattle. It would mean a lot to them."

"Roger that, Dad. I love you. See you Monday."

Uncle Joe and Aunt Ada were at home in Seattle's University District when Ben phoned. They drove to Ft. Lawton in their blue DeSoto and took him home for a late lunch and an afternoon visit. During lunch, Ben told a funny story that he had heard from a young black soldier that bunked with the S-3 section at Chipo-ri. Aunt Ada, a refined lady from Virginia, gasped, "Ben, you slept in the same tent as negrahs!"

Ben just chuckled. He was at a loss for words. His Aunt Ada was from another planet.

Uncle Joe was quiet for the longest time and then said, "Ben, maybe you can help me understand what happened over there. It seemed like every time I picked up the paper, our army was either running away or getting the stuffing beat out of it. What happened to young American boys, in the space of five years, that made it impossible for them to win a war? Why, when we have the atom bomb, did we get pushed around by a mob of hooligans with obsolete weapons?"

Ben bristled a bit, but his uncle sounded more curious than disdainful, so he responded, "Before I went to Korea I had the same impression. I guess the *San Francisco Chronicle* was no different than the *Seattle Post Intelligencer*. The press didn't help us understand the meaning of limited war. It focused on the negative aspects of the conflict and ignored our successful offensive actions. You know, Uncle Joe, I never did see a news correspondent up on the line. I understand that they stayed in hotels in Seoul and picked what they wanted out of communiqués and briefings from army information folks."

"Then too, you need to know that the Chinese soldier is not an untrained idiot. He didn't drop into Korea, earn his thirty-six points and go home. He was there until we killed him or until he died attacking through his own artillery barrage. He's an expert with his old Russian, Japanese and American made weapons, particularly with mortars. He climbs like a mountain goat. He's well-suited physically for Korea. He can hump those steep slopes with his kind of weird sideways walk without stopping and can do it much more quietly than we can. No, sir. Old Joe Chink isn't rabble. He knows his trade."

Uncle Joe didn't look like he was completely convinced but he did make it clear to Ben that he and the rest of the family were relieved to have him home. That said, he rose and suggested that they head on back to Ft. Lawton so that Ben would be well rested for his trip home.

The rain had stopped when they got back to the post. As Ben walked down the hill toward his barracks, the mist cleared and he could see

Seattle's beautiful harbor. He suspected that he was probably going to enjoy spending a few months in the Northwest.

* * *

The train pulled into Davis at the stroke of nine on Monday morning. Ben shot out of his seat and stepped down to the platform. He went to the baggage office and retrieved his barracks bag. The bag weighed heavily on his shoulder as he paced in front of the station. He began to wonder if he had been forgotten.

Finally, around 9:30, he saw Bill Stewart's '46 Chevy pull into the parking lot. His dad still had a problem with punctuality. Grabbing his bag with one hand and holding his cap down with the other, he raced toward the car. By the time he reached his parents, his eyes had welled up with tears. He hugged and kissed them both, threw his bag in the trunk, and joined them for the trip home. He was feeling both relieved and nervous at the same time. As they passed each familiar landmark, he became more and more anxious to get to the old Victorian house on Greenback Lane.

It was raining when they pulled into the garage behind the house. Ben enjoyed the feel of the drops splashing on his face. He was looking forward to getting reacquainted with a benevolent rain. He was too used to a rain that turns roads and the floors of bunkers into muck and nourishes mildew on sandbags.

When he entered the parlor, he dropped his bag and vaulted up the three flights of stairs to his tower bedroom. Nothing had changed. The small marble fireplace was flanked by his record cabinet and bookshelves. He clicked on his bedside radio and found that it remained tuned to KPO, San Francisco. The mirror over his dresser was still plastered with track meet ribbons and several yellowed news clippings. One headline read "Big Ben Stewart Tops High Hurdles."

Ben examined the victorious smile on the face of the seventeen-year-old in the picture and wondered if he would ever feel like that again. He took off his Ike jacket, dropped it on a chair, loosened his tie and flopped down on his bed. Somehow the tragic realization that he could never be a seventeen-year-old innocent again coupled with the relief of being home affected him so deeply that he began to sob. Not wanting to alarm his parents, he quickly got himself under control and wiped his eyes on his sleeve. Then he clicked off the radio. In five minutes he was fast asleep.

JANUARY 1954

BEN FELT more lonely during the Christmas season of 1953 in Orangevale than he had during his previous Christmas on Line Minnesota. He made a few attempts to contact high school friends but the boys were away in the service and any girl, in which he might be interested, was married, going steady or away at school. He was tempted to call Mary Ellen but feared that the contact might be unwelcome. Therefore he slept until noon, moped around the house, drank too much beer, and snarled whenever his mother tried to make suggestions. When the time came to put their eldest son back on the train to Tacoma, Bill and Mary Stewart were somewhat glad to see him go.

When Ben reported to the Second Division Replacement Depot, he was initially assigned to Service Company of the Ninth Infantry Regiment. He spent two boring weeks typing requisitions at the motor pool until an opening occurred at the Regimental Troop Information and Education Office. Ben was happy to be back in a familiar situation. He was put to work conducting another twenty-hour discussion leader's course, advising soldiers who were interested in self-study through USAFI (United States Armed Forces Institute) courses, interviewing lieutenants and captains to determine whether they had met the minimum academic requirements to retain their commissions as company-grade officers, and, whenever he had the time, working on an update of the hundred-year history of the Ninth U.S. Infantry.

One Friday morning, Ben answered the phone with his usual, "TI&E, Corporal Stewart speaking, sir."

"Hey, Ben. This is Grady. How you doing?"

"Grady, where in the hell are you?"

"Down the street. I'm with Medical Company of the 23rd. I've been trying to locate you for the past three weeks. Your personnel guys kept referring me to the motor pool."

"That figures."

"Got plans for the weekend?" asked Grady.

"I was just thinking about heading for Seattle," Ben responded. "You got a better idea?"

"No let's do it."

Ben was about to say that he would check and see if they could bunk at Uncle Joe and Aunt Ada's house and then thought better of it. Aunt Ada wasn't ready for a "negrah" under her roof.

The following morning the two buddies hopped a Greyhound for the city. The YMCA was close to the bus station and they were able to get a room for the night. That evening, after dinner, they walked to the Aloha Club. Ben had spent an evening there two weeks before. They entered and were soon greeted.

"Good evening, gentlemen. May I help you?"

"We'd like a table please."

"Oh, I'm very sorry but we require all gentlemen to wear coats and ties. It's our policy."

"That's interesting," observed Ben. "When I was here a couple of weeks ago, I didn't have a tie on. Nobody mentioned your policy."

"C'mon, Ben," said Grady. I know a better place."

As they stepped out on the sidewalk, Ben exclaimed, "What the hell was that all about? Do you suppose he pulled that policy out of the air because we're obviously G.I.'s?"

"No, Stew, I'm afraid that Jim Crow is alive and well on the West Coast. It's just not obvious. That guy in there pisses me more than some honest old redneck in Alabama who directs me to the drinking fountain reserved for the 'colored'."

"Speaking of which," Grady continued, "What do you suppose ever happened to Lieutenant Stebbins?"

"I could care less as long as he doesn't turn up as TI&E Officer for the Ninth Infantry," Ben chuckled.

"Or CO of Med Company of the Twenty-third," laughed Grady.

They hailed a cab and a few minutes later arrived at the Ebony Club. When they entered, Ben noticed that the regulars were sizing him up. They weren't used to seeing many white boys in their watering hole. He expected to be asked to leave but wasn't. They spent the rest of the evening sipping bad scotch and listening to good jazz.

Sunday afternoon Ben and Grady went to the Orpheum Theater to see a production of Verdi's *Aida*. During the singing of *Celeste Aida,* Ben felt another crush of melancholy. Disgusted with himself, he tried to stifle his sobbing, hoping that he could not be heard above the strains of music.

When they walked out of the theater, Grady said, "What was the matter with you in there?"

"Nothing."

"What were you crying about?"

"Oh, that. I don't know. I guess I got thinking about how there were times last year when I doubted that I would ever see or hear anything beautiful again. It just got to me. No big deal."

"Does stuff get to you very often?"

"Not very often. Once in awhile."

"It might be a good idea if you go talk to a shrink over at Madigan General, Stew."

"Drop it, Grady. I'm not going crazy."

A couple of weeks later Ben and Grady spent a Saturday afternoon in Tacoma. Ben suggested that they try the food at Ronny's Dock on the waterfront. It was only 5:30 and they shouldn't have a problem getting a table. As they expected, when they got there the place was nearly deserted. It was difficult to believe the maitre d' when he informed them that all of the tables were reserved for the entire evening. He was most apologetic.

"What in the hell would he have said if we had made a reservation," asked Ben.

"He probably would have fumbled around for awhile and then would have admitted that there had been an unfortunate mistake, our reservation had not been logged correctly. I've run into that a couple of times because my voice, on the phone, just sounds…well, just like a regular California honky."

"Well, to hell with Ronny's Dork." said Ben, amused at his new name for the exclusive restaurant. "I guess we ought to just head back to Pacific Avenue and join the rest of the doggies in some chicken-fried steak."

* * *

Ben and Grady reported to the Separation Center at Ft. Lewis on Monday, June 4. They were the beneficiaries of a cost-cutting strategy used by the Department of Defense. Soldiers due for discharge in July were released in June before the beginning of the next fiscal year. They were assured that their twenty-three months of active duty would still result in the full thirty-six months of educational benefits under the Korean G.I. Bill.

For two days, they lay on their bunks and read, with one ear tuned to announcements over the PA system. Every two hours or so, they would fall out for a formation and roll call. Threats to keep anyone missing a formation for an additional two days, kept the short-timers in line.

Wednesday afternoon, June 6, everyone dressed in their class-A wool uniforms and reported to an auditorium. Chief Warrant Officer Stumpo read a directive thanking them for their service to their country and then each man had his picture taking receiving his discharge papers from Mr. Stumpo.

Following the separation ceremony, they lined up for their final payment from the U.S. Army. In addition to one week's pay, they received travel pay to their city of residence at the time of induction and payment for any unused leave. Ben and Grady each received around three hundred dollars. Then, wallets bulging with their separation pay, the two comrades set out for California.

Ben had bought a 1950 Chevrolet from a co-worker in Regimental S-3. The two-door sedan had a low-slung rear end, fender skirts and twin tail pipes that roared and popped. Somewhere south of Grant's Pass, Oregon the car began bucking and complaining. Neither Ben nor Grady knew anything about cars so they chose to ignore the problem and pushed on down Highway 99. The car nearly stalled several times as they climbed hills, but the travelers persisted. They were anxious to get home.

Ben left the engine idling roughly as he helped Grady unload at his home in West Sacramento and then headed for Orangevale with his fingers crossed. When he reached home and popped the hood for his father, the older man found a loose spark plug wire which he refastened. The engine hummed sweetly. Ben was so relieved that he was not going to have to spend a big chunk of his separation pay for auto repairs.

A nurse, who lived in the rental unit that Bill Stewart had built off the family garage, encouraged Ben to apply for a summer position as orderly at the new Roseville District Hospital. The hospital administrator, aware of Ben's plans to return to Stanford in late September, offered him a meager salary of $150 a month, free laundry service for his white uniforms and free meals while on duty. Ben readily accepted. He hoped that the hospital experience and a good recommendation from the administrator would help him when he began applying for medical school.

Once he got settled, Ben tried to contact Grady by phone. He left a message with Grady's grandmother. When he had heard nothing in a week, he called again. He was told that Grady had returned to Berkeley to prepare for football season. Ben thought that the situation was a little strange but he didn't dwell on it. He was loving his job at the hospital and was receiving a lot of good feedback from the medical and nursing staff. He would try to get together with Grady in the fall.

FALL 1954

"BEN? Ben Stewart!"

Ben looked at the fellow ahead of him in the bookstore line and saw a familiar face, the big happy-go-lucky face of Nick Shymanski.

"Nick!" The two fraternity brothers shook hands and laughed. Then each waited for the other to speak, neither knowing what to say.

"So," Ben finally said. "Did you graduate? What are you still doing on campus?"

"Yeah, I graduated. I'm in first year law now."

"That's great!"

"Well, it isn't that great. But it makes my folks happy. What's great is seeing you. The last we heard was that you had dropped out of school to work for a while. That was a couple of years ago."

"Yeah I got a job and ended up at a place called Outpost Harry."

"Never heard of it."

"That figures," responded Ben. "It's a long story and your cashier over there is waiting. I'll catch you later." It was a long story and Ben had no intention of telling it to Nick Shymanski or anyone else for that matter. It would be a waste of breath. They couldn't begin to understand.

When it became Ben's turn to move up to the cashier, he found himself staring at the lovely young woman who was punching the cash register. Her face was somehow meaningful to him. It was as if he had finally found the real reason for returning to school. He paid for his books, thanked her and went out into the bright sunlight.

* * *

Ben had found a room in a quiet neighborhood in Palo Alto, but was beginning to experience trouble sleeping. He would fall asleep around nine-thirty or ten o'clock with his face in a textbook. Then he would wake up and go to bed only to wake up about two-thirty in the morning and toss and turn the rest of the night. By early afternoon he was too exhausted to study and frequently took a two-hour nap.

The physician at the Student Health Service listened to his complaints for about five minutes before dispatching him to the Veterans Hospital on the east side of Palo Alto. The VA psychiatrist, Dr. Leibowicz, gathered a history and prescribed chlorohydrate to help him sleep.

"Do you have any free afternoons, Mr. Stewart?" Leibowicz asked.

"Tuesday and Thursday are my free afternoons. Why?"

"Good. I want to try you in a Thursday afternoon therapy group. I think you'll find it helpful."

"Oh, I don't think I need that, Dr. Leibowicz. I just need to get some sleep. But thanks for the offer."

"You're suffering from depression, Ben, and you need to deal with the things that are causing you pain. It's very unlikely that you will get better by yourself. The other men in the group are Korean War vets, too. They know what you're going through and they won't let you get away with any unnecessary suffering. What do you say?"

"Will it cost anything?"

"Not a red cent. Uncle Sam pays for it."

"Okay. I'll give it a try."

When Ben arrived at the hospital on Thursday, he was carrying a clipboard. The VA Hospital was crawling with Stanford medical students and graduate students in psychology who were involved in fieldwork. He wanted to look like one of them. After a few sessions with Dr. Leibowicz's group, the clipboard was no longer necessary.

Ben began looking forward to the therapy sessions. He was intensely interested in the way that Dr. Leibowicz directed the flow of the conversation; reflecting, interpreting, and re-directing questions. When Ben started doing the same thing, Dr. Leibowicz was amused. The other group members weren't. They quickly let Ben know that they needed only one "shrink."

One rainy December afternoon, the group members got around to the subject of guilt. When it was Ben's turn to speak, he talked about Outpost Harry, his loss of his friend, Rudy, and his killing of the young Chinese soldier.

"So what's your problem, Stewart?" growled one of the group members. "We all lost buddies in Fecal-Com. Harry Truman killed your friend. You had nothing to do with it."

"I know that. It's not all about Rudy. I just keep thinking of that Chinese guy and wondering if he really intended to kill me."

"Of course not, asshole," interjected one of the other patients. "He just dropped in to see if you wanted to trade a can of beans and wienies for a rice ball."

"My platoon sergeant searched him," Ben continued, "and found a snapshot of the guy's family and a couple of letters. The moment I looked at that picture, it hit me that I had killed a human being, not just some Chink, some animal. He was a man and had people who loved him and missed him. I remember that he just looked scared and stood there for the longest time without pointing his burp gun at me. I've often wondered whether he just wanted to give himself up."

"If you feel so bad, why don't you write to his old lady and tell her you're sorry?" remarked another man in the group. This idea aroused a chorus of snorts. Ben was visibly angry but didn't respond.

"That's probably not such a bad idea, Stewart," said Leibowicz. "Write her a letter."

"How do I do that?"

"You just sit down at your desk and tell her how you feel. You express any regrets that you might have. Did you keep the letters and the picture?"

"I think I still have the letters."

"Well see if you can get some help from the Asian Studies Department on campus. They'll probably have someone who can tell you whether the letters contain a return address. You might have better luck mailing it through the Republic of China Cultural Office in the City."

"They'll probably just throw a letter away don't you think?"

"They might," admitted Leibowicz. "But her receiving the letter is not the point. Your making an effort to write to her is."

It was "dead week" on campus. Classes were suspended to allow the students to prepare for their final exams. Ben tried to study that evening but couldn't get the absurd idea of writing to Xing's widow out of his mind. Finally he slipped a piece of stationery into his old portable Royal typewriter and began to struggle.

Dear Madam,

You will probably never receive this letter, but, in case you do, I just want you to know that you have been on my mind for many months. On 13 June 1953, I was a U.S. soldier assigned to protect a small mountain-top outpost called Outpost Harry. It was about sixty miles due north of Seoul, Korea.

That night we were attacked by men of the 220th Regiment, Seventy-fourth Division of the Chinese Army. Your husband bravely attacked our fortifications and jumped into a trench very close to me. Without thinking, I ended his life. I've never been sure if he intended to harm me or not. I just did what I was trained to do and he was gone before I could get an answer to my question.

After the battle, my sergeant searched your husband's person and found nothing but a couple of letters and a picture of you and your child. I'm sure that means that nothing mattered

to him but the two of you. He must have missed you terribly.
Please forgive me for taking him from you.

Sincerely,
Benjamin Stewart
Palo Alto, California

Ben kept a file containing his DD214, Report of Separation from the Armed Forces of the United States, and other documents that were required to prove eligibility for veteran's benefits. He found Mei's two letters among the papers. He paid a graduate student in the Asian Studies Department, five dollars to translate his letter into Cantonese and to address an envelope.

On the morning following his last final exam, Ben caught the northbound Del Monte Express at the Palo Alto train station and rode to the end of the line at Third and Townsend in San Francisco. It was a thirty-block walk to the Republic of China Economic and Cultural Office on Montgomery Street but the rain had held off all morning, so Ben decided to hoof it.

When he reached his destination, he had no idea what he was going to do next. He felt foolish and doubted that anyone inside would even care about his predicament. He was wrong. A young receptionist listened to his story, shrugged and said, "I can place the letter in a larger envelope and send it to our office in Taipei. What happens from that point on is anybody's guess."

Ben was relieved and paid her sixty cents to cover airmail costs. Thanking her he left the building and decided to stay and explore the streets of Chinatown for a couple of hours before returning to Third and Townsend to catch the 4:00 P.M. train south.

WINTER 1954

DURING GROUP therapy, Ben had finally admitted that his lack of aptitude for the physical and life sciences would keep him out of medical school. He had also come to the conclusion that he should quit sniveling and get with the program. Half of the men in his therapy group had landed in Korea in 1950. They had seen and experienced horrors that surpassed his by a mile. He really was a fortunate young man and needed to stop manufacturing reasons to feel angry.

In January, Dr Leibowicz, shifted Ben to individual monthly maintenance sessions.

"Doc, I've made a decision."

"Always a good step. Or maybe not always. What have you decided," asked Leibowicz.

"I'm going to go to the Registrar and switch my major to psychology. I aced general psych and abnormal psych. They were really interesting courses."

"Sounds like a good plan, Ben. So what else is going on? How are you sleeping?"

"I'm popping one of those little green footballs at bedtime and usually get about six or seven hours before I wake up. Occasionally I'll take a second one."

"Well, just so it's occasionally. I want you to get off the chlorohydrate as soon as possible. How about exercise?"

"Still manage to work in a swim or a jog around the track most every day…I've been giving some thought to moving back on campus, not being such a hermit. What do you think?"

"Moving back into the fraternity house?"

"No, that's not a good study environment. I was thinking about checking with the dorms that house upper classmen. There are a lot more vets there who have put the days of drinking and puking behind them."

"I would encourage you to do so, Ben. You need more practice getting along with people. What have you learned about you and people in the past few months?"

"Well one thing I've learned is that not every professor is a prick second lieutenant. I'm finding that when I ask for help they seem genuinely interested in me."

"Good, anything else on your mind."

"Well, there's a little brunette at the bookstore, about 5'6", pretty face, kinda skinny but I think she likes me."

"Have you asked her out?"

"I've tried, but so far I always chicken out and end up buying another notebook or Stanford t-shirt or something."

"Well, when I see you next month, I want a full progress report on that. Just a minute." Leibowicz scribbled on his prescription pad, tore off the sheet and handed it to Ben. "See you next month."

Outside Dr. Leibowicz's office, Ben unfolded the prescription order and read, "Spend at least one evening a week with the bookstore clerk until this condition clears up."

* * *

When spring quarter rolled around, Ben moved into Stern Hall, but decided to board at the SAE House. The residence hall director objected mildly but Ben told her that he was hashing at the fraternity so he really should eat there. He didn't tell her that he had fallen in love with Edna's cooking two years earlier and was unwilling to subject himself to the vagaries of a larger dining room.

There were several letters in his mailbox that had come in during the one-week spring break. One was postmarked in Greece and addressed to: Mr. Benjamin Stewart, Stanford University, California, USA. Ben was grateful to the postal clerks who had gone out of their way to find him and deliver Iannis' letter. He read,

> *Dear Ben,*
> *I hope you are there at Stanford. You said that you would be returning there. How are you enjoying civilian life? You will be surprised to learn that I too am a civilian. I was discharged when my term of enlistment was up and have returned to my studies of archaeology at the institute in Athens. I decided that it was time for other young men to take up the fight against the kommunisti.*
> *When I was in hospital at MASH, I met a lovely Greek-American nurse and what do you think? She found my address through the army locator and says she is coming to Greece to learn about her heritage and she insists that I must be her guide.*

*So, poor Iannis will have to take some time off from his studies
this spring.*
*I so hope that this letter will reach you. I would really like
to hear about your new life. Maybe I will be coming to America
someday and maybe I won't be alone. Take care, Ben.*

Warm regards,
Ianni Karsatos

"Lucky Iannis," thought Ben, as he walked to his one o'clock at
Terman Hall. "He damn near dies of hemmorrhagic fever and comes up
smelling like a rose." As he passed the Student Union, he spotted the
young woman from the bookstore, perched on a low wall near the fountain,
having her lunch.

Ben couldn't keep his mind on the professor's orientation to
Psychology 210. He was too busy plotting, what he felt, might be the most
important campaign of his life. He would ask Edna to pack him a lunch on
Tuesdays and Thursdays when he had no one o'clock class.

The following day, he thanked Edna for the lunch, and walked across
Lasuen Street to the Union. She wasn't there. He nibbled at his sandwich
and potato chips for an hour and a half and still she didn't show. At 2:00
he rose, somewhat numb from sitting on the concrete wall and walked
dejectedly back to Stern Hall.

Ben's luck improved on Thursday. She was there, dressed in a plaid
skirt and a yellow, short-sleeve cashmere sweater. There was no one else
in the vicinity. Ben walked over, gestured at the wall next to her and said,
"Is this seat taken?"

"What do you think? Have a seat. Apparently you don't have a one
o'clock at the School of Ed today."

"Who gave you my schedule?" asked a surprised Ben.

"I was here Monday and noticed that you went by and eventually
turned into Terman Hall. I think you were kind of checking me out."

"That's very possible. Oh excuse me, I'm Ben Stewart."

"I'm Bonnie Pereira, Ben. It's nice to meet you. You're a good
customer at the bookstore. I see you there a lot. I've also seen you at
Terman Hall. I'm an elementary ed major."

The two chomped quietly on their sandwiches for awhile. Ben
struggled to think of something to say. He finally came up with, "So how
are things going at the bookstore?"

"Crazy," said Bonnie. "Everyone waited until this week to buy their
books. In fact, I've got to get there right away and help out. Nice to have
met you finally, Ben. Maybe we can get together for lunch again
sometime."

"How about Thursday," he said.

"Okay, see you then." She was away before he could stammer another word.

While they visited on Thursday, Bonnie admitted that Ben was someone that she had hoped to get to know better. He seemed to be a bit more mature than most college juniors.

"I've had some time out," he admitted.

"Korea?"

"Yeah, I hope you don't want me to tell you what that was like."

"Only when you're ready," she answered, smiling.

Such a smile. A smile Ben knew he would kiss some day soon.

EPILOGUE

BY THE FALL of 1967, Sergeant First Class Frank Champion had been stationed at Fort Ord for two years. He was a drill instructor, a good, tough one at that. His bearing suggested that he was outranked by no one, with the possible exception of his wife, Trudy.

Eight-year-old Roxanne Champion was destroying Mrs. Bennett's third grade and Trudy had insisted that Frank accompany her to a meeting with the school psychologist at Hayes Elementary School. He didn't see why he had to go to a school conference just because they were having a little problem controlling his daughter. She certainly toed the line when she was around him.

Frank was all the more annoyed when they were ushered into a cramped conference room and he was confronted by thirty-four-year-old Ben Stewart. "Crap," thought Champion. "They've sent a boy to tell me how to raise my kid." He reluctantly shook Ben's hand and said, "How long is this going to take?"

"I appreciate that you're busy, Sergeant Champion. You DI's work long days."

"What do you know about it?" growled the sergeant."

"I was in the Army. I was here for basic and AIT."

Champion looked Ben over from his brown crew cut down to his powder blue flannel suit and his black wing-tip shoes and said, "How long were you in the Army?"

"Two years," responded the young psychologist.

"Two years! Hell, that isn't long enough to get your laundry back," sneered Champion.

"Right," agreed Ben, "particularly when there were times that I had to wear the same underwear for three weeks. I notice you have a Third Division patch on your right shoulder. Were you anywhere near OP Harry in '52?"

"Close enough. I was with division artillery. We provided supportive fires to Harry. Don't tell me you were with the Fifteenth Infantry."

"Actually, I was with the Fifth RCT. We were attached to the Fifteenth. Those of us with First Battalion logged in a few hours on OP Harry. A few too many."

"Well," said Sergeant Champion, as he began to relax, "your Fifth RCT was a fighting outfit, a fine unit. As you probably know it's now called the Fifth Mech. It's in Nam and operates between Cu Chi in the south and Tay Ninh in the north."

"What's the Fifth Mech?"

"The Fifth Mechanized Infantry," explained the sergeant. "The regiment now patrols in tracked vehicles. They have a fifty-mile perimeter to secure and some heavy fighting to do. Couldn't cover that much ground on foot."

Ben's mind wandered to SFC Rob Palmer. The fighting in Vietnam had really become intense since late summer. His old mentor would have about one more year to serve until he could retire. Hopefully he had a safe berth stateside or in Europe. However Ben was unable to convince himself of that. It was more probable that Palmer was in harm's way somewhere north of Saigon trying to keep a batch of nineteen-year-olds alive.

"Well, I would like to know more about the Fifth Mech," said Ben, "but I didn't ask you here to talk army, Sergeant. I'm interested in Roxanne. I'd like to know more about her. I've observed her in class and on the playground and I've had a couple of chats with her. Let me tell you what I've seen and heard and see if any of it reminds you of her behavior at home."

"Do you have any kids, Doc?" Frank Champion was still not sure that the young man across the table from him had anything to offer.

"Thought you'd never ask," replied Ben. "Yes, we have four girls. The oldest is nine and the youngest is two."

"How are the older ones doing in school?" probed the sergeant.

"So far, so good."

"No behavior problems?"

"Not yet," replied Ben. "We try to keep one jump ahead of them. Now how about Roxanne?"

"OK," agreed Sergeant Champion. "Let's have the scoop."

It was shortly after four when the conferees had finished developing a plan that, hopefully, would get the adults in Roxanne's life working together for her sake as well as theirs. Ben was officially off-duty at five, but he really didn't want to go back to the district office and start returning a bunch of phone calls. What the hell! It was Friday afternoon.

He turned east on Coe Avenue, then north on North-South Road. He wanted to see if there still was a Dog Company of the Sixth Engineer (C) Battalion. Of course, it would now be Delta Company. Ben turned down First Street and then turned right on First Avenue by the old theater where he remembered seeing a Dick Powell and Debbie Reynolds film. He couldn't remember its title or anything else about it. He drove past the warehouse where he was measured for his combat boots and his olive-drab uniform. Then he turned right into block after block of World War II-era barracks. They all looked the same. Every company street was identical.

Realizing that his quest was futile, Ben drove out the Twelfth Street gate and turned south on Highway One. On his right were the rifle ranges. The known distance range was deserted but a company of trainees had just finished zeroing their M-16s at the zero fire range and were joining a formation for the march back to their company area. They had spent a long day preparing for a new war in the highlands of a little country in Southeast Asia.

Ben slowed down to check out the troops. He wanted to stop the car and go over and yell, "Listen up, young troopers. Your parents loved and nurtured you and sacrificed so that you would never know deprivation, but that didn't, in any way, prepare you for what you are going to see and going to have to do. Please learn all you can from the Sergeant Champions in your life. If you do, you increase the chances of your life being long and happy and useful."

But then, he realized, that would probably go in one ear and out the other. "Well, you sure as hell had better listen to the Sergeant Palmers when you get to where you're going." Then he glanced at his watch and stepped down on the accelerator. It was time to head home and begin his weekend with Bonnie and the kids.

GLOSSARY OF ACRONYMS AND MILITARY TERMS

BAR: Browning automatic rifle. The primary squad-level automatic weapon used by U.S. infantry forces in Korea.

CCF: Chinese Communist Forces

CG: Commanding General

CHICOM: Chinese Communist Forces

CIB: Combat Infantryman's Badge

CP: Command Post

EM: enlisted man, regardless of whether he volunteered or was drafted for military service

EUSAK: Eighth U.S. Army in Korea

FAB: Field Artillery Battalion

FEAF: Far East Air Forces

FECOM: Far East Command (dubbed FEcalCom by the men who served there.)

GI: government issue, common slang name for an American soldier.

HBT: herringbone twill, a type of cloth used for making Army fatigue and Marine utility uniforms.

HE: high explosive, a type of ammunition fired by tanks and artillery primarily for use against personnel.

I & R Platoon: Intelligence and Reconnaissance Platoon, generally attached to battalion or regimental headquarters.

KMAG: Korean Military Advisory Group, U.S Army personnel assigned as advisors to ROK units. (Sometimes said to stand for Kiss My Ass Goodbye)

LP: listening post, usually the most forward deployment of soldiers. Their purpose was to detect and communicate information about enemy patrols and probes

KATUSA: Korean Augmentation to the U.S. Army

KSC: Korean Service Corps, South Koreans who served the UN forces as laborers and porters.

LSI: Landing ship, infantry

LST: Landing ship, tank

M-16: Armored half-track vehicle mounting four .50 cal machine guns, frequently called "quad fifties."

M-19: Armored half-track vehicle mounting dual 40mm quick firing cannons.

MASH: Mobile Army Surgical Hospital

MATS: Military Air Transport Service

MLR: main line of resistance, the established line of battle, the front lines.

MSR: main supply route, primary roads and highways used as lines of movement and supply for military units. Usually identified by a number, such as MSR blue 5.

NCO: noncommissioned officer. Enlisted ranks such as corporal, sergeant, etc.

NKPA: North Korean People's Army

NOKO: North Korean soldier

OD: olive drab

OG: olive green

PLA: Peoples Liberation Army (China)

PUC: Presidential Unit Citation

RR: recoilless rifle, was available in 54mm and 75mm bores

R & R: rest and recuperation

RTO: radio-telephone operator

SCR: set, complete radio

S-1: personnel section of a regiment or battalion staff, responsible for personnel management, administration, morale, and discipline.

S-2: military intelligence section of a regiment or battalion staff, responsible for collecting, interpreting, and disseminating tactical information.

S-3: operations section of a regiment or battalion staff, responsible for planning military operations and training.

S-4: logistics section of a regiment or battalion staff, responsible for unit supply, maintenance, and transportation plans.

TF: task force

TO&E: table of organization and equipment, U.S. Army tables that showed the allotment of troops, weapons, and equipment at every level of command, from company through corps.

VT:..Ammunition with a variable time fuse. Explodes in the air to kill and wound ground troops.

ZI: Zone of the Interior (the continental United States)

SOURCES

Barbero, Julio et al. "Clinical and laboratory study of thirty-one patients with hemorrhagic fever," *AMA Archives of Internal Medicine,* February 1953, pp. 176-196.

Dannenmeier, William D. *We Were Innocents: An Infantryman in Korea.* University of Illinois Press, Urbana, IL 1999.

Fifteenth Infantry Regiment. *After-action Report for 10-18 June 1953.* National Archives: College Park, MD.

Fifteenth Infantry Regiment. *S-2/S-3 Journal: 31 May 1953 - 30 June 1953.* National Archives: College Park, MD.

Fifth Regimental Combat Team. *Command Reports: 1 November 1952 - 30 September 1953.* National Archives, College Park, MD.

First Battle Group, Fifth Infantry. *History of the Fifth Infantry Regiment.* Fort Riley, KS. June 1962.

Gould, Dudley C. *Follow Me Up Fools Mountain: Korea 1951.* Southfarm Press, Middletown, CT, 2002.

Murphy, Edward F. *Korean War Heroes.* Presidio Press: Novato, CA 1992.

Rigg, Robert B. *Red China's Fighting Hordes.* Military Service Publishing Co: Harrisburg, PA 1952.

Russ, Martin. *The Last Parallel.* Fromm International: New York. 1999.

Schafer, Elizabeth. "Greek Forces in the Korean War" in *The Korean War: An Encyclopedia.* (ed. Stanley Sander) New York: Garland, 1995.

Sixty-fourth Tank Battalion. *Command Report for June 1953.* National Archives, College Park, MD.

Slater, Michael. *Hills of Sacrifice: The 5th RCT in Korea.* Turner Publishing, Paducah, KY, 2000.

About the Author

Sam Kier was born in Oakland, California in 1932. He grew up in the San Francisco Bay area and the Sacramento Valley. Upon graduation from Stanford University with a degree in psychology, Kier was immediately drafted into the U.S. Army. After completing basic training at Fort Ord, he was assigned to the Fifth Infantry Regiment.

During much of his time with the Fifth Infantry, Kier served as the regimental troop information and education NCO. One of his responsibilities was to update the regimental history and see that it became part of the troop education program.

Following his separation from the army, Kier returned to school and earned a master's degree in psychology at Sacramento State University and a Ph.D. in special education from the University of Arizona. He worked in the public schools of California for forty years as a classroom teacher, school psychologist, director of special education, and finally as professor of education at San Jose State University. He continues to provide consultation to teachers in the area of critical thinking.

Now retired, Sam lives in Pacific Grove, California. He enjoys barbershop singing, military history, writing, travel and Civil War reenacting. During the latter, he portrays an assistant surgeon with the Seventy-first Pennsylvania Volunteers. His first book, *Sons of the Commonwealth: A Story of the Pennsylvania Reserves,* was published in 1999.

Sam met his wife, Betty, while he was stationed at Fort Lewis, Washington. They were married in 1955 and have four daughters and seven grandchildren.